THE ACCOMPLICE:
BUCKING THE TIGER

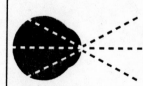 This Large Print Book carries the
Seal of Approval of N.A.V.H.

THE ACCOMPLICE: BUCKING THE TIGER

MARCUS GALLOWAY

WHEELER PUBLISHING
A part of Gale, Cengage Learning

GALE
CENGAGE Learning

Detroit • New York • San Francisco • New Haven, Conn • Waterville, Maine • London

GALE
CENGAGE Learning

LIBRARY OF CONGRESS CATALOGING-IN-PUBLICATION DATA

Galloway, Marcus.
   The accomplice. Bucking the tiger / by Marcus Galloway.
     p. cm. — (Wheeler Publishing large print western)
   ISBN-13: 978-1-59722-798-8 (pbk. : alk. paper)
   ISBN-10: 1-59722-798-6 (pbk. : alk. paper)
    1. Gamblers — Fiction. 2. Large type books. I. Title. II. Title:
Bucking the tiger.
   PS3607.A4196A65 2008
   813'.6—dc22   2008016834

Published in 2008 by arrangement with The Berkley Publishing Group, a member of Penguin Group (USA) Inc.

*This is dedicated to my beautiful wife,
Megan.
You're the best gamble I've ever taken.*

AUTHOR'S NOTE

Keeping up with John Henry "Doc" Holliday was a hell of a job. Anyone who knew him at the time would have told you as much, but that task becomes even more difficult when trying to piece him together from the research we have today. For the same stretch of time, one source might have Doc being chased by a posse through Indian country while another source puts him on an uneventful train ride. This isn't uncommon where notorious figures of the 1800s are concerned, but I thought it was worth mentioning here. For the purposes of this book, I have tried to keep Doc's whereabouts and associations as historically accurate as possible. Documented gunfights and scrapes with the law were also kept more or less intact, but some of these vary, depending on who is telling the tale. I've gone with the versions that make the most sense to me with the intention of staying true to Doc's essence while also telling a good story about the man. In the end, this is a fictional account. For a more biographical read, I'd recommend *Doc Holliday* by John Myers Myers or *Doc Holliday: A Family Portrait* by Karen Holliday Tanner.

Enjoy the book!

1
DALLAS, TEXAS
1875

John Holliday was a young man with a handsome, if somewhat gaunt, face. His blond hair was well kept and his mustache neatly trimmed, but all the fine grooming in the world couldn't blunt the razor's edge of his stare. Holliday, who'd become known more and more as Doc, coughed on some of the dusty air inside the quiet room. His eyes remained steady, however, as they fixed upon a man who wasn't too anxious to look back.

McDowell was the man taking the brunt of that stare, and he did so while shifting on his feet and nervously clearing his throat. He was a stout man dressed in a rumpled suit, which was currently becoming soaked with sweat around the edges. Like most everyone else in Dallas, he'd heard the rumors about Doc and had seen the city's former dentist carousing on numerous occasions.

There'd been plenty of talk about the guns Doc carried, but McDowell tried not to think too much about that. If he got too nervous, he might make a mistake and slip up at a bad time. A mistake like that could cause quite a stir, and McDowell simply wanted to get his job done and go home in one piece.

Doc stared at McDowell and immediately sensed the man's nervousness. Like a shark smelling blood in the water, Doc's gambling instincts picked up on the beads of sweat on the man's face even before they trickled down McDowell's cheek. Just to add a bit of fuel to the fire, Doc smirked at McDowell and nodded as if he'd already read what was written upon his soul.

"We the jury," McDowell said, "in a plea of guilty, assess the punishment as a fine of ten dollars." Once that was out, McDowell let out the breath he'd been holding and lowered himself back into his seat.

The judge sat at the front of the courtroom and smacked his gavel against the top of his desk. "A fine, it is. Ten dollars, Dr. Holliday. Next case."

Doc stood up, beaming as if he'd won a thousand-dollar pot with a ten high. Most of the folks sitting in the courtroom were there on business of their own, but Doc looked straight past them and to his own audience of one. As Doc walked toward the exit, the rough-looking figure from the public seats fell into step beside him.

"If you don't mind, I'd like to depart from this place as soon as humanly possible," Doc said in a smooth, Georgia drawl. "The heat in here is unbearable."

The man who walked with Doc out of the courtroom was of average height and had a complexion slightly darker than one that had been tanned by the sun. His coal-black hair fell in uneven clumps that stopped just short of shoulder length. Although his dark eyes seemed more comfortable in a scowl, they were smiling right along with the rest of his face as he walked with Doc through the newly built Dallas courthouse. His name was Caleb Wayfinder, and it was plain to see that he didn't want to be in the fancy building for one more second.

"I'll say it was hot in there," Caleb said. "That jury foreman looked like he was about to faint dead away."

"He just doesn't take to public speaking, Caleb. Try to show a bit of compassion."

"Compassion, huh? Tell me, how exactly did McDowell pay back that money he owes you?"

Doc shrugged while taking a folded bill

out of his pocket and handing it over to the prettiest of the court clerks. "Why, whatever are you trying to imply? Ten dollars is a standard fine for someone brought up on a gambling charge."

"Last time you were hit for a lot more than that."

"Thanks to a corrupt lawman and several other mitigating circumstances, thank you very much." After getting his slip for the fee, Doc winked at the woman behind the counter and turned on his polished heels toward the courthouse's front door. "Still, a little insurance never hurt anyone."

Caleb chuckled under his breath and stepped outside. It was a fine day, and trying to figure out what deal Doc had or hadn't arranged would only give him a headache. "Insurance, huh? That's fine talk coming from a man who plays cards and drinks all night when he should be resting."

"My condition isn't going anywhere," Doc replied. "That much is insured. Speaking of drinks and cards, how about we pay a visit to the Busted Flush? It's not far from here."

"I remember where it's at, Doc. I used to own the place. It's just not the same as how I left it," Caleb grumbled.

"Did you see that for yourself?"

Caleb shrugged and mumbled something

under his breath, which was more than enough to answer Doc's question.

"Well, I have been there again," Doc said. "From what I saw yesterday, it's still a fine establishment. But if it pains you so much to see it, maybe you shouldn't have come back for this nonsense of a hearing. You weren't even on trial."

"Things went to hell pretty quickly last time we dealt with the law, so I figured it was easier to be here when it started up again rather than have it track me down. Besides, I also wanted to make sure Hank was doing all right with the Flush."

"Is he?"

While glancing down Main Street, Caleb could just make out the Busted Flush itself. He'd seen that saloon built from the ground up, and if he closed his eyes, he swore he could still hear the same old voices talking about the same old things they'd been discussing before he'd left. If he concentrated while pulling in a breath, he could even smell the musty walls of his office, which had closed in around him like a coffin.

"I'm sure he's doing a fine job," Caleb replied. "Probably better than I ever did, in fact."

"Maybe you should pay him a visit before

you leave."

"Nah. The faster I shake the dirt of this town off my boots, the better."

"I recall thinking the same thing when I left Georgia." As Doc spoke, his drawl became a little thicker, as if part of him was already settling back into his former home. "It was partly a necessity in my case, but I was itching to leave. Funny thing is that I couldn't go back now even if I wanted to. Too much has changed in too short a time." Glancing over to Caleb, he added, "There's a stage going back to Denison within the hour. Is that fast enough for you?"

"Maybe just a bit. I probably should pay Hank a visit since I'm here and all. After that, I'll head down to the station myself to see where else I can go."

"Anyplace specific in mind?"

"Anyplace but here."

Doc laughed and patted Caleb on the shoulder. "A man with standards. I like that." Before he could laugh much more, Doc winced and snatched a handkerchief from his jacket pocket. Clutching the handkerchief in a tight fist, he pressed the cloth to his mouth and hacked into it. When he was done, he glanced down at it and then put it away.

"You need to take a moment and rest?"

Caleb asked.

Shaking his head, Doc replied, "Not at all. It seems the western climate has done wonders for my condition after all. I do imagine the mountain air would be even more refreshing."

"Mountain air? Sounds like you've got your sights set on somewhere in particular."

"Why yes. I hear Denver is very nice this time of year."

"And it happens to be on the gambler's circuit," Caleb pointed out.

For a moment, Doc rolled his eyes as though he were tracing the path of a slow bee making its way over his head. He then blinked and nodded solemnly. "Why, what a novel idea. It would be a fine place for a new saloon."

"I'm sure they've got plenty of saloons there already, Doc. Besides, I don't have what it takes to get another place off the ground."

"Not on your own, perhaps. As I recall, we make quite the team." Keeping his eyes fixed upon Caleb, Doc lowered his voice just enough to make it clear he was no longer idly chatting. "You know as well as I do that good partners are hard to find. Taking on the occupation of sport, the first thing I've learned is the value of someone I could trust."

"We got out of a few scrapes, that's for certain," Caleb said.

"Every good venture has its risks. Even dentistry wasn't without its perils. Business is business and that holds true no matter what your business is. Your business is running a saloon and mine is sport. The way I see it, there's no reason for our paths to split just yet."

Caleb shook his head and tried to read the true purpose behind Doc's expression. Doing so was like trying to read what was inside a mountain just by staring at a rock wall. "Already given up on dentistry?"

"I might not have coughed up any blood today, but I'm still not getting any better," Doc said candidly. "Making a living by winning my daily bread puts a fire in my belly that pulling teeth could never do."

"I believe the fire you're talking about is from all that whiskey you pour down your throat. And playing cards with you is hardly sport."

Doc kept up his stony facade for another few seconds before his smile returned. "So long as we're swapping brutal truths, did I mention that you settling into an office and balancing ledgers is about as fitting as this fine suit of mine wrapped around a pig?"

After taking a few moments, Caleb said, "You got a point there, but that doesn't mean I want to run a saloon with you."

"Heavens no! You'd run the place and I'd play cards in it. Just think of the money that could be made with an arrangement like that."

"I may not have known you for long, but I know damn well that you wouldn't just be playing cards with an arrangement like that."

"Well, no. I'd be dealing faro."

"You mean running that game, as well as every other game under my roof, in your favor?"

Doc shrugged and said, "It's called bucking the tiger, Caleb. Everyone knows the odds are stacked against you. The true test is beating them anyway."

As they'd been talking, Doc and Caleb had made their way to the depot where stagecoach tickets were sold. The platform outside the office was empty for the moment, giving them an unobstructed view to the open land beyond Dallas. Caleb shook his head and walked over to a board next to the ticket window where the stage schedules were posted. Even as he quickly examined them, Caleb could feel Doc anxiously awaiting his reply.

When Caleb turned around again, he saw Doc still waiting.

"Well?" Doc asked.

"The stage to Denison should be here soon," Caleb said. "And it just so happens to be one of the only ones out of here today. There's also another stage for Denison leaving tomorrow."

Doc's smile grew a bit when he heard that.

Caleb let out a heavy sigh. "I wasn't planning on spending the night in Dallas, but it's either that or check in on Hank some other time. I might as well head back to Denison in the morning."

"And after that?"

"I'll have to wait and see. I've heard Denver is a hell of a place."

Grinning from ear to ear, Doc slapped Caleb's shoulder good-naturedly. "You can smell the profits just as well as I can. You'll see. This arrangement will work out just fine all the way around. With the two of us working together, we can raise enough money to start up a saloon in no time."

"I haven't agreed to anything, Doc."

Doc nodded and purchased a ticket. "Of course, of course. We'll see where fate puts us. After all, a sporting man has to be able to leave such important matters to the fates whenever possible. It's all a part of our charm."

Even though Caleb was able to keep from sharing Doc's enjoyment of the moment, two ladies waiting on the nearby platform weren't so strong. They whispered to each other and quickly turned their blushing cheeks away from Doc.

Standing there in his expensive suit and fancy gold watch chain, Doc looked every bit the Southern gentleman. Caleb, on the other hand, more closely resembled the cowhands that rode through Texas while accompanying a herd from one ranch to another. Those ladies lost their high spirits when they saw the Navy model Colt revolver holstered under Doc's arm as he opened his arms to take in a deep, excited breath.

Doc didn't seem to notice either one of the ladies' shifting expressions as he stood on the edge of the platform and waited for the stage to Denison. It arrived amid the clatter of wooden wheels and the labored breathing of its horses. The ladies climbed up into the carriage and became quiet when they saw Doc headed for the seat directly across from them.

"Any baggage?" the driver asked.

Both ladies pointed toward a pile of cases stacked at the edge of the platform.

Doc's own case had been waiting for him

at the station. After tossing it up to the driver, he got inside the stagecoach behind the two ladies. All it took was a tip of his hat and a cordial smile for him to put them at ease. "I see the city of Dallas is losing two of its finest assets," he said with a Southern curl to his words. "I only hope you'll indulge me with a bit of conversation to pass these next few hours."

One of the women was shorter than the other and had thick, red hair. "My name's Colleen," she said while offering her hand to Doc. "This is my sister, Jenny."

"Delighted," Doc said.

Jenny nodded in Doc's direction, gazed out the window, and then rolled her eyes as the stagecoach lurched into motion.

Caleb knew exactly how she felt.

2

The last time Caleb had been inside the Busted Flush, it was a clean little saloon with a few gambling tables and a good supply of whiskey. Although the same bar was in the same spot, nearly everything else about the saloon had changed. There were more people drinking, more people gambling, and even a better stage set up at the back of the main room. Caleb stood rooted to his spot for a good few minutes before he finally caught sight of a familiar face,

"Is that you, Thirsty?" Caleb asked as he walked over to a middle-aged man propped up against the end of the bar.

For a moment, Thirsty stared blankly at Caleb. He then smiled widely enough to show a mouthful of yellowed teeth. "Hey Caleb! Where the hell've you been?"

"West Texas mostly."

"That's not what I heard," said another familiar voice.

Caleb turned and immediately found a man behind the bar smiling right back at him. It hadn't been too long since Caleb last saw Hank, but the portly man seemed a bit older than he would have expected. Even so, Hank had a wide smile and plenty of strength in his handshake.

"Good to see you, Caleb! I wasn't sure if you'd be back after handing over the reins to this place."

"Are you kidding? I needed to make sure you didn't run it into the ground."

"I would never do that. I've been trying to make certain everything —"

"Relax, Hank," Caleb said. "I was joking. The place looks great. Just great. When I left, there was just ol' Jed playing banjo in the corner. Now there's a stage and everything. Where are the dancing girls?"

"They don't come on for a few hours. The late show is the most popular."

"I just bet it is." Caleb turned and leaned against the bar. When he settled one hand on the polished wooden edge, he bumped against a fresh glass of beer.

"On the house," Hank said.

Caleb took the beer, tipped it in a quick toast, and drank it down. The fact that it tasted better than he could ever have brewed it didn't settle so well for some reason.

"I changed the recipe a bit," Hank explained. "Hope you don't mind."

"Not at all. Seems like you're doing real well for yourself."

"Speaking of that," Hank said as he reached under the bar, "I've been keeping this aside for you." When he brought his hand up again, it was wrapped around a fairly healthy stack of money. "You haven't been around to collect in a while, so I've been saving it up."

Squinting down at the money, Caleb asked, "What is that?"

Hank blinked and waited as if he expected Caleb to retract the question. "Your percentage. We are still partners, aren't we?"

"You own this place. You run it now."

"But you and I built it. I thought you were just letting me take charge while you were away."

"The Flush is yours now," Caleb said grudgingly. "There's no arguing that."

"If you want to come back and take over, you're welcome to it. It's just that . . ."

"Just what?" Caleb snapped. "Just that you already smoothed it over without me and are doing just fine on your own?"

While Hank may have looked a bit hesitant at first, he now straightened up and furrowed his brow into a firm scowl. "I was gonna say that I thought you were doing fine tearing from town to town with your partner Doc Holliday."

"Is that what you've heard?"

Shaking his head, Hank said, "It's what I know. Saloon owners hear all the gossip, Caleb. You know that. We also know how to separate the bullshit from the truth, and I've heard more than enough to know that you've been having yourself quite a time since you left Dallas. I heard you won more than enough to buy this saloon outright in a game just a month or two ago."

"You heard about that, huh?"

"Yeah," Hank said as he allowed his smile to return. "I sure as hell did. And you know how I knew it was the truth? I knew it because you were miserable as hell in that office and happy as a pig in shit when you were sitting behind a stack of poker chips. All in all, I imagined you were doing pretty well for yourself. If not, say the word, roll up your sleeves, and get to work right now. Things should really be picking up once the show starts and the night's big game gets started."

Hank kept his eye on Caleb for a few seconds and then started laughing. "You've already been a gambler for too long, boy. The thought of an honest night's work gives you the shivers."

"If you think gambling isn't work, you don't know the half of it."

"It may be work, but it's what you'd rather be doing."

"How do you know?"

"Because that's what you are doing," Hank said simply. "Folks do what they want to do, no matter how much they grouse about it. You got up the gumption to strike out on your own and I admire you for it. This was your place, so you're entitled to a percentage of the profits. It's a great arrangement if you'd take a second to look at it."

"I have looked," Caleb grunted. "I just didn't expect everything to work so well once I left."

Hank grinned and pushed the money farther away from his side of the bar. "Sorry to disappoint."

"No you're not," Caleb said as he took the money and stuffed it into his pocket. "And there's no reason you should be."

"You know what would make you feel better?"

"I'm sure you'll tell me."

"Pay a visit to Sarah. She talks about you every time she comes by here."

"Does she still work at the Alhambra?"

Caleb asked.

"Sure does. And she's just as pretty as ever."

"Subtle," Caleb said under his breath. "Real subtle."

Compared to the Busted Flush, the Alhambra was an elegant palace of a saloon. Actually, that was only fair when comparing it to the Busted Flush that Caleb had known before he'd left. Unlike the Flush, the Alhambra hadn't changed much since the last time Caleb had been there. The only thing that wasn't the same was the fact that Sarah was no longer running drinks back and forth from the bar and its customers.

Caleb knocked on the door marked "Private" and waited until he heard a hurried voice from the other side tell him to come in. After pushing the door open, he stood there and took a long look at the woman sitting behind a large oak desk.

She slammed a ledger shut, tossed a pencil down, and got up from her chair before even looking to see who was standing there. The moment she did take a second to check, she smiled and practically jumped over the desk to get into Caleb's arms.

"Good to see you, too, Sarah," Caleb said as he gave the blonde a squeeze.

"How long have you been back?" she asked.

"Not long at all." He held her at arm's length so he could take a good look at her.

The blonde was more than a foot shorter than Caleb, but she had no trouble standing up to him. Her chin was always held high, and there was always a spark in her eyes that only grew brighter when Caleb was around. This time, however, that spark seemed to dwindle a bit after just a few seconds.

"How long were you going to keep me waiting before coming here?" she asked.

"At least a week, but Hank twisted my arm."

She scowled and swatted his shoulder. "That's no way to talk! Without me, you never would have gotten that saloon off the ground."

"I know it. That's why I wanted to come by and thank you for what you've done."

"What are you talking about?" Sarah asked.

"I've been to the Flush. There's a stage, dancers, and I even smelled food cooking somewhere amid all that cigar smoke. Those were all your ideas."

She shrugged and stepped back until she was able to lean against the corner of her desk. "Hank does a fine job on his own. In case you haven't noticed, I've got my hands full right here."

Caleb walked forward slowly, until he was less than a foot in front of her. Reaching out to place his hands against the desk on either side of her, he whispered, "Thanks for doing your part."

Averting her eyes and smirking, she made no effort to put any more distance between herself and Caleb. "My pleasure. So what brings you back to Dallas? Considering how you were run out of here the last time, I didn't know if you'd be back at all."

"I wasn't run out. This place just became more trouble than it was worth."

"That's right. Speaking of trouble, how did Dr. Holliday's trial turn out?"

"Ten-dollar fine. That's it."

"If he sticks around you for much longer, he should be expecting a lot more trouble than that."

Turning so he could sit on the desk next to Sarah, Caleb laughed and asked, "So I'm a bad influence now?"

"You and I both know Doc ran a crooked game when he dealt faro at the Flush."

"There's plenty of cheaters making the rounds, Sarah. You know that."

"Bucking the tiger is hard enough. You

can't tell me that you didn't know those odds were being swung even more in your favor."

"And everything here is aboveboard?"

She shrugged and stepped in front of him. Now she was the one to lean forward and drop her voice to a whisper. "I don't take a percentage of cheaters' profits."

"Everybody cheats at some time or another," Caleb replied. "The only difference is who gets caught and how many times they're called out for it."

Slowly, Sarah's smile returned and she started to nod. "You've grown up, Caleb Wayfinder. When we first got into the saloon business together, you said you wouldn't tolerate a cheat at your poker tables."

"Poker's different."

"I believe you said anyone who'd swindle a man at a card table deserved to be —"

Sarah was cut off when Caleb took hold of her waist and pulled her close. His lips touched against hers for a moment before she leaned in closer to make the kiss even more passionate. In no time at all, her hands had found their way around him and her fingers were sifting through his hair.

As he continued kissing her, Caleb could feel every inch of his skin warming up. Soon, it seemed as if Sarah's body was melting into his own. When their lips parted, it was out of sheer necessity to draw a breath, and even so, they were reluctant to give in to such simple demands.

As Caleb was starting to lean in again, Sarah turned away and backed off.

"What's the matter?" he asked.

Sarah crossed her arms and walked over to the door without opening it. "You're not staying," she said. "Are you?"

"No."

"Why not? Things are back to normal around here. The only ones looking for you or Doc anymore are just asking out of curiosity."

"This place . . . Dallas . . . it's not . . ." As Caleb struggled to find his words, he found himself moving closer to Sarah. "There's a lot outside of Texas that I haven't seen."

"From what I've heard, you've been making the rounds to card tables rather than taking in any sights."

"What would you rather I do? Stay here and rot in some office?"

"You mean like me?" Sarah asked.

"No. What I mean is there's plenty more out there than just Dallas, and there's nothing stopping me from going out and taking it. You could come with me. Doc mentioned heading up to Denver. After that, I was thinking about seeing California or maybe Canada. Hell, I could go see New York City for the hell of it."

"Sure beats staying here and rotting with me."

Caleb took her in his arms and brushed the hair away from her face. As much as he wanted to tell her what she'd said wasn't true, he just couldn't. Not even Doc could have gotten away with a bluff like that.

"I'm sorry," she whispered. "I shouldn't have said that."

"You can come with me, you know. There's nothing stopping you, either."

Glancing around at her office and the shelf full of ledgers, Sarah nodded. "Yes there is. I've got this place and this job. I already own most of the Alhambra and will own it all in a few years. Dallas is getting bigger every day and there's so much more for me to do. I'd ask you to stay, but —"

"I can't," Caleb said before she could. "So, I guess that leaves us in a bad spot." Pulling her close, he added, "But I won't be leaving until tomorrow."

Sarah allowed herself to be drawn into his embrace one more time.

3

The stage pulled into Denison right on schedule. Jenny was asleep while Doc amused Colleen with general chatter and the occasional card trick. Without missing a beat, Doc winked at Colleen and climbed out of the carriage door the moment the stage came to a stop.

"Everyone getting off here?" the driver asked.

"The ladies are heading on to Denver," Doc said. "And I may be joining them."

"Getting along pretty well, huh?"

"You can say that."

Doc was heading for his hotel when he heard a vaguely familiar voice calling for him. Stopping, he turned and saw an old man standing in the door of the post office.

"Dr. Holliday!" the old-timer shouted. "You got some letters here!"

"Keep it down, I'm right here," Doc said through gritted teeth.

"This just came for you," the old-timer said as he waved an envelope at Doc. "Sitting with the others, in fact. Ain't you ever gonna read your mail?"

"Is it from the same place as the others?"

"All the way from Georgia, yes sir."

Doc looked at the letter in the old man's hand. Although it was an effort to do so, he managed to shake his head and turn his back on the old man. "I'll read it later, when I've got the time."

"Just take them now. I can fetch the others and —"

"When I've got the time," Doc snapped. "Thank you very much."

Rather than walk the rest of the way to his hotel, Doc went straight to the little saloon next to the stagecoach platform. It was a place no bigger than a horse stall and smelled just as bad. The man behind the bar recognized Doc on sight and immediately filled a shot glass with whiskey.

After downing the shot without so much as a wince, Doc removed the flask from his pocket and handed it over. "Be a good man and fill that for me."

The barkeep did as he was asked and said, "Didn't know you were back in town, Doc."

If Doc even heard the barkeep, he gave no indication. Instead, he simply drained a good portion of the flask and then handed it over again to be refilled. Once another portion of whiskey went down, Doc let out a few short hacking coughs, which eventually tapered into a wheezing sigh.

"You feeling all right?" the barkeep asked.

"I'm right as the mail," Doc said, which brought a wry grin to his face as well as the flask back to his lips. This time, he took a bit less of the liquor before twisting the flask's cap back in place. Placing down more than enough money to cover the amount of whiskey he'd been given, he said, "Be so kind as to forget this visit."

The barkeep made the money disappear with a deft swipe of his hand. "Anyone in particular I should keep an eye out for?"

"No."

"Long as there ain't no trouble nipping at yer heels."

"With any good fortune," Doc said as his more familiar grin returned, "all the more interesting troubles are in front of me."

Doc left the little saloon with a tip of his hat. True to his word, the barkeep returned to his business as if nobody had stepped through his door.

By the time Doc returned to the stagecoach, the horses had been replaced with a fresh team and the driver had climbed back into his seat. When he saw Doc coming, the driver leaned down and asked, "Still no luggage?"

"There are stores in Denver, aren't there?"

"I suppose so."

"Then who needs luggage? Let's put this town behind us."

As Doc settled into his seat, he was careful not to disturb Jenny. Soon after the wagon got moving, she was snoring loud enough to cover the sound of the horses. Colleen and Doc engaged in a bit more chat, but it wasn't nearly as spirited as when they'd left Dallas.

Doc soon crossed his arms and gazed out the window, allowing Colleen to drift off to sleep. Even though Denison wasn't more than a smudge on the horizon behind them, Doc couldn't help but feel as if he were still standing on that boardwalk with those letters in arm's reach.

Part of him wondered what was in those envelopes.

Part of him already knew.

After he'd taken a healthy swig of whiskey from his flask, every last one of those parts quieted down and allowed Doc to nod off and catch a bit of sleep.

Doc's eyes came open grudgingly and then

he immediately squeezed them shut.

Pulling in a ragged breath, he leaned forward and stretched his back as best he could within the confines of the carriage. He forced his eyes open again, took a look around, and saw the same two faces that had been there when he'd dozed off. The view outside the window, however, wasn't quite as familiar.

"Where are we?" Doc grunted. Just to be on the safe side, he blinked and rubbed his eyes a bit before taking another look out the window. It didn't help.

Since she'd been the first one to fall asleep, Jenny was already awake. She looked out the window, but didn't seem half as perplexed by what she saw. "Are we there already?"

"Already?" Doc asked. "Feels like I've been asleep for a week." Seeing the sour look on Jenny's face, he quickly added, "That doesn't look like Denver."

Jenny scowled and looked at Doc as if he'd suddenly sprouted horns. "That's because it isn't Denver. It's Weatherford."

"Weatherford? But that's . . . that's . . . a hell of a ways from Denver."

"Yes," Jenny said calmly. "It is."

Since he was getting as much help from Jenny as he was from trying to talk to the back of his hand, Doc used the back of that hand to wipe the sweat from his brow. "Looks like we're coming to a stop. I do hope there's some decent food in Weatherford."

Not only was Doc able to get a hearty dinner in Weatherford, but he acquired a neighbor as well. Walter Barry was a tall man in his early fifties with a full head of black hair that was evenly spattered with gray. The same pattern covered a good portion of his face with a thick, well-maintained beard.

Walter was a good enough sort, who took to Jenny almost immediately. The two of them laughed and joked about mundane things while Doc rolled his eyes at just the right moments to make Colleen laugh.

After a while, Walter glanced over at Doc and said, "You don't have any luggage."

Doc blinked and seemed genuinely confused. "Pardon?"

"When I boarded at Weatherford, I gave my own bags to the driver. I saw the ladies check on theirs, but that means you have none. How can that be?"

"I'm certain you and the driver had a long, involved conversation about that very thing. He also seemed quite fascinated with the matter."

Although Walter laughed, he would not relent. "Seriously, though. You look like a man who is well traveled."

"Do I also look like a man who wants to talk about luggage?"

"I don't suppose so."

"How about we discuss something more interesting? I know. What about gardening?"

Walter shrugged and crossed his arms like a child who'd been unceremoniously put in his place. "Just making conversation. It's a long ride and I wondered how anyone could travel without proper preparations."

"Whatever I need, I can get in Denver," Doc declared. Softening his tone a bit, he winked at Colleen and added, "Besides, you can't deny there's a certain thrill that comes from throwing caution to the wind and jumping before you pack a bag."

"You mentioned that you wanted to go to Denver for the clean mountain air," Walter pointed out.

"There's that, too."

"I think that sounds very exciting," Colleen said.

Jenny gave a choppy laugh. "You would."

"You see?" Doc said as he leaned back to close his eyes. "The lady thinks it's a marvelous idea."

■ ■ ■ ■

As they traveled through Jacksboro and Fort Belknap, Doc and Colleen talked more and more about where they'd been and where they were headed. Actually, Colleen did the lion's share of the talking after switching places with her sister so she could sit directly in front of Doc.

Her voice was like a smooth ride down a steep hill. The longer the conversation went on, the faster she talked. Doc wound up nodding and adding the occasional word here and there, but little else. Once they learned they would be stopping in Fort Griffin, Doc asserted himself once more.

"Since we won't be leaving there right away, we might as well continue this conversation," Doc offered. "I could meet you after you've had a chance to settle into your room."

"That would be great," she said. "Perhaps we could have some dinner as well."

"I believe we could work that into the equation," Doc said in his most charming Southern drawl.

Although Jenny didn't voice any disapproval regarding her sister's flirtations, she shifted in her seat and let out another short, skeptical grunt.

The ride lasted a little more than one hundred and fifty miles, most of which was filled with constant jostling and the increasing tedium of Walter's never-ending small talk. Soon, more and more of that talk was interrupted by Doc's coughing fits. They started as a scratch in the back of his throat, but soon escalated to a painful, all-consuming hacking. Most of Doc's good acquaintances were accustomed to those fits.

The sisters in the carriage, however, hadn't yet fallen into that category.

"Are you all right?" Colleen asked as the coughing got progressively worse.

Doc waved her off and pressed his handkerchief to his mouth. As the fit grew in intensity, he started taking pulls from his flask to take the edge off. Walter glanced over and caught a glimpse of blood on Doc's handkerchief.

"Oh my goodness," Colleen said as she reached out to pat Doc's shoulder. "Maybe we should —"

Doc flinched away and ripped his shoulder from beneath her hand. In a haggard voice, he snarled, "Just leave me be. I'll be fine."

Even though Colleen was kind enough to keep her distance without getting angry at the tone in Doc's voice, she was more than a little put off at the sudden paleness that had crept into his skin and the sunken aspect of his eyes.

"You want me to talk to the driver?" Walter asked.

Shaking his head, Doc folded his handkerchief and took another drink. The whiskey seemed to clear his throat enough to take a few easy breaths, which was enough to bring some of the color back to his face. After another sip from the flask, he looked more like his normal self. "No," Doc said. "I'm feeling better." Glancing at the sisters across from him, Doc smiled and slipped his flask back into his pocket. "Now, where were we?"

4

Caleb's ears were ringing as the stagecoach pulled to a stop in Fort Griffin. Compared to the quiet of sleeping under the stars for the last few nights, the rattle of the stage's wheels and thunder of its horses made him feel as if he'd been put into a sack and shot out of a cannon. Judging by the way Doc looked as he stepped down out of the coach and onto the muddy street, he felt much the same way.

Jenny and Colleen couldn't get out of the coach fast enough and began climbing down well before Doc turned to offer them a hand. Colleen took the help with a quick smile and Jenny soon followed.

"It will be nice to have some fresh air," Colleen said. Despite the politeness in her voice, her actions spoke twice as loud. She and her sister both hurried away from the coach without so much as a glance over their shoulders.

"What the hell was that about?" Caleb asked.

Clearing his throat, Doc said, "They're from St. Louis. I find people from there tend to be a bit more excitable." Stretching his arms and legs, Doc strolled toward the nearby boardwalk. After working a few of the kinks out of his neck, he took a look around. "What are you doing here, anyway?"

"I checked the schedule and saw the stage was due to stop here for a bit on its way to Denver. Thought it might be a good spot to say hello. Also, the horse I bought wouldn't have made it another day before keeling over."

Doc smirked and patted Caleb's shoulder. "Did you at least get a chance to pay Sarah a visit?"

"Sure did."

"And?"

"None of your business." Craning his neck to get a look around before Doc could respond, Caleb said, "Jesus Almighty, will you look at this place?"

Fort Griffin was teeming with so many sights and smells that the place felt as if it had a pulse all its own. The ground rattled under Caleb's boots thanks to the constant flow of horses and people making their way from one place to another. There was music coming from several different angles, and though none of it was particularly good, it beat the ruckus that had filled Doc's ears for the last one hundred and fifty miles or so.

Doc's eyes quickly turned upward to the balconies that were almost as crowded as the streets below them. Several men in suits leaned against rails like kings overlooking their domain, but most of the space on those balconies was occupied by women of all shapes and sizes in varying stages of undress.

"What about her, Doc?" Caleb asked as he nodded toward a plump woman with long dark hair who wore her blouse open more than enough to expose her generous breasts. "Do you think she's from St. Louis?"

"If she is, I'll have to seriously reconsider visiting that place."

Both men laughed and made their way to the closest saloon like two leaves drifting along the same current. They were stopped by a gruff voice calling from directly behind them.

"Hey," the stagecoach driver said. "Don't wander off too far. There's another stage coming through that's bound for Denver.

It'll be leaving in a few hours."

"If you could tear yourself away from a place such as this in just a few hours," Doc said, "then you are more ill than I will ever be."

The driver winced at that and hopped down to the street. Before he could say anything, he caught a glimpse of the generous breasts swaying more or less over his head. "You got a point there, mister. No need to hurry off so soon."

"That's the spirit!" And with that, Doc strode into the saloon he'd chosen simply because it was first in his line of sight.

Caleb remained outside for a few moments to take a better look up and down the street. In the space of those few moments, he spotted more and more gambling halls, saloons, and bordellos than he'd ever dreamed could be crammed into a single stretch of land. A few gunshots rang out in the distance, but they weren't followed by much commotion, so he assumed they were fired at the sky rather than at anything with a pulse.

Gunshots or no, Caleb couldn't help but smile at Fort Griffin. And he wasn't the only one to find something of interest there. As far as he could tell, the place had swallowed up the stagecoach driver along with every one of its passengers. The driver was gone and the sisters from St. Louis were nowhere to be seen. A few words of caution came to mind, but it was too late to say them now. All Caleb could do was hope those two ladies knew when to keep their heads down.

Feeling like a fresh gust of wind had just filled his sails, Caleb headed into the saloon that had already claimed Doc. As soon as Caleb stepped into the place, he was quickly shoved right back out again by the slender dentist.

"No gambling tables in there," Doc said as he brushed past him. "Let's take a look at what else there is."

"Don't you at least want a drink?"

"Already got one."

"Well, I didn't. Where the hell are you headed, Doc?"

"I just remembered a friend of mine might be around here somewhere. Fellow by the name of Owen Donnelly."

Before Caleb could ask who Owen Donnelly was, he realized that he didn't much care. "You go on ahead. Just be sure to find your way back to the stage before it leaves."

But Doc was already making his way down the street and was almost out of sight. Caleb watched him disappear and shrugged to himself. He knew Doc could handle himself, and if he couldn't, it wasn't Caleb's job to do it for him. Besides, Fort Griffin was a place that deserved to be soaked in, and this saloon was as good a place as any to start.

The front of the saloon was tall and narrow. While some places seemed bigger on the inside than they looked on the outside, this wasn't one of them. It was every bit as narrow as it appeared to be and was even more cramped due to the fact that its upper floor was closed off and only accessible by a narrow set of stairs. Lanterns swung from hooks at odd spots along the walls, giving the place a dim glow.

Standing at the bar, there were mostly cowboys being tended to by working girls sporting velvet ribbons tied around their upper arms. Caleb quickly found the stagecoach driver being romanced by a little brunette with her hair tied into a braid.

When he spotted Caleb at the door, the driver lifted his drink and shouted, "Hell of a town, ain't it?"

Caleb put on a smile and walked over to the driver's side. Leaning in close to the man's ear, he said, "Keep an eye on your valuables. Looks like your new lady friend is doing the same."

Immediately, the driver's hand shot toward the pouch that had been slung over his shoulder since the beginning of the ride from Denison. And, twice as quickly, the brunette's hand slipped out from where it had just made its way beneath the pouch's flap.

Since he was too slow to feel the woman's hand where it shouldn't have been, the driver smirked and chucked Caleb on the shoulder. "I think I'll keep an eye on this pretty lady's valuables, if it's all the same to you," he said.

"Suit yourself." With that, Caleb tipped his hat to the working girl and let her get back to her job. If some men were too stupid to take care of themselves, they deserved whatever they got. All concerns he might have had for the driver losing more than just his shirt flew out of Caleb's mind once he got a look at the small table in the back corner of the saloon.

Caleb couldn't see much, but he could just make out the pretty face of a redhead sitting on one side of the table. She was looking out and smiling at four other men who were sitting across from her. Between them, on the table itself, was a faro layout where all sizes of bets were being placed.

"You want to buck the tiger, mister?" came a voice from Caleb's left.

Considering what was going through Caleb's mind at the time, he didn't put that phrase together with playing faro right away. He chuckled and forced himself to look away from the redhead so he could see who'd asked the question. The man he found was as tall and narrow as the saloon itself and displayed a smile as crooked as the game to which he was referring.

"I thought there wasn't any gambling in here," Caleb said to the barkeep.

The barkeep's smile wavered a bit as he asked, "Who told you that?"

"A friend of mine who was just in here."

"You mean that skinny fellow with them fancy clothes?"

"That's the one," Caleb said.

"He was asking about poker. Didn't seem to want to hear about faro, but we do have plenty of that." Leaning forward on his elbows, the barkeep added, "I see you took a shine to Lottie over there. She deals a straight game and looks even prettier up close. Why not take a look for yourself?"

"Actually, I thought she was someone else."

"If there's another one as pretty as Lottie around here, I'd like to meet her."

The fact of the matter was that Lottie was a whole other animal compared to the redhead that had shared Doc's stagecoach into town.

"Lottie, huh?" Caleb said under his breath. "Maybe I will introduce myself."

"You want to talk to her, you gotta have a drink."

"Didn't my friend buy enough whiskey for the both of us?"

Although the barkeep didn't seem too happy about it, he soon started to nod. "Yeah, you're right. Go on ahead."

"Come to think of it, I am a little thirsty," Caleb said. "How long ago did you brew your beer?"

"Just this morning," came the practiced response. After he saw a critical glare from Caleb, the barkeep said, "Actually, you may want to try something else. This morning's batch don't exactly taste so fresh."

"Why? Because it's been sitting around for a few months?"

The barkeep didn't say anything, but he did roll his eyes just enough to answer the question.

"Thanks for the warning," Caleb said. "I'll have a whiskey."

"Coming right up."

When he got his glass full of whiskey, Caleb carried it across the room toward the faro table. He sipped the liquor and felt it burn down his throat. Once the taste hit him, it was much easier to bear when he was jostled enough for more than half of the whiskey to be spilled onto the floor.

5

Caleb fought the tide of drunks and working girls until he made it to Lottie's table. He stood there for all of two seconds before the redhead glanced up and made eye contact with him. It was worth the wait.

Lottie wore a dark green dress with a plunging neckline that displayed a generous amount of cleavage. Her skin was smooth and pale, accented here and there by the occasional freckle. She sat with perfect posture and her arms situated nicely on the table. Her lips curled into a seductive smile before parting just enough to let out a few words.

"Care to have a seat, stranger?" she asked.

"I think I'll just watch for a while," Caleb replied.

"If you're watching to check up on me, you don't have to worry. Ask anyone and they'll tell you this is an honest game."

"Maybe it's not the cards I'm watching."

Smiling as she laughed under her breath, Lottie started shuffling the cards in flowing, easy motions. "How many times have I heard that today, Earl?"

A slender man with an unkempt beard shifted in his seat next to the abacus at the corner of the table and scratched his chin. "Today? At least two. I'd say it's been a couple dozen times this week, though."

"Well, if you want to stop hearing compliments," Caleb told her, "you're going to stop looking so pretty."

Turning over the last card and settling up on the bets, Lottie grinned and shifted her eyes back to Caleb. "That wasn't as smooth, but it was newer than the rest of the lines I get around here."

"Hey, now!" blustered a gray-haired fellow who wore the dust of a weeklong ride on his face. "I take exception to that!"

"All except for Jordan," Lottie corrected. "He's got the tongue of an angel."

"And the hands of a devil," Jordan said, which elicited a round of bawdy laughter from all the other men gathered around the table. Despite all the encouragement, however, Jordan kept his hands over his money and his backside attached to his chair. His eyes, on the other hand, were glued to the pale, supple curves of Lottie's breasts.

Caleb joined in and laughed with all the rest, but also made a point of taking another look around the table. It was then that he spotted a few men who weren't laughing. In fact, those men grew more stern as more attention was being drawn to Lottie's table.

When one of those men with the sour expressions took a seat around the table, Lottie lost a bit of the warmth in her smile. It came back once she noticed that another seat had just been filled.

"Maybe I will try my luck," Caleb said as he scooted his chair up close to the table.

Lottie nodded to acknowledge all the players as she shuffled up the cards and spread them on the table. Every one of her movements flowed like steam drifting along the edge of a bathtub. When she placed the cards into the dealing box, Lottie pulled the edge of the first card out, but kept enough of it inside the box to keep the one beneath it from being seen.

"Enough with the soda," Jordan grunted, referring to that first card by its slang name. "I'm ready for the hard liquor!" To punctuate his words, he slapped down a silver dollar beneath a penny onto the ten displayed on the table.

"All that talk and you're only coppering one little bet?" Lottie asked in a sweet yet teasing voice.

"And this on the little lady to win," Jordan added as he slapped another five dollars onto the queen on the table's layout.

While this was going on, the rest of the men at the table placed their bets for what they thought would win or lose. Bets were placed on a display of the cards, all of which were shown in the suit of spades. If they thought a card would lose, they placed a copper token, or sometimes a penny, on that card. The bets came quickly and with plenty of cross talk between the gamblers before they were all stopped by a subtle wave of Lottie's hand.

Lottie pulled the soda from the box and set it aside. She then removed the next card as well and laid it beside the box. All of these motions were done with such a quick fluidity that both the card she'd removed as well as the one displayed through the rectangular hole cut in the box were revealed at approximately the same time.

The card she set next to the box was the loser. It was the five of clubs.

The card showing through the hole in the box was the winner and it was the jack of spades.

"You know I love you, Jordan," Lottie said. "But I'm going to have to take that money away."

Jordan made a show of being mad, but knew better than to make a move toward the money.

As he played that hand along with a few others, Caleb watched the way things at the table moved. He could see how players were kept on their side of the layout and how well the dealer's box and stacks of money were controlled. He also watched the frowning man at the end of the table, which was more difficult than it should have been, since Caleb wanted to keep his eye on Lottie more than anything else.

Even though the redhead never moved from her seat, her body shifted as if she were wriggling through calm waters. She tossed her hair from one shoulder to the other with little twitches of her head as she snapped the cards from the dealer's box with deft twists of her wrist. When she spoke, it was always in a luxuriant tone. When she looked at Caleb, it seemed that she was making him a sinful promise with her dark brown eyes.

As they worked their way through the deck, every man at the table tried their luck with gaining the dealer's favor. Some of the flirtations were innocent enough, while others drifted more toward heartfelt and even desperate. Lottie deflected most of them with as much skill as she used in handling the cards, and none of the exchanges ended on a harsh note.

None of them, that is, except for one.

The frowning man at the end of the table had his hands flat upon the felt and his eyes fixed upon Lottie. He hadn't even made a move toward the small pile of chips that had been pushed his way.

"What the fuck is this?" the frowning man growled.

Although the other gamblers were no strangers to such language, those words were very much out of place at that particular table. A few of the men even seemed offended.

"No need to speak to the lady like that," Jordan said.

Caleb shared that sentiment, but he knew all too well that saying as much wouldn't do a lick of good.

"It's all right," Lottie said while patting Jordan's hand. "He's just a little upset. What seems to be the problem?"

Flicking a few fingers toward his chips, the frowning man said, "This is the problem. It's short."

Lottie's brow furrowed as she went over the last several moves she'd made. Finally, she pointed out, "But you won. I paid you."

57

"You paid me, but it's not enough," the frowning man insisted. "You shorted me and I want the rest of what you owe."

"I paid you the proper amount. Just take it and if you want to win more, you should probably bet more than five dollars a hand."

"I bet fifty dollars on that hand, bitch, and you know it." Even though he hadn't taken his hands off the felt on top of the table, the frowning man took on the disposition of a wolf that had just bared its fangs.

The other men around the table could feel the tension in the air on an instinctual level.

Caleb was more concerned by how close the frowning man's hand was to the gun holstered at his side. "If you've got a problem, maybe you should take it up with me," Caleb said.

The frowning man's eyes shifted in their sockets just enough to get a look at Caleb. "And who the fuck are you supposed to be?"

"He's not a part of this," Lottie interrupted. Shifting in her seat, she squared her shoulders and fixed the frowning man with an intent gaze. "If you have a problem, you speak to me. This is my table and you know that well enough."

But Caleb and the frowning man's eyes were locked in a fierce test of wills.

The frowning man's eyes were close-set

and dark as two nuggets of charred iron. His face was a tough mask of leathery skin, which barely moved as he stared Caleb down. It normally took emotion to change a man's face that way, but there was none to be found in this man's expression.

"Whoever you are, mister, you'd be wise to let this pass. It don't concern you."

"That's right," Lottie said as she glared at Caleb. "It doesn't. This is my table," she added while shifting her gaze over to the frowning man. "Since I don't want it disturbed any longer, I'll set these matters straight right here and now."

The frowning man didn't attempt to smile, but he did take some of the edge from his glare when he said, "Finally, the voice of reason."

Caleb's first instinct was to get back into the confrontation before Lottie bit off more than she could chew. On the other hand, she seemed to know more about what was happening than he did. She also wasn't short on backup since Earl was subtly reaching for something under his section of the table.

"Any of you assholes feel like you got a wild hair up your ass, make your move now," the frowning man said. "Otherwise, back off and let me and the lady here take

59

care of our business."

Before any of the gamblers could say a word, Lottie glanced around the table and spoke in a voice that was as calm as it was convincing. "It's all right, fellas. This is just a misunderstanding. I'll take care of it and we can get right back to the cards as soon as I'm done."

That seemed to be enough to convince the men to pursue their entertainment elsewhere for the time being. Once the table had been cleared, however, one seat was still occupied.

"Go on," Lottie said to Caleb.

"Are you sure?"

She nodded and gave him another one of her promising winks. "Don't worry. I won't forget about you."

Caleb got to his feet and took one more look at the frowning man. After that, he tipped his hat and headed to the bar. There wasn't a spot open where he could still keep an eye on the faro table, so Caleb pushed aside a few drunks and made a spot for himself.

"Who's that man?" Caleb asked the barkeep.

The moment the barkeep spotted the frowning man at Lottie's table, his eyes widened and he pulled in a quick, reflexive breath. "Oh . . . I don't know."

"Don't give me that," Caleb said. "He's been waiting to stir up some shit from the moment he sat down.

"He's probably just drunk. A lot of times drunks need a while to screw up their courage."

"He's not drunk and he's not looking for any courage," Caleb said with certainty. "He's just been waiting for his opening. Now he's got it." Although he didn't want to take his eyes from the table, Caleb did just that so he could get a better look at the barkeep. "You know who he is."

"He's trouble, mister, and you're better off not knowing him. We all are," Seeing that Caleb wasn't about to back down, the barkeep sighed and said, "His name's Boyer."

"And what's his problem with Lottie?"

"It's got something to do with the game she runs. I don't know the details because I just rent her the space and take a small percentage of the winnings."

"How small?"

"Ten percent," the barkeep said in a wavering voice. After a stern, unfriendly glare from Caleb, the barkeep shifted his eyes away and added, "More like twenty percent. I swear that's all."

It was only then that Caleb realized he was starting to lean over the bar and stretch his hand toward the gun at his side. At least that explained why the barkeep had suddenly become desperate to get away from him.

"All I want is to . . ." Caleb's words trailed off as he twisted around to look back toward Lottie's table, only to find it empty. After looking around quickly, he caught a glimpse of her long red hair as she tossed it over her shoulder while making her way around a corner and into another section of the saloon. Boyer was close behind.

"What's over there?" Caleb asked.

The barkeep glanced in that direction and replied, "Just some storage space."

"Aw, hell."

6

Lottie walked with a bounce in her step and a smile on her face as she made her way through the saloon. Several of the men glanced at her to trade a few quick words, and several more glanced at her just to catch a glimpse of one of the prettiest faces in the place. She played up to every last one of them, expertly keeping at least a few people watching her as she led the way to one of the back rooms.

If Boyer noticed any of the attention she was getting, he made no indication. He was aware enough to know when nobody else was able to see her because that's precisely when he made a move of his own.

Lottie had just stepped into a small hallway that led to two doors facing each other in a cramped space. Positioning himself so he filled up most of the end of the hall, Boyer moved forward while dropping his hand to the gun at his side. Before he could clear leather, the woman in front of him wheeled around and raised a small gun of her own.

"You must truly think I'm stupid," Lottie said as she held the derringer at just above hip level. "And that, more than anything, truly pisses me off."

Boyer's hand didn't waver from its position. His expression didn't change. He didn't even stop moving forward as he said, "I don't think you're stupid. I do think you're a bit too confident for your own good. Otherwise, you would have accepted the more than generous offers you've already been given."

"Generous offers? Is that what you call them? And here I thought I was being threatened and pushed out of my business."

"Gambling isn't your business around here. If you don't know that by now, then maybe you are stupid."

"You're the stupid one if you think half of these men would drop half of the money they do if it was someone else but me dealing those cards," Lottie said.

"Which is why you were offered nearly twice the amount given to the other dealers in this town."

"If I'm gone, those gamblers will find somewhere else to go. Also, it's not like you can just kill me and dump me somewhere. I've got protection of my own, you know."

Boyer instantly picked up on the shift in Lottie's tone as well as the flicker of her eyes as she took a split second to look at something behind him. In a sudden burst of motion, he swiveled at the hip and grabbed hold of the man who'd just stepped into the hall.

With that grab, Boyer got hold of Earl's sleeve. It wasn't the best way to control another man, but Boyer tightened his grip and put enough muscle behind his movement to nearly take Earl off his feet and shove him toward one of the nearby doors. Earl's shoulder slammed hard enough against the door to force it open, revealing a cluttered supply closet filled with brooms, buckets, and extra chairs.

Even though Earl was shocked by how quickly he was pulled off balance, he managed to regain his composure just as fast. The knife he'd been carrying was almost knocked loose on impact, but he cinched his grip around it and made a quick slash with the blade.

Boyer leaned back just enough to dodge the swipe, while wearing a look on his face that barely seemed concerned with the weapon he'd so narrowly avoided. Once

Earl's hand flew by, Boyer reached out and grabbed hold of the man's shirt, pulled him forward, and then followed up with a swift knee below the belt.

Earl let out a wheezing gasp and thanked his lucky stars Boyer's knee had landed just north of his groin. Even so, the impact was enough to drive most of the wind from his lungs and cause his vision to fade for a second or two.

With everything happening so quickly, Lottie was barely able to move toward the storage closet before Earl was dropped to the floor. Standing in the doorway, she lifted her derringer to take a shot. Unfortunately, that was the very moment that Earl got enough breath to straighten up and lunge at Boyer like a charging bull.

Taking half a step back, Boyer tensed his stomach and was more than prepared to catch Earl on his way in. One arm snaked under Earl's arm while his other snagged the knife from Earl's hand. Boyer viciously pounded his knee into Earl's chin and chest again and again, until he was the only thing holding Earl up.

"I warned you, too, asshole," Boyer whispered. "Is that pussy worth dying for?" With that, Boyer flipped the blade in his hand so he could drive it into Earl's belly. Gritting his teeth, he pulled the blade through Earl's flesh until it snagged against the bottom of the man's rib cage.

Lottie stood in the doorway with her gun in hand and her jaw hanging open. When she saw the blood pour from Earl's wound to soak into the floor, she could barely keep from fainting dead away. When she saw Boyer set Earl down and then turn around to look at her, she knew she was about to experience her last moments on this earth.

A rough hand clamped down on her shoulder and nearly pulled her off her feet, but Lottie wasn't pulled into the blade that had just ended one man's life. Instead, she was pulled out of the doorway and into the hall until her shoulders knocked against the opposite door.

"Get the hell out of here," Caleb said.

That was all Lottie needed to hear. She bounced off the door and turned toward the saloon's main room. Some of the men looked away from their drinks or women long enough to show her a concerned glance, but none of them seemed to realize what had happened. Rather than explain it to them, Lottie headed for the front door.

Caleb watched her just long enough to know she was out of harm's way. From there, he was able to twist all the way back in order to clear the path for the blade that was coming straight at him.

Lunging forward to extend his arm as if his shoulder were spring-loaded, Boyer gritted his teeth and cursed under his breath the instant he realized he'd missed his target. Even before his lunge was completed, he was tensing for another strike.

Using his own momentum, Caleb continued to step back until he was able to turn and pivot all the way around. He then snapped his arm out and down like a cracking whip to make contact with Boyer's elbow. The move didn't do much damage, but it was able to wedge the incoming knife into the door right next to him.

Boyer tried once to pull the blade free, which was more than enough to realize it wasn't going anywhere. By the time he swung around to get a look at what Caleb was doing, he was just in time to see a set of rough knuckles coming straight at him.

Caleb punched Boyer in the face so hard that he knocked the frown right off him. "Jesus," he grunted while trying to shake out some of the pain that immediately flooded his hand.

After recovering from the punch, Boyer snapped his head forward to butt it against the bridge of Caleb's nose. That impact filled both men's heads with a dull roar. Boyer shook off the effects, while Caleb staggered back as though the entire floor was being tilted beneath his feet

Just as he was about to right himself, Caleb was pulled from the hall by a rough set of hands.

"That'll be enough of that!" said the burly man who was practically dragging Caleb out by the scruff of his neck. "Take this shit outside, both of you."

When he heard that last part, Caleb knew the fight wasn't over. Sure enough, a few seconds after he was tossed out the front door, Boyer came out after him. Nobody seemed to be dragging Boyer, however. The frowning man was charging out on his own steam.

Still reeling from the knock he'd taken to his nose, Caleb started to take another swing at Boyer and was cut off by a short jab to the chin. While the first shot to the nose had dimmed his lights, the punch to the chin made Caleb see nothing but red.

When Caleb reared an arm back and balled up his fist, he had every intention of taking Boyer's head off. He was so intent on that purpose that he didn't even react to the fact that Boyer had already drawn his gun. Caleb went right ahead and threw his punch. The stupidity of that move worked in his favor, since Boyer was too shocked to see it coming,

Caleb's fist slammed against Boyer's face and twisted his head around as far as it could go. He followed that up with another punch to the ribs. When that second fist landed, he felt at least one bone break against his knuckles.

Despite the pain that accompanied every breath, Boyer remained in position to deliver a definitive killing shot when he lifted his gun and pointed it directly at Caleb's midsection.

A shot cracked through the air, which made Caleb hop back and reflexively grab at his stomach. He'd seen the gun in Boyer's hand and could guess where it was aimed. There was no pain in his gut, however, and no blood on his hands when he took a quick look down. When he looked up again, he saw the redhead standing in the street with a smoking derringer in her grasp.

"Drop the gun, Boyer," Lottie said forcefully as she lowered the gun to make it clear the next shot wouldn't be aimed at the sky.

Turning so he could keep both Lottie and Caleb in his field of vision, Boyer said, "You only got one more bullet in that derringer."

"And it's got your name on it. You want it now or should I save it for later?"

Slowly, Boyer let out a breath and lowered his gun. As he shifted his eyes to get a better look at Caleb, Boyer found him squared off and staring right back at him with blood trickling from his nose.

The men regarded each other for a few seconds before Caleb's hand flashed to his holster and took his gun from its resting place. Boyer responded with a quick move of his own before they were both startled by another shot. This shot made the previous one from the derringer sound more like a champagne cork.

"Get the hell away from my place," the barkeep said as he brought down the shotgun he'd just fired in both Caleb and Boyer's direction. "That goes for both of you!"

Boyer nodded slowly and holstered his gun. Even though he could see Caleb's pistol was still in his hand, Boyer didn't seem to care too much about it. "You'll be hearing back from us, Lottie. Don't you worry about that."

Lottie watched Boyer turn his back to her and walk away. Just when her eyes narrowed and her finger started tensing around her trigger, Boyer turned a corner and shoved his way into a milling crowd of people.

Reaching out with one hand, Caleb eased her derringer down until it pointed at the ground. "Easy now."

She looked over at him with a fierceness in her eyes and dropped the derringer into a pocket that was completely hidden by a fold in her dress. "That animal is a killer."

"I know, but we can't do anything about it if we're in jail. We can do even less if that shotgun goes off right about now."

Lottie let out the breath she'd been holding and took another look at the barkeep. It seemed as if she'd just realized he was standing there. Seeing the smoking shotgun in his hand was even more of a shock to her system. "You're right," she whispered. To the barkeep, she said, "Check your storage room when you get a chance. Then come and talk to me about who should have been run out of here."

The barkeep didn't seem interested in any of it, so Caleb put his arm around Lottie's shoulders and led her in the other direction. Once they got a certain distance from the saloon, everyone else who'd been standing around lost interest in them.

"Earl might not even be found for a while," Lottie said. "Those assholes will be so busy drinking that they won't even bother to look. They didn't even bother looking in on the fight until —"

"He'll be seen to," Caleb said. "Even if I have to do it myself."

She looked into his eyes and managed a weak smile. "You shouldn't have gotten tangled up in this."

"I don't mind. Faro's not really my game."

"No, I'm serious. It was a great thing to do and I appreciate it, but the smartest thing would be for you to just forget you ever saw me."

"Way too late for that."

"Obviously you don't know who that was."

"You mean the rat who started this whole mess?"

She nodded. "If you did, you would have known better than to cross his path the way you did. Hell, I should have known better."

"If that wasn't about someone being a really sore loser, then what was it about?"

They were walking along a busy street and headed for an even busier one. The boards under their feet ranged from new and placed perfectly together to rotten and crooked. Lottie kept her head down as if she was watching every one of her steps, while Caleb tried to keep from falling on his face in front of her. People moved along on either side of them, chatting among themselves and generally adding to the bitter stench in the air.

"I hope you don't think I'm rude," Lottie finally said, "but telling you any more would just pull you in even further. After seeing what happened to the last man who tried to protect me, I'd rather just fend for myself."

"I can make my own —" Caleb started to say, but it was too late.

Lottie gave him a quick kiss and then allowed herself to be swept into a flow of people crossing the street.

7

It didn't take much for Caleb to realize that Griffin Avenue was the main street as far as saloons and entertainments were concerned. There, all manner of diversions could be found, ranging from women and gambling to anything else that would make a man's toes curl. As he made his way from one saloon to another, Caleb wondered if he would ever be able to find Doc again. He'd already given up on looking for Lottie.

Fort Griffin seemed to attract every kind of rowdiness, from some of the roughest characters Caleb had seen. And that was saying a lot considering how long he'd owned his own saloon back in Dallas. Before leaving that place, he'd heard more than a few things about Fort Griffin. Apparently, more of those stories were true than he would have guessed.

As Caleb stuck his head into more and more doors along Griffin Avenue, his blood started to cool off and the pain in his face started to fade. Then, he began seeing Fort Griffin through new eyes. Rather than seeing it as a giant, noisy haystack in which he'd lost a few needles, Caleb looked at the town from a businessman's perspective.

For a man in the saloon business, Fort Griffin was a gold mine.

It took a while for the shine to wear off, but eventually Caleb recalled one name from when he'd been tending to his own place back in Dallas: the Beehive. More than once, he'd heard that name tossed around as one of the places a man had to go if he was in Fort Griffin. At the time, Caleb had ignored those comments. Things had changed, however, and in ways he never would have guessed.

Rather than reflect on all the different turns he'd taken over the last few months, Caleb asked around until he got directions to the Beehive. All he needed to do was continue down Griffin Avenue until he found one of the rowdiest places on that main street.

While looking through the Beehive's front door, Caleb felt the hairs on the back of his neck stand on end.

". . . dead man found in a saloon," said a voice from somewhere not far from where

Caleb was standing. Although he wasn't able to catch every word of the conversation, a few phrases most definitely caught Caleb's ear.

". . . still looking for the killer" was one.

". . . string him up" was another.

Without turning to see who was talking, Caleb walked calmly into the Beehive and headed for the first table he could find that allowed him to circle around and get a look at the door without being too obvious. The saloon was crowded enough to cover his tracks until he was certain that nobody had followed him inside. Only then was he able to take a breath and get a look at where he was.

As far as saloons went, it was pretty standard fare. There was a small raised stage in the back with a pair of girls doing a dance routine being accompanied by a man playing guitar. The bar wasn't huge, but it did take up a good portion of the room. Scattered throughout the front half of the room were card tables as well as a roulette wheel and a few faro setups.

"Hell of a place, wouldn't you say?" Doc asked as he walked up to stand beside Caleb at the bar.

Caleb turned and reflexively balled his fist. "Don't sneak up on me like that, Doc."

"I was about to ask why you're so high-strung, but then I got a look at you. What on earth did you get yourself into? We've only been in town a short while. You need to pace yourself."

"I need to pace myself?" Caleb asked in disbelief. "I'm not the one who tore off like some kid at the county fair."

Doc smirked and leaned against the bar. In his hand was a cup that was big enough to hold a generous amount of drinking water. It didn't take a genius to deduce that it wasn't water inside that cup. The smell of whiskey hung around Doc's head like a fog, but it didn't affect him in any other way. In fact, he stood up a little straighter and talked with a bit more refinement than he had the last time Caleb had seen him on the street.

"I was a bit anxious, I admit," Doc said. "But you've been able to see some things around here. Haven't you felt your blood moving a bit faster just being in the middle of all this? Speaking of which, what happened to your nose?"

Caleb let out a sigh and reached up to tentatively feel the spot where he'd been hit. His hand came back bloody, so Caleb quickly cleaned himself off. "Got into a scrape over at another saloon."

"Which one?"

"I don't even know the name of the place. It was the one closest to where we were dropped off."

"Oh, that's right. You should have asked me about that place before going in there. They don't host any poker games, but I do hear that Lottie Deno runs a faro game in there."

"She does. I met her."

"I hear she's a beaut."

Smirking as he thought back to Lottie, Caleb was distracted enough from the rest of it that the pain in his nose faded for a bit. "Yeah. She sure is."

"You didn't play at her game, did you? I've told you that bucking the tiger is a sucker's bet."

"There was another man there, Doc. His name was Boyer. Ever hear of him?"

Doc's brow furrowed and he mulled that over. Finally, he shook his head and replied, "No, but it may come to me later. Why?"

"He was at her game. He killed a man in the back of that saloon. I saw it."

Suddenly patting the bar and shaking his head, Doc looked around at the other people nearby. "Don't advertise, Caleb. That is, unless you'd rather spend your first night here in a jail cell rather than a hotel room."

Since he didn't have much of an answer to that, Caleb shrugged. Suddenly, he blinked and said, "Wait a second. First night here? What about Denver?"

Doc waved that off dismissively. "There's plenty of action right here. I can feel it. Besides, Denver isn't going anywhere."

"A man's dead, Doc. Pardon me if I'm not thinking about playing cards right now."

"Who was he?"

"The lookout at Lottie's table."

"And he was killed by this Boyer person?" Doc asked.

Caleb nodded. "Stabbed. I stepped in and Boyer tried to take me out as well. We tussled and it was split up outside the place."

"Hopefully, he looks worse than you do right about now."

"This may be a joke to you, Doc, but I saw that man die and there wasn't anything funny about it."

Shaking his head, Doc said, "I don't think it's funny either. But if you want to do something about it, you can pin a badge to your chest, become some sort of vigilante, or look into it to the best of your abilities. Either way, we'll have to stay here. I won't mind lending you a hand if you need one, but a man's still got to eat. Can't you ply your new trade and fight the good fight as well?"

"I suppose so."

Doc closed his eyes and pulled in a long breath. The deeper he inhaled, the wider his smile became. When he opened his eyes again, he said, "This place reeks of opportunity. It reeks of other things as well, but it's the opportunity that interests me."

Caleb couldn't help but chuckle.

"Remember that friend I mentioned?" Doc asked.

"Oh . . . wasn't it Donaldson or something?"

"Donnelly," Doc corrected. "Owen Donnelly and he's standing right behind you."

When Caleb turned around, he saw a man of slightly more than average height and slightly heavier than average weight. Most of that weight seemed to be packed in layers around a solid frame, making it difficult to distinguish the muscle from the rest of it. The friendly nature of the man's smile was unmistakable as he gripped Caleb's hand and shook it painfully.

"Pleased to meet ya," Donnelly said.

Doing his best not to wince, Caleb said, "Likewise."

"So you're a friend of John's?"

"We've stirred up some trouble here and there," Caleb said.

That caused Donnelly's smile to grow and his handshake to speed up a bit. "He's good for that, if nothing else. I hear some of that trouble was in Dallas."

"No need to bring that up so quickly," Doc said with a definite edge in his voice.

"Can't hardly deny what I've been hearing lately."

"And what did you hear?" Caleb asked once he got his hand back and was shaking some of the blood flow back into his fingers.

"I heard John killed a man in cold blood," Donnelly said as he took a glass from under the bar, filled it with beer, and set it in front of Caleb. "But I don't believe that. At least, not the cold blood part."

"What's the matter, Owen?" Doc asked. "You don't think I can handle myself?"

"Courage was never a problem with you, John. Or should I call you Doc?"

Doc shrugged and sipped his whiskey.

"I heard there were shots thrown all over some saloon," Donnelly continued, "as well as a posse that chased you halfway across Texas and back."

For a moment, Doc and Caleb merely glanced at each other. Then, they started laughing.

"How big was this posse supposed to be?" Caleb asked.

"A dozen men."

"Why stop there? Why not make it an army?"

"So it ain't true?"

"No," Doc said. "There was no posse. That is, unless it was chasing behind the stagecoach I took from Dallas. Did you see a posse, Caleb?"

"Not as such."

"What about the man you killed in Dallas?" When he asked that question, there was a subtle shift in Donnelly's eyes. He was studying Doc carefully, as if sizing him up for the first time.

Doc didn't so much as twitch under the scrutiny. Instead, he swirled the whiskey around in his glass and said, "I'd rather not discuss such matters at length. I've already stood trial for the disruption and beat the charges, so I'd rather not push what little luck I have. I will say that there is some truth to the rumors you've heard."

"Just like them black fellas you killed around that watering hole back home, huh?"

Caleb started to laugh at that, but saw that Doc was nowhere close to laughing. The smile he already had on his face was stale as month-old bread, but was tapered and controlled so it didn't give away much of anything on the subject at hand.

"I'd rather not talk about that, either," Doc said.

Whether or not he picked up on Doc's sudden discomfort, Donnelly moved on to the next subject without skipping a beat. "Speaking of back home, how's Mattie?"

"I don't really talk much to the family any longer." Glancing up from his whiskey, Doc fixed a stare on his face that would have split a boulder in half. "And I'd appreciate it if you didn't talk about them, either."

"Just trying to catch up, John," Donnelly said as he raised his hands. "Maybe you should let me know what you do want to talk about."

Doc nodded and slipped right back into his normal, easygoing mannerisms. "To put any other rumors to rest, I'm still sick as hell and fiercely averse to the evil temptations of the flesh. Now let's talk about more current matters."

Looking at the whiskey in Doc's hand and the natural way he fit into the atmosphere of the saloon, Donnelly slapped the top of the bar and began laughing boisterously. "You always were a hoot, John. Tell you what, I'll call you Doc just as soon as you help me with this pain I got in the back of my jaw."

"And I'll fix you up for no charge whatsoever if you allow me to set up a faro table in this saloon."

Donnelly blinked and cocked his head to one side. "You sure you want to do that? It can be pretty rough sometimes."

"I realize that. It was fairly rough in Dallas, as well."

"True. Still, I'd rather not have any killings in my place if you can help it."

"I can handle myself, Owen. Right now, I just need to get a start in my new profession."

"No more pulling teeth?" Donnelly asked.

"Only on special occasions." When he saw that his joking tone was no longer bringing a smile to Donnelly's face, Doc added, "I'm a sporting man now. Just give me some time at my own game and I'll start turning a profit for you."

"I don't run no crooked games here."

Doc scowled enough to make the barkeep start to squirm.

"Well . . . you know what I mean," Donnelly amended.

"Yes, I do. And any complaints you get in that regard will be handled by me and will not put a smudge upon this establishment."

Pulling in a breath, Donnelly rubbed his

chin and grumbled to himself. "We go back a little ways, John. I'd hate to have you get hurt on account of this. Especially since you're not in the best condition. No offense or nothing."

The look on Doc's face showed that he took plenty of offense from the inference that had just been made.

"Then again," Donnelly said, "if you had your own security, I might reconsider the offer."

Before Doc could say anything, Caleb nodded and said, "He's got it."

"And you know how to handle yourself?"

Shifting so his hand drifted toward the gun holstered at his side, Caleb nodded once more. "That posse couldn't bring me in, so I think I should be able to handle watching over a faro game."

Although Doc was close to smirking, he held back long enough to see how Donnelly would respond. Amazingly enough, the barkeep was nodding with more and more confidence. "I can only pay five dollars a shift to start. That goes for each of you."

"And when the profits justify it, I hope the rate will go up accordingly?" Doc asked.

"If you bring in enough, I can raise the rates," Donnelly agreed. "But I don't care how far we go back, I won't tolerate anything that makes my place look bad."

"Of course," Doc said. "And what about poker games? Will I be able to organize a few of those?"

"You'll need to use one of my dealers, but I do allow men to deal their own cards for friendly games. I got no problem with poker just so long as you kick back a piece of that action as well." Donnelly leaned against the bar and stared both men dead in the eyes. "I ain't stupid, so don't treat me like a fool. You want to make a living playing cards, you best know that it ain't a life with any guarantees and it ain't the sort of place where friendship amounts to much."

Doc extended a hand over the bar and said, "That's why I came to speak with you, Owen. You're someone I can learn from."

"Save it until you been livin' that life awhile, John. Maybe by then, you'll curse me for letting you into this line of work."

"I'm gambling every day I step outside," Doc said. "I might as well start making some money off it."

Finally, Donnelly's smile returned. "I suppose so. All right, then. You can set up at the table in the back over there. That way I can say I didn't see whatever bullshit you're trying to pull if some angry cowboys come my way looking to complain. It'll be open in a few hours."

"That will give me some time to get situated. I truly appreciate this."

Donnelly turned and walked off. The moment he started talking to one of his customers, he regained his cheery disposition and began telling loud jokes as if he were celebrating rather than working.

"And I do appreciate what you did," Doc said without meeting Caleb's eyes. It took some effort, but Doc eventually looked at Caleb directly. "If you could act as lookout for a few days, that would be fine. After that, I should have gained enough trust for —"

"A few days, my ass," Caleb interrupted. "You said we worked well together, so that's what we're going to do."

"And here I thought you were bent out of shape about not heading to Denver."

"Denver's not going anywhere," Caleb replied. "And this place has potential. I can feel it."

Doc chuckled and lifted his glass. "You've got good instincts. I've even thought of a few good ways for us to make even more than five dollars a shift."

"Yeah. I've had a few ideas of my own."

8

One of the few things Doc had brought with him from Dallas was his faro setup. The case was waiting for him at the stagecoach office, where it had been left when the driver finally headed off to Denver, and was small enough to have been missed by nearly everyone on that stage. Caleb didn't know how long the driver had waited or if he'd waited at all, but it seemed more than a little fortuitous that the one item was waiting for them when they checked for it at the station.

Since Donnelly provided a room for each of them at a sorry excuse for a boarding-house not far from the Beehive, Caleb and Doc didn't need much money those first few days in Fort Griffin. Both of them quickly realized they were missing something very important to a professional gambler, however: a reputation.

Nobody knew Caleb from Adam and what

little they knew about Doc revolved around the increasingly wild rumors that were coming out of Dallas. Reports had Doc doing everything from shooting a group of Indians full of holes to being chased down by the same posse Donnelly had mentioned.

Doc took it all in stride, denying whatever rumors he didn't like and embellishing a few that would help ease him into the gamblers' circles. The next few weeks passed fairly quietly as Doc and Caleb settled into the lives of sporting men. While Doc perfected his shuffle and card-handling skills, Caleb became acquainted with the people he considered to be his competition.

As he studied names and faces, Caleb kept on the lookout for one face in particular. It wasn't too long before he spotted that pretty face on Griffin Avenue.

"Lottie!" Caleb shouted. When he saw her glance his way, he waved at her and crossed the street.

She met him with open arms and quickly pressed her soft lips against his in a way that nearly stole all the breath from Caleb's lungs. Even after she'd ended the kiss, Lottie held him at arm's length as if she didn't want to let him go.

"If it isn't Caleb Wayfinder," she said. "Aren't you a sight for sore eyes!"

"You remember my name?" Caleb asked, thinking back to if he'd introduced himself fully or not.

"I've been hearing about you and Doc Holliday. I've heard even more about the game you two run."

"Hope you're not taking any losses because of it."

Lottie nudged him with her elbow and stepped back so Caleb could get a full look at the way her black satin dress hugged her hips and wrapped around her body like a tangle of expensive sheets. "Doc may know his way around a card table, but I've got assets of my own."

"That you do, Lottie. That you do."

"Sorry I haven't tracked you down, but I didn't know you were going to stay in town after what happened the last time we met. Once I started hearing about you working at the Beehive, I found myself engaged in some business of my own."

"Nothing dangerous, I hope."

"Not too bad, but not too good either," she said with a wink.

"Did they ever find the asshole who killed Earl?"

She shook her head and continued walking along the side of the street. The sun was on its way down, which marked the time of day that had started to become like dawn to Caleb and Doc. As with most other gamblers, it was the time when work started and the real customers started to show their faces. The last time Caleb had seen an actual sunrise was at the tail end of a forty-eight-hour-long poker game.

"Aren't you worried he might come back?" Caleb asked.

"He may or he may not."

"If he does, you should have someone looking out for you."

"Someone like you?" Lottie asked.

"Maybe."

"I thought you had your hands full keeping Doc out of trouble."

"Doc can handle himself," Caleb said. "Besides, I'd much rather look at you than at him."

She smiled at the compliment and then tucked it away with all the others she'd gotten during her walk down the street that evening. "You're sweet, Caleb, but I can take care of myself, too, you know."

"All right then. Do you play poker?"

"Does the sun set in the west?"

"How about you come by the Beehive when it sets tomorrow?"

Lottie stopped so she could turn and square her shoulders to Caleb. Even though

Caleb had thought about her more than once, he was still surprised by how good she looked just then. Every move she made was a show and every shift of her feet got the rest of her body wriggling in an almost sinful way.

"I had plans for tomorrow, but I'll see what I can do about canceling them," she said.

"If there's anyone else you'd like to bring along, feel free."

"The more, the merrier, huh?"

"That's the idea."

"I'll try to make it, Caleb. I truly will. In the meantime, would you like to have a drink with me? I've got a bit of time before I need to open my table."

It took every bit of strength that Caleb could muster for him to shake his head and say, "Not right now. There's some errands I need to run."

"Picking up Doc's laundry?"

"If you're trying to get that invitation revoked, you're on the right path."

She showed him a pouting lip before mouthing the words "I'm sorry." After that, Lottie blew him a kiss and headed down Griffin Avenue toward the saloon where Caleb had first laid eyes on her.

After watching her go for as long as he

could without actually following her, Caleb reminded himself of why he'd been out and about at that particular moment. Despite the more practical side of his brain nagging at him to move along, Caleb took another lingering glance in Lottie's direction and then put his nose back to the grindstone.

Although he'd been in Fort Griffin for a little while now, Caleb still didn't know the saloons by name. Even considering how often he made the rounds visiting each and every one of them, there were still too many for all of them to rank equally in his mind. If he picked a favorite other than his base of operations, he might be tempted to start taking some of the offers he'd been getting to work there and not the Beehive.

Also, not knowing those other places by name made it a whole lot easier to steal from them.

Caleb's first stop was a place he'd labeled Red in his mind simply because of the color of the walls inside. After nodding to several of the regulars, Caleb got a few dollars in hand and walked between the roulette wheel and a faro game. As he went from one to the other, he managed to snatch at least two chips off each table, pocket them, and then fuss about with placing a bet using his own money.

Most of the money he got was from care-less gamblers, but the roulette spinner made the mistake of talking to a serving girl for a few seconds too long, which gave Caleb an opening he couldn't resist. Just to look like he belonged, Caleb placed a bet and actually won another couple of dollars before cashing in all his chips and moving on.

The next place he hit was an out-of-the-way shit hole at the west end of town. Caleb liked it because it was the first place a lot of cowboys saw when they were done turning over their cattle. Caleb stood at his favorite spot at the edge of a faro bank and waited.

Sure enough, it wasn't too long before two dirt-faced cowboys got on each other's bad side and started tossing obscenities back and forth. But short-tempered cowboys were harder to predict than the weather, and sooner rather than later, they were slapping each other on the back and laughing once more. Before they could get too close, Caleb tossed a log onto the dying fire by saying, "What did you just call him?"

"I didn't call him nothing," one cowboy replied.

"Oh, you must have been talking to your friend again."

"What?" the second cowboy snarled.

"What the hell did you say to me?"

From there, it was a short road back to another fight. This time, it came to a few blows before either of the cowboys stopped to think about why they were even fighting. By that time, Caleb had used the distraction to help himself to a few dollars off the top of the banker's stack and made his way out the door.

"Too rough for me in here," Caleb said as he left.

Even though he was still feeling lucky, Caleb went back to the Beehive and met up with Doc at a table near their faro spot.

"You make the rounds?" Doc asked.

Caleb's reply was emptying his pockets of over a hundred dollars in folded up or wadded bills. "I nearly got spotted at a few places."

"It's my turn next, so I'll keep my eyes open." Wincing, Doc hacked into his hand and tried to pass it off as if he were just clearing his throat. "If too many people are watching, we can lay off the skimming for a while. This was a good idea, by the way. I'm just surprised you came up with it."

"Why? Because only you get to hatch every scheme we pull?"

"No," Doc replied. "As a former saloon owner, I'd have thought you would have more loyalty to your fellow businessmen."

"You don't seem to have any trouble stealing from other gamblers," Caleb pointed out.

"Point well taken."

"Besides, I learned my best lessons through making mistakes. These saloon owners will either get smarter or find another business they're better suited for." After finishing counting up the money, Caleb added, "Looks like we've got enough to stake us both in our upcoming game."

"A stake can never be too big. And we need to win big if we're going to make a name for ourselves. Otherwise, we won't get much farther than Fort Griffin."

"Seems like we've already got a name around here."

Doc nodded as he used one hand to hold a deck of cards and flip one from the top, to the bottom and back again. "Things are coming along, but that's only because of the small size of this place. Word travels quickly."

When Doc fanned the cards onto the table, Caleb reached out and selected one. "That's not the only thing adding to what folks are saying. More than once, I've heard of an incident at a swimming hole when you were a boy."

The shift on Doc's face was barely notice-able to the commoner's eye, but caught Caleb's attention like a flare from the sun. Oddly enough, the small coughing fit that followed slid right under Caleb's notice. "The only reason I mentioned that was to establish a foothold," Doc said.

"A foothold in what?" Caleb asked as he showed the card he'd taken to be the five of diamonds.

After clearing his throat loudly, Doc fanned the cards once more and pointed to them. Caleb slipped his card in with the rest so Doc could gather them up and shuffle. "You saw the way Owen looked at me. He saw an invalid standing in front of him. A walking dead man. I needed to give him cause to think otherwise."

"That's not the first time I've heard that story, Doc." Once more, the cards were laid down and Caleb selected one. He flipped it over to once again show the five of dia-monds. With another flip of his wrist, he produced another card he'd palmed and tossed it on top of the rest.

Doc nodded approvingly. "You're getting a lot better, but mechanics are just another tool of the trade. So is padding the truth from time to time in order to put certain people's minds at ease." Shuffling the cards in three different ways before fanning them out as if he were putting on a show, Doc said, "There was a bit of trouble at a swimming hole back in Georgia. I barely even recall what happened, since it was so close to nothing at all and I wasn't more than a boy at the time. A few colored kids were flapping their gums and I was flapping mine even more. We scuffled as boys are known to do and I took it further than it should have gone."

"You killed one of them?"

"Lord, no," Doc replied with a subtle laugh. "I fired a shot over their heads, they ran off, and that was that. To be honest, I believe we ran into each other a few times after that and conducted ourselves with a bit more respect for one another, as boys are also known to do."

"Yeah," Caleb said as he skillfully palmed the five of diamonds while taking another card. He then showed the five and replaced the hidden card into the deck. "Waving a gun around will do that."

As he laughed, Doc gazed down at the table wistfully. "I was sent off to live with an uncle after that and forgot about it. That is, I forgot until it came up again in various bloated forms of retelling. Since it seemed to garner some bit of respect from certain sorts of crowds, I stopped discouraging it. The way I see it, we're already well on our way to building a reputation that has nothing to do with exaggerated exploits from a dubious youth."

"You're right about that. I ran into Lottie today and she accepted an invitation to our game. She accepted pretty quickly."

"Was she where I told you she would be?"

Caleb nodded. "And at the time you said. Just like clockwork."

"Good. The gambling circuit is tough to break into, but well worth the effort. You must show yourself to be wheat and not chaff."

"A professional and not a sucker, you mean?"

Doc grinned and nodded. "Exactly. And once we're in the proper circles, my guess is that we won't have to track down that killer who crossed your path on our first day in this fine town."

"I haven't heard a damn thing about him since then," Caleb said with a steely tone in his voice. "And it's like Earl never even existed. He got half a sentence in the obituaries, a pauper's burial, and that was that."

"The matter is not resolved, I assure you. It's just a matter of patience," Doc said as he flipped over the top card to reveal the five of diamonds, "and waiting for the proper time to make a move."

Caleb twitched and immediately took the card he thought he'd replaced and flipped it over. It was the nine of clubs. "Dammit," he said under his breath.

"You're getting better," Doc said with a grin. "Just keep practicing."

9

It was ten o'clock the next morning when someone knocked on Doc's door. The sound was just enough to make it through the flimsy wood, but not quite loud enough to make it through the fog that filled Doc's head at the moment. When the knock came again, it was strong enough to rattle the door on its hinges.

"Come in before I start shooting through that door," Doc snarled.

The door opened, allowing Doc's nose to immediately pick up on the smell of potatoes, cooked buffalo meat, and something else that put a fond spark in his eyes.

"Did someone finally hunt down some grits?"

The man holding the tray of food stepped in and set the tray down on the small table normally reserved for a washbasin. He took a quick survey of the room using intent, close-set eyes and then shut the door behind him.

Doc sat on the edge of his bed, wearing trousers and an undershirt. He held a newspaper in his hands, but lowered it when he saw that the man was still in the room. "Is it fair to assume you're not just here to deliver my breakfast?"

"Yes, Holliday. It is."

After lowering the paper, Doc asked, "And would it also be fair to assume your name is Boyer?"

The surprise on Boyer's face registered as something slightly more than a twitch in the corner of one eye. He twitched again when he noticed the gun holstered beneath Doc's arm.

"You're not the only one who remembers a name or two," Doc said. "Since you didn't pay for that food, why don't you step aside so that I may indulge myself?"

"Be my guest," Boyer said as he clasped his hands like a preacher and stepped to one side. "I hope you don't mind a little company while you eat."

"A guest who doesn't expect to be fed? What better situation is there?"

"A better situation for you would be to pay your dues like the rest of the gamblers in Fort Griffin before some bad luck befalls you."

Doc crossed his room in less than two full steps and took the fork from the side of the plate. He cut off a hunk of tough buffalo meat, dipped it in some of the grits, and wolfed it down. "Bad luck? Oh, you mean like the luck that was dumped on the head of Lottie Deno's unfortunate lookout?"

Without a flinch or even a spark of emotion, Boyer said, "You're a smart man, Holliday. Is it true you used to be a dentist back in Dallas?"

"And other places. I've been looking around for a spot to hang my shingle here, but these cowboys don't seem to be concerned with oral hygiene."

Boyer couldn't help but smirk at the thought of any one of the dirty cowpokes squirming in a dentist's chair. "You're not like the other men I talk to, Holliday. You seem to have a head on your shoulders that's good for something other than counting cards."

"Why, thank you."

"Because you seem like a friendly sort, I'll pay you the compliment of being honest with you. The people I represent take a piece from all the gambling operations in Fort Griffin as well as many other spots on the circuit. Some might say that we're the reason there even is a circuit."

"I've always wondered about that," Doc said as he continued eating his breakfast. In between bites, he poured some of the contents of his own flask into the cup of coffee that had already been sitting at his bedside.

Boyer nodded, picking up on the smugness in Doc's tone and not approving of it one bit. "By keeping on our good side, gamblers like yourself can set up shop in saloons, run things the way you see fit, and conduct your business with a minimal amount of trouble from the law."

"How generous."

"All we ask in return is a small percentage of your profits."

"And when there are no profits?" Doc asked.

"A small fee, which many consider to be the simple price of thriving within your chosen profession. Other folks pay their taxes and such. There's no reason why you should be any different."

Doc's eyes widened as he got to his feet and straightened up. "Oh! You're a representative of the government? I did not realize, sir. I do try to keep up on paying taxes and the like. After all, it is what keeps this grand country of ours —"

"I've allowed you a certain amount of

slack due to your condition," Boyer interrupted. "But don't think, for one moment, that I will extend you such a courtesy if you try my patience."

Doc kept right on eating his breakfast and sipping his coffee.

"Do you want to make a name for yourself on the circuit?" Boyer asked.

"That's the idea."

"Then you'll have to abide by the rules. You pay us five percent of your profits, which will be collected on a monthly basis."

"And I just hand over the money to yourself or someone else who claims to be collecting a gambler's tax?"

"You'll know us because we'll claim to represent the Tiger."

"How colorful."

Boyer nodded without a hint of humor. "When you hear that, you'll pay what you owe or you won't be allowed to run a game or play in one that's anything more than gin rummy dealt in a sewing circle."

By this time, Doc had continued eating while also managing to get himself situated so the table was between him and Boyer. Within the confines of that cramped room, it made him feel a whole lot better.

"I suppose everyone pays this outrageous fee?" Doc asked.

"In time, the tributes can be lowered. That is, if you prove to be worthy of such a consideration. If you have a particularly fruitful month, we'll accept less than our percentage."

"Just so long as you get more than normal on those months," Doc pointed out.

"We're not being unreasonable, Dr. Holliday. Merely requesting a fee for a valuable service. Within our good graces, you'll find it a whole lot easier to get into games or even open your own in practically every saloon on the circuit.

"Fall out of our graces," Boyer added, "and we'll see to it that your name is uttered in the same breath as words such as amateur, untrustworthy, poor cheater, and high risk. Things like that won't bode well for a sporting man's career."

"Ironic, but true."

"So, do we have a deal?"

Doc sipped his coffee and let the whiskey-soaked brew roll around in his mouth as he furrowed his brow thoughtfully. After setting the cup down, he picked up his plate and moved some of the food around. He set that down as well, but not on the table.

"A man doesn't get a good reputation by having vermin like yourself speaking on his behalf," Doc said.

"And I suppose lying about your own exploits is any better?"

"At least I'm making my own way."

"A very short way if you make the wrong decision right now."

Nodding as a bit of fire glinted in his eyes, Doc said, "Let's find out, shall we?"

With that, Doc bent at the knees and slapped his left hand against the bottom of the table. As the table upended and landed noisily on its side, he dropped down behind it while making a quick grab for the pistol holstered under his arm.

Boyer was caught off his guard by the sudden move, but was quick to react in response to it. While dropping to one knee, Boyer drew his own pistol and fired a quick shot at Doc. The gunfire exploded within the little room and punched a hole through the table directly in front of him.

Doc could feel the lead whip past his knee after it had cut through the table like warm butter. He'd cleared leather by now and fired a shot of his own, which chipped off a healthy chunk of wood as it tore through the edge of the tabletop. Rather than pick his next shot with the same patience Boyer was displaying, Doc focused his gaze on his target and pointed his gun as if he were pointing his own finger.

Three more shots blasted through the room.

One of them came from Boyer as he straightened up to shoot over the table.

The next two came from Doc, both of which drew blood.

For a moment, Boyer stood his ground and blinked a few times in quick succession. He kept hold of his gun, but wasn't quite able to raise his arm enough to point it at the slender man who now walked calmly around the table.

As the burnt black powder drifted into his nose, Doc felt it irritate the tender strip at the back of his throat. When he started coughing, it seemed as if he wouldn't be able to stop until the taste of blood welled up on the back of his tongue.

"This is precisely the sort of thing . . . my physician warned against," Doc said in between vicious coughs.

As Boyer dropped to his knees, he reached with his free hand to his own bloody torso. There was a blackened spot on his side, but it was the dark pool of blood soaking into his gut that concerned him even more. When he took his next breath, it was accompanied by a powerful, jabbing pain.

While keeping his gun trained on Boyer, Doc reached out with his free hand to take hold of the coffee that he'd saved by placing it on the edge of his bed. He sipped it and let out a relieved breath as the warm, liquor-laced brew went down his throat. "I'm a great admirer of irony. Considering the facts, I'd say it's ironic that you're on the floor coughing while I'm still on my feet."

Boyer tried to get up, but the effort of doing so brought another agonizing stab into his gut. When he dropped down, he landed with his hand pressing down on top of his gun just to keep from falling over.

"And considering what I've heard about what you did to Miss Deno's lookout," Doc continued, "this becomes ironic on another level."

"Shut . . . up," Boyer snarled through gritted teeth.

Doc holstered his gun and squatted so he could get down to Boyer's level. "Tell me more about this Tiger," he said while calmly taking Boyer's gun out from under his trembling hand.

"You're a . . . dead . . . man."

"I knew that already. Tell me something else."

"You won't . . . get away . . . with this."

As Boyer said that, Doc heard footsteps and excited voices outside his room. He stepped over the fallen man and glanced

110

out into the hall. After stepping out for a minute or so, Doc returned and grabbed hold of Boyer under both arms.

"You're going across the hall," Doc said as he dragged the man out the door. Fortunately for him, his words and actions were enough to get Boyer kicking and struggling again. That kicking made it a little easier for Doc to move the man the short distance from one room to the other. Even though Boyer was fairly slight of build, the effort of dragging him brought a layer of sweat to Doc's brow.

"Tell me whatever you need to tell me," Doc said. "In my professional opinion, you haven't much time left."

Boyer was glancing around in disbelief. Judging by the look in his eyes, he was having just as much trouble accepting that he'd been shot as he was in believing who'd shot him. "There are . . . others . . ."

"How many others?" Doc asked.

The footsteps outside were getting closer as the folks inside the boardinghouse were gathering enough courage to approach the spot where they'd heard the shots.

Doc stepped across the room to the window and pushed it open. It wasn't until then that he spotted the saddlebags propped in one corner and the dirty shirt crumpled near the bed.

"Who's your connection with the law?" Doc asked. "Who's the crooked one wearing the badge?"

Boyer shifted and looked at Doc with confusion as more and more of the color drained from his face.

Once it was obvious that no more shots were forthcoming, the owner of the boardinghouse made her way up the stairs and down the narrow hall. She was a lady in her early sixties and had eyes that rarely missed a thing. She didn't make ends meet, however, by pointing those sharp eyes too long in the direction of the people who were put up in her rooms by the saloon owners. Of course, she wasn't about to be a party to murder, either.

"Hello?" she called down the hall. "Were those gunshots?"

She knocked on one door and then another while working her way down the hall. Most of her boarders had fled, but she knew it would take an act of God to get the blond consumptive out of his room before noon. Before she could knock on his door, she saw it come open and Doc stick his head out.

He wore a baffled expression as he asked, "Who's renting that room?"

"Some young man in on a cattle drive," she replied.

"I don't know what he's up to, but those noises came from in there. Stand aside, ma'am," Doc said as he stepped into the hall and placed his hand on his holstered Colt. "Better let me see to this."

Boyer was nothing but a husk, and Doc did a fairly good job of acting surprised at having found him.

10

Doc was paler than normal as he walked into the Beehive later that afternoon. The summer was quickly approaching, turning the air into a thick, warm stew. It was a hard day for most folks to bear, but Doc took the change of seasons a little harder than most. He was wheezing and hacking into his handkerchief so much that he could hardly take a breath.

"Jesus, Doc," Caleb said as Doc made his way to their usual table. "You look like hell."

"And yet, I still manage to outperform you at making the rounds." As he said that, Doc reached into his pocket and removed a bundle of cash that was nearly the size of his fist.

"You take more risks than I do," Caleb pointed out. "You always do that when you're feeling your worst."

"Spare me the bargain diagnoses."

Without needing so much as a wave from

either of the men, a dark-haired serving girl brought over drinks for them. "Plenty of people asking about the game tonight," she said while setting a beer down in front of Caleb and a bottle of whiskey in front of Doc. "We haven't hardly heard about anything else."

Keeping his eyes locked on Doc, Caleb said, "That's good. Especially since there's been plenty more going on."

"Really?" she asked. "Like what?"

"I don't know. Why don't you ask Doc? He's been around more action than I have."

Nudging Caleb and winking, she said, "That's not what I heard."

Doc glanced up at Caleb and laughed under his breath. "Now, this is something I do want to hear."

Caleb peeled off some of the money from the stack on the table and handed it to the girl. She took it and pranced away without so much as acknowledging the question that had yet to be answered.

"Like what?" Doc asked with a vague impression of the girl in his voice. "Tell me all about it."

"After you tell me about the man you killed in your boardinghouse."

As he took hold of the bottle, Doc reached into his pocket and removed a small, dented cup with a bent handle. "She always remembers the bottle, but never the glass."

"Don't change the subject, Doc. Who was it?"

"Some fellow by the name of Boyer." When he saw the look of surprise that had sprung onto Caleb's face, Doc said, "Oh, I see you've heard of him."

"The same Boyer that killed Earl?"

"I didn't get around to asking as much, but I'd say that's fairly safe to assume."

"How'd you find him?"

"I didn't. He found me."

Since it was easy enough to see that Caleb was bursting at the seams to hear the whole story, Doc didn't wait any longer to tell it. He gave a short yet accurate account of the confrontation while counting up the money he'd stolen and splitting it up between them. When he was done, he'd already found a deck of cards and was practicing his fancy shuffles.

Caleb leaned back in his chair to digest what he'd heard. "The Tiger?" he asked. "Are you sure you heard that right?"

"Dramatic, to be certain, but that is what he said."

"You think he was right about the gamblers being taxed?"

Doc nodded, split the deck in half, and

practiced manipulating the cards in both his left and right hand simultaneously. "I asked around about that very subject as I visited the other saloons. I even went to a few places that we don't usually pay much attention to. We should start going to that place by the opium den. It may be dirty, but the dealers do a piss-poor job of watching their —"

"The taxes," Caleb said to get Doc back on track. "What did they say about the taxes?"

"They said just what Boyer claimed they would. Apparently, the professionals either kick some back to this Tiger person directly or they chip in to a pool that's held by the saloon owner. Doing the latter makes it easier to fudge some of the numbers." Shaking his head, Doc mused, "Isn't it amazing how many ways there are to steal the same bit of money?"

Caleb leaned back and ran his fingers through his uneven hair. "And you're sure he's dead?"

"Oh, yes. I checked on it myself. My specialty may be dentistry, but I know a corpse when I see one. On that same note, he did have excellent teeth."

"How long before the law shows up?"

"About Boyer? They already made their

appearance."

"What?" Caleb asked with a start. "When?"

"A deputy or two came by the boarding-house and asked what sort of noises I heard and what I was doing. I gave as accurate an account as I could, since I was eating breakfast in my room after just waking up at the time."

Caleb couldn't help but admire the way Doc spoke those words without the first hint that he was lying. Then again, that same quality also worried him about the man. "And they bought that?" he asked.

"Oh yes," Doc said with a nod. "To tell you the truth, they seemed rather relieved to have it wrapped up so neatly for them. Perhaps they didn't take too kindly to being shoved around by that miserable asshole, any more than I did. Although, I couldn't help but think about those others that Boyer was talking about."

"You mean the Tiger?"

"Precisely. If what he's saying is true, there must be plenty more where Boyer came from, and they still may pose a problem. Then again," Doc added with a sideways glance in Caleb's direction, "they might also prove to be our way directly inside the very circuit we've been trying to break into."

"Gamblers will gamble with anyone, Doc," Caleb said with a sigh. "And the circuit is just a bunch of saloons favored by the gamblers at the top of the heap. All we need to do is follow the track and we're set."

"That's a saloon owner talking. That's years of you trying to get your place favored by those gamblers."

"Is it?"

"A man can follow the track and go to all the spots on the circuit, but that doesn't mean he'll be invited to all the biggest games or even be regarded as an equal by the others on that very same circuit. It takes experience and a certain word of mouth to gain that sort of respect."

Caleb looked at Doc and then asked, "When did you figure all of this out? We've been making the same rounds and playing cards for a living for the same amount of time."

"Apparently, I've been doing a better job of watching how the rest of the sporting men in this town operate. I also stay awake for the end of more of the longer poker games than you do, which you desperately need to work on, by the way. You'd be amazed at what bits of wisdom you get when someone's too tired to keep from saying too much."

"They probably assume you're too drunk to remember any of it," Caleb pointed out. "Most mortal men would be."

Taking a silver dollar from his vest pocket, Doc began rolling it over the backs of his fingers as he said, "I'd like to see how many people pay tribute to this Tiger. Even if the system is half the size of what Boyer was boasting, it's still something to be considered. I know for a fact that there are at least two other spots on the circuit where collections are made."

"How do you know that?"

"It was a final confession from Boyer himself."

There was no mistaking the tone in Doc's voice. He was dead serious. Caleb would have bet his own life on that.

"What other towns pay the tax?" Caleb asked.

"Cheyenne and Denver. It's hard to say how deep it runs, but plenty of others in our chosen field know about it. That means they would also know when the taxes no longer had to be paid."

Having leaned forward to catch every word Doc was saying, Caleb had a ways to go when he dropped back against his chair once more. "Are you talking about hunting these men down?"

"Nothing quite so dramatic," Doc said with a shrug. "Just butting heads with a few of them until they back down." When he met Caleb's disbelieving stare, Doc had a fiery glint in his eyes. "The best outcome possible would be putting this Tiger out of business. The worst would be staring these extortionists in the face and telling them where to stuff their taxes."

Shaking his head, Caleb said, "No, the worst would be us marching up to the wrong man and getting shot full of holes for our troubles."

"Either way, don't you think we'd gain some amount of respect with everyone on the circuit? If I've learned anything so far, it's that a man's reputation will follow him to the grave. In this line of work, respect gets us invited to the real money games. It allows us to operate wherever we please and, depending on how we play it up, it can put people off their guard or on their toes as we see fit. If you can't see the promise in all of that, then you have no business gambling for a living."

Caleb shook his head. "These men are killers, Doc. Going up against one or two is one thing, but going up against a whole gang of them is another. Before you declared war on them, maybe you should have thought about anyone else who might have gotten pulled into it. Just because you're in a race to die doesn't mean the rest of us are."

Even as those words came out, Caleb felt the pang of regret stabbing straight down into his chest And, no matter how true they were, he felt like an ass for saying them out loud.

Doc simply raised his eyebrows and kept rolling the silver dollar along the backs of his fingers. "You can join in on this or not," he said plainly. "All I'm telling you is the benefits for doing so."

"I've learned plenty in my experience," Caleb said without as much of an edge in his tone. "And one thing for certain is that there's always someone out there who's better than you. That doesn't mean you should run away from it, but that also doesn't mean you should ride straight into it."

The next few moments ticked by like hours. In that time, Caleb didn't hear the other conversations going on around him or any of the other various sounds that filled a saloon at any time of day. All he heard was the ring of that silver dollar as it knocked against Doc's knuckles before making another pass along the back of his hand.

Finally, Doc ended the silence by asking,

"Have you slept with Lottie yet?"

Caleb had to pause and wonder if he'd truly heard those words. When he couldn't decide for certain, he asked, "What did you say?"

"Anyone can see the spark between you, but if you intend on making a move on her, you'd best do it quickly. I hear she has a weakness for roguish gamblers who know their way around a tooth extractor."

As the laugh built up in the back of Caleb's throat, it seemed to push out all of the tension that had been building inside of him. Doc quickly gave in as well, and when the laughter was over, things were back to normal between them.

No apologies were needed.

"Whatever hell there is to be caught for Boyer's death will land on my shoulders," Doc said. "You were nowhere to be found, so your name shouldn't come up."

"That's some real dandy logic," Caleb said sarcastically.

"You could always go and complain to the law about their lack of interest. Just give me enough warning so I can put on clothes more suitable for laying on a cot in a cell."

"I was thinking more along the lines of thanking you. Even though I would have preferred to kill that asshole myself, I'm glad it got done."

Flipping the silver dollar into his other hand, Doc tipped his hat and said, "Don't mention it . . . please. Gaining notoriety may have its advantages, but being hung for murder isn't one of them."

"The law can't be done with this so quickly," Caleb said. "Even if they did want him out of the way, there's got to be repercussions."

"Perhaps more questions would have been asked if it was someone more respectable laying on that floor. As it was, the law seemed fairly relieved to find who they did. At the very least, they weren't surprised."

"And they didn't ask around for the whereabouts of the folks who weren't in their rooms?"

"Maybe you're not cut out for a sporting life, Caleb. You worry too much."

"Just waiting for someone to come looking for the guilty accomplice."

"No accomplices were needed this time."

"What about at tonight's game?"

"Now, there's a different story," Doc said. "We have some planning to do in that regard."

11

Owen Donnelly was more than happy to host the poker game at the Beehive, since it was being held on a regularly slow night. While the roulette wheel was seeing its fair amount of action, most of the customers were lounging in the back where they could watch a trio of can-can girls kicking up their skirts to show the lacy underthings they wore beneath them. As the night wore on, the girls would be wearing even less under those skirts, which always drew more of a crowd.

Caleb stood at the front door, where he could spot the invited players and direct them to the proper table. Leaning against the bar with a well-practiced smile on his face made him think back to his days running the Busted Flush. It wasn't that long ago, but it felt like a whole other lifetime.

At Doc's insistence, Caleb had purchased a suit of clothes that were several steps above the normal jeans and work shirt he preferred. It was a black suit with a waist-coat over a starched white shirt. He managed to keep the sleeves down for all of two minutes before the material felt as if it were wrapping around his arms like a pair of snakes. Once he'd rolled up the sleeves, the shirt was a bit easier to bear. That way, he was able to return the cuff links for a full refund.

An old pocket watch was nestled in his waistcoat with a chain that was hooked through one of the buttonholes midway up his chest. While he was standing there, a tall blonde in a purple silk dress made her way beside him and slipped an arm around his waist.

"Looking good in that suit," she whispered.

"Don't talk like that unless you're willing to back it up," Caleb replied. When he didn't hear an answer right away, he turned to find her sizing him up with stunning blue eyes. Her face was elegant and trim, accented only slightly by powders and cream.

"And you shouldn't give a girl a hard time when she pays you a compliment," she told him.

Caleb couldn't help but let his eyes wander over the rest of Trish's figure. She had a dancer's body, but with a good amount of curve in all the right places. When she walked, it was with practiced elegance, and even when she stood still, she seemed to be gliding closer to him.

Although the ribbon tied around her forearm matched the color of her dress perfectly, it still marked her as one of the girls on Donnelly's payroll. That took a bit of the excitement out of seeing her look at him the way she was, but not much.

"Some deputy was asking about the game," she said. "Can you believe that?"

"I can if it's the deputy I invited."

Trish pulled back a bit as if to make sure she was talking to the right person. "You invited a lawman to your game? Does Doc know about that?"

"Not yet," Caleb said with a smirk. "But he's always talking about staying sharp and being ready for anything. I figure this will be good practice for both of us, especially considering what's in store for the night."

"You still plan on soaking that dandy Lottie's bringing with her?"

Lowering his voice a bit, Caleb nodded and said, "Right down to the bone."

That brought an excited smirk to Trish's face and also brought her a bit closer to Caleb's side. Her hands moved along his hip before wandering in toward his inner thigh In no time at all, she'd found what she was looking for. "Maybe if you win tonight, you'll have enough to afford the grand treatment."

Caleb didn't exactly move to accommodate Trish's roaming hand, but he didn't move away from it either. "The grand treatment? I've only heard stories about that."

"They're all true," she whispered. "I'm even considering giving you a discount."

"Which is?"

"Let me in on the game. I can help in plenty of ways. I've read cards for plenty of other players. Just cut me in on a percentage and we can both celebrate afterward."

"And here I thought you were interested in me," Caleb said sarcastically.

"I am. You want me to prove it?"

Just as he was about to respond to that, Caleb straightened up and took a step away from Trish. "You won't be any help if everyone sees you all over me like this," he said.

Trish glanced toward the front door and saw what had caught Caleb's eye. She looked at Lottie Deno as if she'd caught sight of a slab of cold, half-chewed steak. Slowly easing her hand off of Caleb, Trish said, "If you're more interested in redheads, you may be out of luck with that one. From what I've heard, she's not interested in much of anything else besides playing cards."

"And I suppose you're an expert on the subject?"

"Maybe not, but the men that come running to us when they get turned away by ones like her sure got no reason to lie."

Caleb smiled, knowing full well just how many ways Lottie would be able to dash a man's hopes into dust. "Hopefully I won't be one of those men."

Shrugging, Trish finally backed all the way off him. "What about the rest?" she asked. "Can I help you during your game or not?"

"Ask Doc about that," Caleb said as he straightened his waistcoat and stood tall.

Before walking away, Trish leaned in and whispered, "Don't blame me if I'm too busy to fit you in when your balls are about to burst from all that pressure." With that, she walked away amid a flutter of skirts and one last brush of her hand against Caleb's chest.

Lottie took her time making her way from the front door. From the moment she'd stepped into the Beehive, she'd been swarmed by waves and greetings of all sorts. Most of them were from men, and a few of them bordered on the inappropriate. Lottie handled every last one of them with style, even rebuffing the few rude drunks with a properly timed icy stare as well as some choice words. The expression on her face had shifted to genuine warmth by the time she made it to where Caleb was standing.

"Am I the first one to arrive?" she asked.

"Anders is here and so is Doc. I will say that you're the first one to cause such a stir."

"If Sheriff Jacobs hears about one of his deputies playing in this game, there may be a bigger stir, but I'll accept the prize for now."

Having taken Lottie's hand out of courtesy when she'd first walked up to him, Caleb had yet to let go of her. She was known for wearing green as a way to accentuate the redness in her hair. This evening was no exception, and she wore a dark green dress with embroidery that was simple yet as elegant as the lady who wore it.

Lottie's hair fell in a cascade of thick, wavy curls that bounced with every step. There was plenty more bouncing as well since the neckline of her dress plunged down just past a respectable level. Even that indulgence wasn't enough to tarnish the sophisticated package that was Lottie Deno.

"If you stare at me any longer, I'll be forced to charge for a ticket," she said.

Caleb shook himself out of his stupor and shrugged. "Sorry about that. I'm sure you've been getting that every step of the way over here."

"Yes, but this is the first time I've been reluctant to put a stop to it. Where's Doc?"

Caleb hitched a thumb over his shoulder. "Back at the big table."

Lottie stood on her tiptoes so she could look farther into the saloon's main room. "I don't see him."

Turning on his heel, Caleb took a look at the spot where he'd left Doc. All he could see was a bottle of whiskey in front of an empty chair. "He probably just got up to stretch his legs."

"Either that, or the sheriff's come around to haul him in for killing Boyer."

As Caleb turned around, he was careful to measure every last one of his movements. "What are you talking about?"

Her eyes narrowed while studying him carefully. "Boyer was around a while ago and he mentioned to a few people that he knew about the new players in town. That means he was going to expect taxes from you and Doc, which means he must have come to see you. Word has it that he went to see Doc and nobody's seen him since."

"Your sources must be better than mine. Seeing as how you were higher than me on Boyer's shit list, I can only guess you're bluffing right now."

After a slight pause, Lottie winked and said, "Fishing is more like it."

"While we're on the subject, what exactly brought on that situation between you and Boyer?"

"He expected me to pay double for running my game so close to where the stagecoach is unloaded, and I refused. He also expected me to let him under my skirts whenever he pleased, and I refused that as well."

"That explains why he was so fussy."

"Either that, or it was the time my boot was introduced to his balls."

Caleb let out a surprised laugh.

"That was the first time Boyer tried to put his hands on me," she explained. "I paid my dues and put him down. He never did like me very much after that."

"Why bother paying him at all?"

Lottie studied him a little more closely while chewing on her bottom lip. When she started speaking again, her tone was back to its normal melody. "You must have really not talked to him if you're asking that question."

"I've heard some things, but I never thought to believe them."

"You should. At least, you should believe what he says about Fort Griffin and Cheyenne, I know him and his friends have plenty going on there."

"Like what?"

Lottie sighed and eyed the empty card table as if it were calling her name. Reluctantly, she said, "Folks here and in Cheyenne pay the tax because it's more trouble to refuse. It's not that expensive and we usually short the Tiger's cut anyway."

"So there really is a Tiger?"

Narrowing her eyes as if she'd just seen through Caleb's mask, Lottie said, "There's always someone coming around to try and use muscle to get a piece of what we earn. That goes whether you work at a bank or at a poker table. And in both of those instances, men can get gunned down if they say no to the wrong man."

"Who's gotten killed?"

Lottie stopped short and forced a calmer facade onto her face. "Have you already forgotten about Earl?"

Caleb hung his head and felt his stomach twist into a knot. "That's not what I meant, Lottie. I was just . . ."

"Fishing," she said when she saw Caleb

struggling. "I know." Reaching out to place her hand on top of his, she added, "Here's some advice from someone who's been making her way in a tough business for a long time. You don't have to pay everyone who sticks their hand out, but you'll stay alive longer if you keep the real tigers at bay. If it was just Boyer, he wouldn't be such a problem. But there's more out there. Plenty more, and they make Boyer look like a kitten in comparison." Lottie's eyes darted toward the door, where she spotted an older man in a dark blue suit step in from the street. He looked around and nodded toward the bar as he slowly made his way through the crowd.

"Looks like one of my own prospects is here," she said. "I think I'll go see what kind of mood he's in."

"Once he sees you in that dress, it won't be difficult to guess his mood."

Lottie crinkled her nose at him in a playful scowl and then pointed toward the back of the room.

Caleb turned and saw Doc stepping out from a narrow hallway leading to the rooms used by the Beehive's working girls. Trish was right behind him, and she was dabbing at the corners of her mouth with a frilly handkerchief.

134

"Great," Caleb muttered. "Looks like we've got a new partner."

12

Caleb sat at the table with Lottie on his left and Deputy Anders to his right. The deputy was a man in his late twenties, which made him old enough to be confident in himself after collecting a few notches on his belt, but still young enough to be ruled by emotions at the worst possible time. To a professional gambler, that was the perfect age for an opponent.

Anders dressed like a rancher with a badge pinned to his chest and sat in his spot as if that badge was enough to earn him free drinks. It wasn't.

Doc sat on Lottie's other side. Apart from his dapper gray suit, he wore a smile that nearly went from one ear to the other. Although Doc always looked happy and a bit anxious at the start of a game, Caleb knew the real reason behind that smile was the blond woman who circled the table like a shark.

So far, Trish seemed to be keeping her distance well enough. She moved with a swivel in her hips, and none of the other men seemed ready to complain if she drifted a little too close. Lottie warned her away with a deadly stare.

To Doc's left was a man Caleb had seen once or twice around town but hadn't yet had a chance to speak to. The man was dressed in a simple set of clothes, which didn't do much to separate him from any of the other cowboys wandering the streets of Fort Griffin. Caleb acknowledged the man with a nod before introductions were made, and that was that.

"I assume most of us know each other," Doc said. "Deputy Anders, I must say I'm surprised to see your face. I didn't think you were the gambling sort."

"Always up for a friendly game," the lawman said. "Especially on the piss-poor salary I get." That elicited a round of half-hearted laughter, which Anders soaked in like he was receiving a standing ovation.

Gesturing to his left, Doc said, "This here is Mike Lynch."

"My game's normally faro," Mike said with a shrug. "Thought I'd give this a try."

"Be careful of our deputy friend, Mike," Doc said with a friendly nudge. "He's heeled and he doesn't like to lose."

"Gotchya."

"Hope you don't mind losing, Doc," Anders said. "I see you and most everyone else at this table is heeled as well."

Doc shrugged in a way that caused the Colt under his arm to disappear beneath his gray jacket. "A man in my condition can't be too careful."

"Or too drunk," Caleb muttered.

Unlike Anders's earlier attempt at humor, this one got some genuine laughs from the rest of the table.

"Now, now," Doc said. "Let's not make our guests feel uncomfortable. This fine gentleman next to Mike is Robert Taylor. I assume more proper introductions are in order?"

Those that hadn't been named just yet introduced themselves to Mr. Taylor, who took it all in with cordial nods and an offhanded greeting of his own. Like most men with a pulse, Taylor's eyes lingered on Lottie, who just so happened to be sitting directly across from him.

Taylor rose from his seat and extended a hand across the table. He wore a dark blue suit without a single thread that was out of place. Gold cuff links glittered on his wrists, and fine white silk extended from beneath his sleeve. "Always a pleasure, Miss Deno."

"Likewise," Lottie said with a little grin.

"Even so, Dr. Holliday is doing such a fine job of starting off a civilized game that I thought I'd continue the tradition." As he spoke, Taylor's hand wrapped around Lottie's and didn't ease up until the last possible moment.

"I'm all for being civil," Anders said, "but I came to play some cards. If you folks plan on talking any longer, I'll go watch them French ladies kick their skirts up."

"From what I've seen, it looks like Doc knows plenty about paying to have a woman lift her skirts," Caleb grunted.

Doc's eyes flashed at Caleb as a grating cough rumbled in the back of his throat. "Let's not bicker," Doc said. "We're here to play a civil game."

Caleb rolled his eyes and drummed his fingers as Lottie shuffled the cards and dealt.

After coughing once into the back of his hand, Doc pushed in a few chips. "I believe that's the minimum?"

"Sure is," Mike said as he tossed in a few chips of his own. "And so's this."

"Raise you ten dollars," Taylor said.

As he tossed in his cards, Anders muttered, "Forget all of you."

"Them girls are still dancing if you want to watch," Mike offered. "It'd cost you less to watch them."

The lawman's nostrils flared as he leaned forward in Mike's direction. "You getting lippy with me?"

Mike held up his hand and shook his head.

"Easy, now," Caleb said in a pacifying voice that had been honed from years of running his own saloon. "We just got started. I call."

"Me, too," Lottie said.

Doc tossed in a card and got another from Lottie. Mike, Taylor, Caleb, and Lottie all drew two and fanned their cards in a closely guarded grip.

"Since it's good luck to play the first hand," Doc said, "I'll bet five."

Reluctantly, Mike matched the bet.

"Call," Taylor said confidently.

"Since Doc's betting on his luck," Caleb said without hiding the biting sarcasm in his voice, "I'll raise it another five."

"Ten to me," Lottie announced, "and another ten."

Doc tossed fifteen into the pot while staring across at Caleb. His eyes darted over Caleb's shoulder and then he said, "Let's make the bet an even fifty."

Mike couldn't throw in his cards fast

enough. "Fifty's way too much to bet on a stinking pair of eights."

While looking around the table, it was hard not to notice the tension crackling between Doc and Caleb. That tension flared up even more as Trish settled in behind Doc and rested a hand on his shoulder.

"Fifty seems like an awful lot to bet in a friendly game," Taylor said.

"I'm one of the friendliest sorts you're likely to meet around here," Doc replied.

Taylor looked down at his cards and threw in enough money to cover the bet. He had yet to take so much as a dent out of the chips he'd brought with him.

Caleb looked at Doc and then at Trish. When Doc reached back to brush his hand along the side of Trish's face, Caleb bristled. "You're not going to push anyone around, Doc. I don't care what you're trying to prove or what you think you're doing," he said, "but I won't be pushed around."

Doc's face was pale, but had less expression than the wall behind him. "How admirable."

"You want to see how well I know this game?" Caleb asked. "You're full of shit, Doc. You're bluffing."

"That's not against the rules."

"I call," Caleb said defiantly.

Lottie had her cards facedown beneath one smooth hand. While reaching out to rub Caleb's shoulder, she looked at Doc and said, "You two need to calm down. We're not out for blood here." Seeing that she wasn't getting much of anywhere with either man, she said, "I call, also. At least that should put an end to whatever this is that is bugging you two."

"You heard her, Doc. Let's see what you've got."

Clearing his throat, Doc laid down a two of diamonds, a three of clubs, then the four and five of spades. He slid the top card back to reveal the four of diamonds.

"Fours?" Caleb snorted. "You stayed in with fours?"

"Jesus Christ," Mike said. "I could've beaten fours."

"Perhaps," Taylor said. "But you couldn't have beaten queens." With that, Taylor showed the queen of spades and the queen of diamonds along with the ace of spades for a kicker.

Dropping a pair of nines onto the table, Caleb stared daggers across at Doc. "Had you beat and called you out just like I said, Doc. How's that for teaching a lesson or two?"

Doc sipped from his whiskey and lifted

his glass in Caleb's direction. "You have my admiration. Unfortunately, you lost just as much as I did. Perhaps I can seek solace elsewhere," he said while leaning back so Trish could rub his shoulders.

Although he seemed to be intrigued by the sight of Trish leaning forward in her low-cut dress, Taylor shifted his eyes toward Lottie. "What about you, ma'am?"

Apologetically, Lottie shrugged and turned over a pair of kings.

Taylor gave her a friendly nod and leaned back so he could fish a cigar from his vest pocket. "A pleasure to lose to such a fine lady. I'd only hoped to see a smile."

She gave him one while raking in the chips and then passing the deck over to Doc.

The next few hands passed without incident as the chips made their way from one person to another. Caleb didn't miss the irony as he lost with a busted flush and managed to see more and more of his chips get taken away by Doc. Lottie seemed content to keep flirting with Taylor while Anders and Mike sparked a rivalry between themselves.

Just over an hour into the game, Doc was dealing and stayed in the hand until it was raised beyond the limit he was willing to go for the crap he was holding. Mike raised, and was eventually raised again by Taylor. Anders pushed in every cent he had with a glorious smile on his face.

"Ain't none of you beating what I got," the lawman said.

"You're worse at bluffing than Doc," Caleb grunted. "I'll raise another hundred."

Wincing, Lottie folded her hand.

Since he was healthy enough to cover the bet, Mike did just that.

Taylor studied his cards for a good, long time. After a fair amount of shifting in his seat, he folded, despite the fact that he had more than enough chips to cover the bet.

After tossing in his wedding ring to cover the raise, Anders won the pot by showing his cards. "Full house," he said victoriously.

"Beats me," Caleb said.

Mike slammed his fist against the table and let out a vicious snarl. "Fucking flush and it still ain't enough!"

"What can I say?" Anders beamed. "Some of us are just luckier than the rest of you."

13

The night wore on and the Beehive became packed to the rafters with gamblers, drunks, and working girls. Most of the crowd was still gathered in the back of the saloon, where all of the French dancers were on-stage kicking their legs up amid a flurry of raucous music. By now, the only thing beneath their skirts was what God had given them, and every time they gave the crowd a good look, they were rewarded with yet another furious round of cheers and applause.

The front half of the saloon might have been slightly quieter, but it still had more than its share of activity. In fact, another couple of tables had been set up to take advantage of the newcomers who wanted to spend some of their money when the French dancers took their breaks.

Every sort of poker that could be played was being dealt somewhere in that saloon, but Doc and Caleb were a tough act to follow. When they weren't bickering among themselves, the pair managed to keep their stacks of chips at a fairly healthy level. Lottie was doing just fine for herself, but Mike and Anders had broken just shy of even. It was difficult for any casual observer to gauge how well Taylor was doing since his pile of money was never less than impressive. The man in the dark blue suit also did a good job of keeping his emotions in check. That became very apparent when he called a bet from Doc without batting an eye.

"Was that five hundred?" Caleb asked.

"Sure enough," Doc said. "I believe Mr. Taylor must have a dandy."

Anders fanned his cards after having drawn one. He looked at them again, rearranged them, and shifted in his seat. Finally, he looked around the table and set his cards down. "I think you got me beat."

Having been dealt a nine, ten, and jack in mixed suits, Caleb had drawn two cards in the hopes of making a straight or at least a good pair. His optimism was promptly dashed by a two and three of different colors. "Take it," Caleb said and then threw in his cards.

Lottie had no trouble raising during the

first round of bets. After drawing one card, she still took a moment to think things over before moving her chips. Freshly painted nails slid up and down along the stacks of chips as the sound of baked clay knocking together rippled through the air. She locked eyes with Taylor, but did not return his smile. "Raise one fifty."

Even though Doc had drawn one card, he had yet to look at it. Instead, he looked over to Lottie and studied her for a few silent moments. Eventually, the silence was broken by a series of coughs.

"Take a drink and make your move," Caleb said impatiently.

As always, Trish reached down to rub Doc's chest when she saw him set down his glass. Doc took hold of her wrist and moved it away. "Save it," he told her. "I'm in the middle of something."

"Sorry, Doc," Trish said.

"I said be quiet," Doc snapped. "I need to think."

Hearing that was enough to get Trish moving away from Doc. She moved around the table behind Mike's, Taylor's, and Anders's chairs. When she made it to Caleb, she sat on his knee and glared defiantly at Doc.

"Maybe you should leave," Taylor said to

the blonde. "It's not proper to have someone walking behind the rest of us like that."

"I'll stay right here," Trish snapped. "Where I'm wanted."

Caleb slipped a hand along Trish's leg and said, "That's right. No need to go any farther."

"For the love of God, just shit or get off the pot!" Anders groaned.

"Here's Lottie's one fifty and another three besides," Doc said as he pushed in a good amount of his chips.

"Fine by me," Mike said as he called the bet.

Taylor kept his cards on the table and used the edge of his hand and his thumb to bend them back so he could take another look at them. After the French dancers let out another wave of yelps from the stage, Taylor nodded and separated a few neat stacks from the rest of his chips. "I call, Holliday. Time for the moment of truth."

"The kings seem to like me tonight. The sevens are warming up to me as well," Lottie said as she showed a pair of each.

"Jacks don't quite live up to those kings, Lottie," Doc said with a drawl that had become as smooth as the expensive whiskey he'd switched to hours ago. "But these aces hold up just fine." With a subtle move of his

148

hand, he spread his cards out to show two pair of his own.

Lottie gave a tight-lipped smile, but still nodded gracefully.

Mike's eyes snapped back and forth between Lottie's and Doc's cards. "Don't get too excited just yet," he said. " 'Cause I got three eights, which is enough to bury all four of them pairs."

"My, my," Doc said. "Look who's learned how to play."

"Up yer ass, Doc," Mike said jokingly.

"This is all very entertaining," Taylor said. "But I believe this round goes to me." Without another bit of fanfare, Taylor laid down three tens. "I must say, you had me quite worried, Holliday."

"That's a fine bit of playing," Doc said. "You shouldn't be worried about a thing."

For the first time all night, Taylor's stack had noticeably changed in size. Unfortunately for everyone else at the table, it had done so thanks to all of their chips adding to the pile. Doc poured himself several fingers of whiskey and downed it all in two swigs. When he refilled his glass, his hand was trembling just a bit.

"Maybe you should ease up on that stuff, Doc," Caleb said.

"And maybe you should mind your own

damn business," Doc snapped.

As the deal was passed around the table, the cards started moving more toward Lottie and Taylor. Anders was making increasingly bolder bets, and when he lost, Mike didn't hesitate to rub his nose in it.

Taylor dealt the cards and the deputy beside him hastily went for his chips.

"That all you pushing in?" Mike snapped. "With all the big talk you've been doing, I had you pegged as a real professional."

After taking a quick look at his first couple of cards, Anders doubled his bet. "How's that grab ya?"

Mike shrugged and shook his head.

As Caleb sifted through the mess he'd been dealt, he felt Trish's hand slip between his legs. Her fingers drifted close to a spot that was very distracting, but Caleb managed to toss in enough chips to call before he started losing his breath.

Lottie folded and excused herself from the table.

When Doc looked at his own cards, he did so by merely flipping them up with the corner of his thumb so he could take a quick glance. "Call," he said in a scratchy voice.

Mike held his cards and got to look at them for about a second and a half before

Anders spoke up.

"Come on, asshole." The deputy taunted him. "You wanna talk big, you'd best make the play to back it up."

Letting out a sigh, Mike shook his head and worked a few kinks from the back of his neck. His eyes were on Caleb and Trish for less than a second. When he looked back at Anders, Mike smiled and raised the bet by four hundred dollars.

Since he was sitting behind a wall of money, Taylor didn't shock anyone when he called. That left the next move solely up to Anders.

"What's the matter?" Mike teased. "I thought you were the lucky one."

Anders nodded and pushed in a call of his own.

As much as it pained him to do so, Caleb called as well.

When it was his turn, Doc didn't even touch his cards. "I need a refill," he said while taking hold of the half-full whiskey bottle. "I suppose I'll have to pass." As he stood up to leave, Doc flipped the cards so they landed perfectly on top of the pile of deadwood.

At the draw, Anders took two cards. Caleb drew two in the hopes of filling in a straight, but only got a few more mismatched numbers to add to his collection. When Taylor looked at him expectantly, Mike waved him off.

"I'm fine just the way I am," Mike said in a voice that was solid as stone.

Taylor nodded approvingly and took three cards for himself.

"Two hundred," Anders said quickly.

Caleb took a few moments, which was just long enough for him to feel another couple of rubs on the inside of his thigh. After a glance up at the blonde sitting on his lap, Caleb got a little wink from Trish in return. After that, he tossed in his cards. "I better not wager any money on this load of garbage."

"Not until you get some more blood flowing above yer belt, huh?" Anders sneered.

"Exactly."

Mike chuckled along with everyone else and took a look at Trish for himself. The blonde was wriggling on Caleb's lap and only looked across the table for a moment before shifting all of her attention back to him.

"You want a woman, go get yer own," Anders snarled. "Bet or fold."

Without taking his eyes off what Trish was showing him, Mike shoved in some chips. "That should be another four hundred."

Looking at his cards, Taylor seemed reluctant to look away. All he needed to do was glance back and forth between Mike and Anders to change his mind. "I like the way these look," Taylor said as he lowered his cards and added them to the top of the deadwood pile, "but not enough to get in between you two."

Anders nodded quickly and stared a set of holes through Mike's face. "You been trying to pull this shit on me all night long. Make it another four hundred."

Before all of Anders's chips were even in the middle of the table, Mike fixed him with an answering glare and waved at all his money. "Whatever I got left, it's in the pot."

The deputy flinched as if he'd been jabbed in the stomach. The longer he thought about what had happened, the sicker he looked because of it. Before too long, the muscles in his jaw tensed up and the corner of his mouth started to twitch. "You're cheating," he wheezed.

"One way to find out," Mike replied in a steady voice.

After pulling in enough breaths to fill his lungs with the smoke from other men's cigars, Anders looked at his cards and then looked back at Mike. He looked over to the seat next to him, only to find Caleb with his face pressed against Trish's neck and the blonde giggling quietly in his ear.

Counting up his money, Anders muttered to himself and threw his cards away as if they'd bitten his fingers.

Mike nodded and raked in the sizable pot.

Leaning forward, Anders reached out to slap one hand down flat upon the pile of chips. His other hand drifted to the vicinity of his gun as he growled, "I want to see your cards."

"What?" Mike asked.

Taylor scooted back a bit, but remained in his chair. "I'm afraid I'll have to side with Mr. Lynch," he said. "There's no cause for him to show you what he was holding."

"Stay out of this," Anders snapped without taking his eyes from Mike. "This is between me and him. I'm not asking for my money back, but I want to see what he was holding."

"Why?" Mike asked.

"Because I want to make sure you weren't cheating."

That brought Caleb back into the conversation in a heartbeat. "That's a serious accusation. Why do you think Mike was cheating?"

"Because he knew how that hand was gonna end before the cards were even dealt."

Even though Mike was smaller than Anders and had both hands reaching for the middle of the table instead of being anywhere near his gun, Mike held his ground without one hint of letting it go. "It's called confidence and knowing how to play," Mike said. "Perhaps you should look into it."

Choking on an obscenity, Anders stood up and knocked his chair behind him.

"Hold on, now," Caleb said as he got Trish off his lap and shuffled her to one side. "If you saw him cheating, let us know. Until this last hand, I've been getting soaked a whole lot more than you."

The longer he went without saying anything, the more it looked as if Anders was about to chew off his own tongue. Finally, he forced himself to say, "I didn't see him cheating, but I know he did."

"You're not broke," Mike said. "You've got more than half of what you came here with, so just take it and be on your way."

"I'm a lawman. You can't get away with this."

"This is just poker," Mike pointed out. "It doesn't respect any law."

Since there wasn't anything else left for him to do, Anders turned on his heel and stormed away from the table.

"Why don't we all stretch our legs and cool off?" Caleb offered. "I'll round up Lottie and Doc. Where the hell did they get off to, anyway?"

14

Considering how much attention she normally drew, it was nothing short of impressive when Lottie decided to blend into the background. For the redhead with skin that looked like poured cream, succeeding in such a feat was something close to a miracle. Sitting at a small table with her hair hanging straight along her back, Lottie sipped a drink and kept her head down while watching Caleb's game from afar.

Doc sat between her and most of the rest of the room, further blocking her from most folks' view. "How's he doing?" Doc asked.

Lottie nodded and took another sip. "Pretty well. I don't think he has a future in theater, but I've seen worse."

"Is your friend Taylor looking too scared?"

"Not from what I can see. If Mike and that deputy start getting rough, though, that might change. Was that a part of your plan?"

"Not exactly, but I should have expected

as much. Caleb does enjoy his surprises."

"You don't think he's trying to sabotage this, do you?"

"Not at all," Doc replied without hesitation. "He's just keeping everyone on their toes. Speaking of which, you're playing one hell of a game, Lottie."

She lifted her glass in a toast. "Thanks, Doc. The same goes for you. I only picked up on your mechanics once so far. I hope you haven't been dealing me seconds."

"I wouldn't risk fixing the deal unless it was absolutely necessary. So far, I've mostly dealt in people's favor."

"Did you learn anything?"

Nodding, Doc said, "I've seen how Taylor reacts to a good hand and how he reacts to a splendid hand. I've even got a fairly good grasp of how he reacts to hands that tend to give a man nightmares."

"Like that one where you were dealt four to a straight flush?"

Doc shifted in his chair and looked over at her to find Lottie wearing an attractive, mischievous smile. "You did that?"

"I certainly knew you had something and that's what I put you on. Looks like I was right." After sipping her drink, she turned to watch the stage for a few seconds. "You do learn something every day. One thing you should learn is to stay away from women like Trish."

"She has her charms."

"I know, but her signals are sloppy and she is way too obvious when she looks at everyone's cards."

"She looked at our cards?" Doc asked in shock.

Lottie glanced over at him with a shake of her head to let him know she wasn't buying what he was trying to sell. "If you truly couldn't tell that much on your own, I wouldn't have considered working with you on this."

"If I may be so bold," Doc said, "why are you working with us?"

"Pardon me?"

"Caleb and I have been trying to get a partnership with some of the others for a while now, and nobody's seemed interested. I could understand being hesitant at first, but I dare say we've proved ourselves to be good earners."

"There's no question about that," Lottie replied. "But some of the others are a little wary of you and Caleb. You two seemed to have built up a hell of a reputation back in Dallas."

"I see."

Patting Doc's arm, Lottie added, "I'm

only saying this because it's something you should know. The saloon owners didn't have many good things to say about you, but that was because they were worried about some sore loser knocking you over and taking his money back. As for Caleb, there's been a whole other problem."

"Go on."

Lottie took a sip of her drink. Once the liquor worked its way through her system a bit, she seemed to find it a little easier to continue. "Caleb's a good soul and Lord knows he's stepped in for me when I needed it. When I heard the things I've heard, I knew better than to believe them."

"What things?"

"Things like he's too dangerous to work with," Lottie said. "And that he's a little too quick to draw his gun at the wrong moments. Apparently, there's been some other trouble in Dallas that doesn't sit too well with folks on the circuit. There are stories about cardplayers winning big in the place he used to own and never being seen again. Gamblers have long memories, Doc. That goes for faces and rumors just as it does for tells and odds."

"And what's he supposed to have done that is so bad?"

"Killing that penny-ante hustler for one."

Doc froze with his glass raised halfway to his mouth. After thinking for a solid couple of seconds, he shook his head. "That's something I've never heard of. Do you have a name to go with that?"

"No, but there's been a few more. Enough for us to have heard about it in Fort Griffin. If you're truly trying to make a way for yourself in places like Denver and California, then you might want to get some distance between yourself and someone like him." When she saw Doc grin and finally start to laugh, Lottie asked, "What's so funny?"

"This whole conversation. We're taking a breather while fleecing a rich man for all he can lose and you're worried about the ethics of my partner."

"For right now, I'm your partner as well, Doc. If you want to be known in a town and set up a game without having to fight for the right to do so, you should choose your company a little more wisely."

"You've spent a bit of time with Caleb. Do you believe he's some coldhearted killer?"

"No, but this isn't about what I believe. There's talk on the circuit and I thought you should know what it is. Boyer isn't even cold in the ground yet and his people are spreading word all the way into Cheyenne."

"Ah." Doc breathed into his whiskey glass. "The infamous Tiger rears its ugly head."

"Caleb was asking me about that," Lottie said, "and I don't think he appreciates what I told him. Killing Boyer earned you some praise, but it'll cause you a whole lot more grief."

"It will if the Tiger is only wounded and left alone," Doc said. "Any animal becomes more dangerous in that situation."

Lottie shifted and leaned forward so she could be heard when she lowered her voice. "The Tiger isn't just some legend and he's no joke."

"Then maybe he should have picked a more adult name."

"Joke all you want. More folks around here listen to the Tiger than they do to you."

"Things can change," Doc said. "They always do."

"Nothing needs to change right now," came a voice from behind Lottie, which was followed by a hand dropping onto Doc's shoulder.

Caleb stepped up to the table and pulled up a chair for himself. "Mike just took out Deputy Anders. It was beautiful."

"Then I guess I'd better get back to the game," Lottie said as her familiar smile

162

returned. When she stood up and tossed her hair over one shoulder, she practically beamed with a radiant beauty that was impossible to duplicate. "You boys better not keep me waiting."

After Lottie was gone, Doc shook his head and emptied his whiskey glass. "Women like that make me yearn for the girls I knew in Georgia."

"Is Mattie the one you're talking about?" Caleb asked.

Doc's head snapped around and his eyes narrowed. "What are you saying about her?"

"Easy, Doc. Just taking a guess. After all those letters she sent you in Dallas, I figured she had to be someone special. Speaking of which, I'd wager there were a few of those waiting for you back in Denison."

"Right. And that's where they'll stay."

"Is she someone who might pull you back into Georgia and away from this life of sin and debauchery?"

Doc chuckled once under his breath and then let out a full-fledged laugh. "Now, why on earth would I want to leave behind a perfectly good slice of sin and debauchery? Now that you mentioned sin, I have been thinking about one in particular."

"If it involves you and Trish before the game started, then I don't want to hear about it."

"Not that, although that was fairly . . . Never mind. The sin I was thinking about was murder."

"Huh?"

Putting a steely edge into his voice, Doc said, "As in, I should kill you for inviting that badge-wearing son of a bitch into this game. That prick could ruin everything."

"That lawdog's been sniffing around a lot of the games in town trying to get in on one of them," Caleb explained. "Soon as I invited him to ours, he backed off the rest. It's caused a hell of a lot of goodwill around here. Besides, you're the one who's always talking about expecting the unexpected and all of that. What better way to practice your mechanics than when you're being watched by a lawman? It's bound to happen sooner or later."

"Actually, it wasn't as bad as I thought it would be."

"And he won't even be there for the rest of the game."

"Mike cleaned him out?"

"He got him out of the game, and I doubt he'll be wanting to get into another one anytime soon."

"He was just looking for a percentage of the profits, Caleb," Doc said. "You should have paid him off and been done with it."

"I don't like being shoved around, Doc. Especially by the law."

"I know how you feel. Too late to fret about it now. Mike was all too eager to divert that deputy's attention. Now that he's gone, we can get right back to the business at hand. That is, unless Taylor has left us."

"He hasn't," Caleb said. "In fact, he seemed to enjoy watching the fireworks when Mike and Anders locked horns."

"Probably just the sort of thing he was looking for. I'd imagine having a lawman at the table even lent our game that much more credence in his eyes."

"We'll see."

"Does he suspect that we're not actually about to throw punches at each other?" Doc asked.

"I don't think so, but he might be suspicious if he catches us talking like this."

"Nice touch with the whore, by the way," Doc added.

Caleb averted his eyes and tapped his boot against the table leg. "Yeah. She worked out pretty good."

"She was a perfect reason for us to bicker. She also did a good job of tipping me to a few of the hands Taylor was playing. I've got a real good eye for the man by now."

"Looked to me like you had your eye on something else before the game."

Shrugging, Doc said, "I am only human, after all. She offered to help and I accepted after a bit of convincing."

"Since you got the convincing, you can pay her out of your cut."

"Are you serious?"

Caleb cocked his head and fixed Doc with a look that showed him just how serious he was.

When he leaned forward to meet that glare, Doc wheezed slightly and forced himself to hold back the coughing fit that was scratching at the back of his throat. "And whatever money of ours that deputy walked away with will come out of your cut."

"That's fair."

Doc offered his hand and Caleb shook it. Even after all the whiskey Doc had ingested and all the coughing he'd done, his cool, bony hand was still able to maintain a powerful grip.

"Now," Doc said, "let's play our parts and fleece this lamb that Lottie was so kind to bring to our table."

15

Hours passed and the music inside the Beehive finally started to fade. Even after the dancers got tired and found other things to keep them occupied, there was always some sort of commotion in the back half of the saloon. As the first rays of the sun broke across the sky, nobody at Caleb's table noticed. They were too busy managing their cards and guarding their chips.

The chair between Taylor and Caleb was once again empty, but it hadn't been that way the entire night. After Anders had made his exit, a few other brave souls sat down there, only to be snapped like a dry twig in a hurricane. The gamblers had played together for too long and were too intent on their purposes to be affected by a new face. As morning turned into afternoon, the saloon was quieter than it had been all night. By that time, the gamblers and drunks were the only ones there, and music didn't do much to soothe their souls.

Lottie and Mike were doing fairly well for themselves and had a decent amount of chips to prove it.

Caleb wasn't so lucky and had fought tooth and nail to stay in the game during some of the bloodier skirmishes. The main reason he was still in the game at all was the increasing skill shown in Doc's dealing. Even as Doc unleashed a series of brutal coughs, he still managed to get his hands on the right cards and send them Caleb's way when they were needed.

But Doc wasn't completely unselfish in that regard. Knowing what to look for, Caleb spotted some of Doc's fancy mechanics used to fix the deal. But that didn't explain how he won so many hands that he didn't deal. Doc's skill at the game shone through all the whiskey he drank and all the blood he coughed into his handkerchief.

And yet, somehow, Taylor's winnings rivaled Doc's. At times, they even eclipsed his.

Caleb looked down at his cards and had to blink away the fog that came from lack of sleep. They'd been playing for the better part of a day, and those hours were wreaking havoc on Caleb inside and out, top to bottom. At first, Caleb thought he had a straight, but then he blinked and saw another batch of the same crap that Taylor had been dealing him all night.

"I'll bet twenty," Caleb said without flinching.

"Sure you can afford that much?" Lottie asked.

Caleb actually looked down at his chips before he realized she'd been kidding. "I can afford it," he said. "Especially when I take this hand."

She tossed her chips in and gave him a consoling rub on the shoulder.

Without looking at his cards, Doc said, "Make it three hundred more."

Caleb didn't have to do one bit of acting when he glared across at the other man's sunken face and growled, "That's all I got left."

"I believe you're thirty-five dollars short, but I'll let you float if you want to call. That is, if nobody objects."

"Don't matter what I say," Mike said as he pitched his cards lazily in Doc's direction rather than to the dealer. Although he got a stern glare from Taylor, Mike appeared to be too close to keeling over from exhaustion to notice.

"No offense, Caleb," Taylor said, "but considering your luck these last few hands,

I'd call whatever bet you made and would take any marker you offered."

Lottie covered her mouth and shook her head when Doc looked her way.

While mulling over his decision, Caleb went through the motions that had become second nature after so many hours of playing in that particular spot. He drummed his fingers, fidgeted with his cards, and worked out the kinks in his muscles, all of which were signals to Doc as to the exact cards he was holding. "Ah, to hell with all of you," Caleb said as he tossed his cards onto the pile of deadwood near Doc's left hand. "I'm out."

"Out of turn, but accepted," Taylor said as he pushed in enough chips to match Doc's raise. "What about you, Lottie?"

After taking a moment for consideration, Lottie shook her head and said, "I do have a debilitating sense of optimism, so I'll stay in to see how my hand can improve."

Once the money was in the middle of the table, Taylor took the deck and looked at Lottie.

As she pondered her decision, she ran the tip of her tongue along her bottom lip. She could feel eyes being drawn to her from every section of the room. Taylor wasn't as lecherous as some of the drunks scattered nearby, but he found it just as difficult to look away from her.

"I'll take three," she said softly.

"Two for me," Doc added. When he didn't get his cards right away, Doc tapped the table with his discards. "Excuse me. If you'd prefer to be alone with the lady, by all means fold and do your business."

Taylor shook his head as if to snap himself from a dream and flipped two cards at Doc. Once Lottie had looked away from him, Taylor said, "Dealer takes one." After filling in his own hand, Taylor reached out and gathered up the deadwood.

"I'll bet fifty," Lottie said.

Clearing his throat, Doc asked, "You make that pair, Miss Deno?"

"You'll have to pay to see them, just like everyone else, Dr. Holliday. Well," she added while winking at Taylor, "maybe not quite everyone."

"For your sake, I hope it's one hell of a pair," Doc said. "I'll raise it to five thousand."

Although it was already quiet in the place, those words somehow made it get quieter. The only sound that could be heard was a subtle wheeze in the back of Doc's throat. As he sipped his whiskey, the wheeze dwindled away.

"Did you say five thousand?" Taylor asked.

"Yes," Doc replied while shoving in several stacks of chips. "Is that a problem?"

"Why settle for that, Doc?" Taylor asked with a nervous chuckle. "Why not just push it all in?"

"Table etiquette denies me that honor since I've already made my bet," Doc said in a whiskey-soaked Southern accent that was thick as peach cobbler.

"Then let me do the honors." As he pushed in his own chips, Taylor lost every bit of discomfort or even friendliness in his voice. "Ten thousand more . . . Actually . . . make it ten thousand fifty-five. I believe that would put you all in."

Letting out a slow whistle, Lottie set her cards down and slid them away from her as if they were rigged to explode. "You boys can fight this out among yourselves. Count me out."

Taylor acknowledged her fold with a nod. He leaned forward a bit with both arms on the table as if to physically guard what little of his chips remained. "What about it, Doc?"

Despite all the money in the middle of the table, all the time that had been devoted to the game, and all the tension that was in the air, Doc sat in his seat as if he were watching a dog cross the street. Refilling his glass from his own flask, he seemed to be more interested in the way the whiskey swirled at the bottom than whatever else was going on.

Taylor may have been showing a bit more anxiousness in his posture and eyes, but he wasn't chomping at the bit half as much as Caleb.

After a subtle cough, Doc said, "You must either think I don't have the fortitude to make this call or you've got one daisy of a hand."

"I wouldn't cast aspersions on your fortitude, Holliday."

"And there's always the third option," Doc continued as if there were nobody else in the room. "You think I'm bluffing."

"That is something that's happened from time to time at a poker game."

"Indeed."

"You want a lesson in gambling, Caleb?" Doc asked, completely dropping the previous ruse that he could barely tolerate his partner's company. "This is what you call a strong-arm tactic. Mr. Taylor here wants me to call so badly, he can no longer contain himself. What a pity. He's been doing such a good job until now."

Caleb didn't say anything in response to

that. In fact, he was so tired that he had to strain to think back to when he and Doc had agreed to fight and squabble at the table as a way to make the targets think they weren't running anything. Doc had been the one to suggest running that act during this game as a way to get some practice. They'd pretty much dropped it once Anders was gone, but Caleb didn't like having Doc speak so frankly while there was still work to be done.

"Sure, Doc," Caleb said. "Thanks for the pointer."

"We can pick this up some other time," Mike offered. "We could all use some sleep."

"Nonsense!" Doc said a little too loudly. "It's just getting good. I've had to wait for hours and hours and . . ." Wobbling in his seat, Doc removed the watch from his vest pocket, flipped it open, looked at it, snapped it shut, slipped it back into his pocket, and said, ". . . and hours just for this moment."

Without saying a word, Caleb craned his neck so he could look straight into Doc's eyes. Once he saw what he needed to see, he said, "You're drunk, Doc. That's no way to piss away this much —"

"I don't need a wet nurse!" Doc snarled as he viciously swatted at Caleb, while almost hitting Lottie in the process.

174

Rolling his eyes, Caleb leaned back in his chair so he could watch from a safe distance.

"Are you going to move your chips in, Doc?" Taylor asked.

"Yes," Doc replied. "In fact, I believe I'll raise."

Taylor eyed him cautiously. "Raise with what? I'd rather not accept a marker."

"No marker needed. I believe this will be sufficient." As he said that, Doc removed the gold and diamond stickpin that was with him almost as much as his rasping cough. He took it from his collar reverently and set it against his chips.

Caleb had to keep from wincing when he saw that, knowing well enough that Doc was wagering with something that was much more to him than just a piece of jewelry.

"That was a gift from my father," Doc explained. "And if you question its value, you'll need to defend yourself."

"I'm not questioning anything," Taylor said as he studied the stickpin. "I can see from here that it's a fine piece. I must be honest when I tell you I didn't think this would go this far."

"It's poker," Doc said with a fond smile. "There is no *too far* in this game. You can either call the bet or fold."

"Fine, then," Taylor said as he pushed in the remainder of his chips. "I call."

"That's not enough to cover the diamonds alone," Doc said. "You'll need to find something else to bet or fold."

"All I've got is out there. Surely we can come to an arrangement if this hand goes your way."

"Afraid not. I'd rather not accept a marker. I'm sure you understand."

Although there was a bit of nervous laughter coming from Mike and Caleb, Taylor wasn't quite so appreciative of the way Doc threw his own words straight back at him.

"You still feel like you can lead me around by the nose, Holliday?"

When Doc sat up straight, he wavered slightly and then held his chin up high. "Whatever are you trying to insinuate, sir?"

"Cut the shit," Taylor snapped. "You're a hell of a card handler, I'll give you that much. But you're a little too big for your britches. If you wouldn't have been so full of yourself, I might have been impressed with what I've seen so far."

"And what have you seen?"

"A couple of wet-behind-the-ear hustlers who bit off more than they could chew."

Glancing back at Caleb, Doc said, "I

prefer to think of us as up-and-comers within these prestigious ranks."

"You want something more to cover this bet?" Taylor asked. Reaching over his shoulder and behind his neck, he removed a slender blade and slapped it onto the table in a smooth motion that was over in nearly as much time as it took to blink. "That should cover it."

Doc glanced down at the blade before reaching out to take hold of it by the handle. Since Taylor didn't make a move to stop him, Doc turned the blade around in his hands so he could examine it from end to end. The handle was smooth wood polished to a black sheen, which closely resembled ebony.

"I'm no judge of knives," Doc admitted, "but the craftsmanship is impressive. I especially like the blade. Here, Caleb. See what you think."

Engraved upon the blade, running from handle to tip, was a tiger with its tail stretched out and one forepaw extended. Every claw could be seen within the engraving, along with the feral look in the animal's eyes.

"Did you think no one would notice when Boyer turned up dead?" Taylor asked.

Just then, four of the remaining customers

scattered throughout the saloon turned to face the card table. Their guns were already drawn.

16

"So, am I to presume you're this Tiger we've all heard about?" Doc asked as if there weren't currently several gun barrels pointed in his direction.

"I'm a representative," Taylor replied. "Just like Boyer was before me."

"Whatever happened to him?" Doc queried.

Taylor shook his head slowly. "Don't make this into a joke, Holliday. I assure you, none of us think it's funny."

"So what's going on here?" Caleb asked. When he started to scoot back from the table, two of the gunmen shifted their aim toward him and cocked their hammers back as a none-too-subtle warning. Staying where he was and keeping his hands in sight, Caleb said, "I thought all you people wanted was a percentage."

"We do," Taylor replied. "And we still haven't gotten it yet. At least, not from you and Dr. Holliday here."

"The game's not over yet" Doc said in a steady voice.

As a few of his men started getting restless around him, Taylor nodded and waved for them to settle back down again. "If you want to pay your tax, betting everything you own on a hand of poker isn't the smartest way to go about it."

"Betting is how fortunes are made," Doc said.

"You want to play through this hand?"

"Isn't that why we're here?"

"Yes. It is." After taking a bit to think it over, Taylor shrugged. "All right, then. But if you lose, I'll still expect our tax. In fact, I'll need interest seeing as how it's late and all."

"That's bullshit," Caleb snarled as he jumped up from his seat. Even the sound of those other two gunmen jumping to their feet and stepping up to surround him wasn't enough to back Caleb down. "All of this is bullshit. What happens when the law takes a look at you assholes? Will you have enough taxes to pay off every one of them?"

"Give it a try," Taylor said. "Who do you think is keeping the law from checking on every last one of the decks that are used in these saloons? Or from taking a good, long look at the faro games being run by you people? The law gets a good deal out of this because they don't want to waste their time policing dregs and vagrants like the lot of you. With the exception of Miss Deno, of course."

Suddenly, Mike pushed back from his own spot while drawing a pistol that had been tucked under his belt. The moment his gun came into view, a shot from one of Taylor's gunmen blasted through the saloon and knocked Mike off his feet. He landed with a pained grunt, but still struggled to get up.

The same gunman who'd fired that shot was also the one to come rushing up to snatch the pistol from Mike's hand. He turned that pistol along with his own weapon back around so both guns were pointed in Mike's face.

When he tried to prop himself up, Mike winced and flopped down again. He grabbed at the source of pain, which was a fresh, bloody gash in his shoulder. Just one touch was enough for him to feel the gristle of exposed bone beneath the flesh that had been shredded by the passing bullet.

"Jesus," Mike gasped as he went pale and lay down.

Ignoring the guns being waved around, Lottie got up and rushed over to Mike.

"Hold on," she said. "It looks a lot worse than it is. We'll fetch a doctor for you."

"Nobody's fetching anyone," Taylor said. With a nod over one shoulder, he motioned for one of his gunmen to stand by the front door and prevent anyone from passing through. There were a few folks trying to get a look inside after the shot had been fired, but their curiosity wasn't great enough to overcome the murderous intent in the gunman's eyes.

Doc looked down at Mike and asked, "You feeling all right?"

Mike nodded weakly and pulled in a breath. A bit of the color was returning to his cheeks, but he'd since broken into a sweat.

"Get something to hold against that wound," Doc said. "Help yourself to some of this, Mike," he added while handing down his flask. "It'll hold you over just fine until we can get that looked at."

"Things will get a whole lot worse if you two keep insisting on going against the grain," Taylor said.

"If you want to shoot this place up, then we can do that," Doc said. "But I thought we were going to play through this hand."

This time, Taylor didn't even try to keep the smirk from his face. In fact, he even chuckled a bit as he nodded slowly. "You're a tough man to figure out, Doc. Just when I think you're acting more drunk than you are, you go and start talking like a damned fool again. You want to see the cards? Fine. Since I'm bound to get all of this anyway, I might as well go through the motions."

Doc eased his flask into the inner pocket of his jacket.

When Taylor turned over his cards, he revealed a whole lot of red. "Flush," he declared. "I know there are bigger hands out there, but I also know this one's bigger than yours."

Every eye shifted toward Doc. Some of those eyes were narrowed in suspicion and others were tainted by mean-spirited smiles. Others, like the ones belonging to Lottie, Mike, and Caleb, were anxious. None of them were hopeful.

"I wouldn't speak so quickly," Doc said as he placed his cards on the table while keeping his hand over them. "But remember that we're all gentlemen here. Please, no swearing in front of the ladies."

With that, Doc removed his hand and cleared his throat.

Initially, Taylor hardly even spared a glance toward Doc's cards. Suddenly, however, the smugness on his face evaporated.

"Wait a second," he said as he jumped to his feet and leaned forward with both hands on the table. Like a vulture gazing down at a stretch of desert floor, Taylor eyed Doc's cards before reaching out to spread them a bit farther apart.

"This isn't right," Taylor muttered. "I know it isn't."

Doc's cards were all clubs. Although they were a bit lower than the ones Taylor had shown, they were in order.

"Straight flush," Doc said. "This will be of some use to me," he added while taking hold of the knife by its handle. "There are some letters waiting for me in Denison that need to be opened."

Caleb couldn't help but laugh at that. The feeling passed, however, as he saw the gunmen creeping in on them from all sides.

"This can't be right," Taylor said. "Those aren't the cards I dealt to you."

Putting on a confused and somewhat hurt expression, Doc asked, "Are you saying that you cheated? How deceitful. And to think this was just a friendly —"

Taylor's hand leapt from the table and drew his pistol in the space of a heartbeat. Before he could take aim, he was staring down the barrel of Doc's gun. With wide eyes, Taylor shouted, "Somebody shoot this skinny son of a bitch!"

Upon hearing that, Caleb grabbed the closest thing he could find, which just so happened to be the glass that he'd been drinking from all night. Some beer sprayed through the air as the glass flew, but that was quickly joined by a bloody mist as the glass slammed into the face of the closest gunman.

As the man that had been standing over Mike turned to fire at Doc, he saw a sudden burst of motion from Lottie. The redhead yelped in surprise as she was pulled down by Mike, who then stuck his hand in her skirt.

"Pardon me, Lottie," Mike said as he found her derringer, aimed it at the gunman standing over him, and pulled the trigger.

The derringer didn't let off much more than a pop as it sent a bullet through the gunman's rib cage. The gunman crumpled over and twisted to bring his pistol to bear on Mike. The derringer popped again. This time, the little gun punched a hole through the gunman's head and dropped him into a dead heap on the floor.

Lottie was still gasping in surprise when her gun was handed back. The moment she felt the familiar iron in her grasp, she fished in another pocket for two fresh rounds.

Caleb took one step toward the man with the shattered glass on his face, planted his foot, and then brought his other knee up to bury it deep into the gunman's stomach. That doubled the man over, allowing blood from his nose to drip onto the floor, accompanied by the spatter of glass shards hitting the wooden slats.

One look toward the door allowed Caleb to see the gunman guarding the entrance point his weapon toward the card table. Caleb dropped reflexively as the gun went off. Lead hissed over his head and buried itself loudly into the table behind him.

"Goddamn!" Donnelly shouted as he stomped in from one of the back rooms. "What the hell's going on here?"

He was answered by random shouting as a few of the real customers tried to get out of there, only to stop short when they noticed the guard at the door. A few of the working girls had been watching the whole thing and went over to report what they'd seen to Donnelly.

"You made a big fucking mistake, Holliday," Taylor snarled.

Cocking his head slightly, Doc flipped the knife he'd been holding so he could grip it by the blade rather than the handle. "Did

I?" he quipped, before snapping his wrist and sending the blade right into its owner.

Taylor reflexively grabbed for the knife protruding from his upper torso. The moment his hand found the weapon, he winced in pain and practically threw himself to the floor.

Doc took advantage of the show by getting to his feet and drawing his pistol. Before he could take a shot, the room filled with a thunder that could only have come from a shotgun. Everyone in the saloon either turned or dropped to the floor. The members of that former group were able to see Donnelly stepping forward with the smoking shotgun in his hands.

"The law's on their way!" the saloon owner shouted.

That was all that needed to be said to get the remaining gunmen as well as the gamblers up and moving.

Doc held his Colt in one hand while offering his other to Mike so he could bring the gambler up off the floor.

"You just signed your own death warrant, Holliday," Taylor grunted.

"That was done long before I ever laid eyes on you," Doc replied.

"Nobody draws a gun on us. You're finished! You better pray you die of that sickness, because it'll be a walk through the roses compared to what's in store for you."

Doc gritted his teeth as his finger tightened around the trigger. Suddenly, from the corner of his eye, he spotted someone coming at him like a charging bull.

The fourth gunman took one step and extended his arm to point his gun at the side of Doc's head. Just as the gunman was about to pull his trigger, he heard a shot and felt a burning pain flood through his chest. When he looked down, he saw blood soaking into the front of his shirt.

Doc stood in the spot where he'd been before, only one of his hands was extended beneath the other. In that hand, Doc held his second pistol. It was still smoking from the bullet it had just delivered.

As Taylor staggered toward the door, he pulled the knife from his body and let out the snarl of a wounded animal as the blade slipped from between his fingers. He spotted Caleb rushing toward him, but was too weak and disoriented to think of anything to do about it. Fortunately for him, the gunman Taylor had posted at the door had already lined up a shot of his own.

The shot cracked through the air, adding to the smoke that hung in the room like an acrid fog. The bullet drilled into Caleb's back and dropped him to one knee.

As Caleb's vision started to fade, he felt Taylor shove him down and then watched as the man in the dark blue suit and his remaining guards headed out the door.

17

When Caleb woke up, he was surrounded by feathery pillows that were thicker than his head. Soft, downy comforters were wrapped around him and the smell of lilacs filled the air. As he shifted, he felt his legs and back rubbing against what he guessed to be satin or silk.

"Am I . . . in . . . ?" he asked groggily.

"Not quite heaven, but you're close," Doc said from somewhere that was nearby but out of sight. "You're in Lottie's bedroom."

Caleb opened his eyes and tried to sit up. Any thoughts of a glorious afterlife were erased when he felt pain lance all the way from his shoulder blades to the front of his chest. "Jesus!" he grunted as he dropped back down again. He felt another stab of pain as he hit, and he clutched two fistfuls of sheets until the pain died down a bit.

As something cool was pressed to his forehead, Caleb heard another voice. This one was also familiar and matched his surroundings much more than the scratchy drawl that had come before it.

"Sit still, Caleb," Lottie said. "The doctor said you shouldn't move unless it's absolutely necessary."

"It is necessary," Caleb groaned. "My mouth feels like baked leather."

"I don't exactly know what that means, but I bet you're thirsty."

"That's exactly what it means," Caleb said. As the pain faded a little more, he soon felt another cold touch against his skin. A tin cup was being placed in his hand and he took it gratefully. The first sip of water hurt like hell, but the second was a blessing. After that, he felt as if he'd never be able to drink enough.

When he finally came up for air, Caleb rubbed his eyes and took another look around. "How long have I been here?"

"Two weeks," Doc said.

Almost immediately, Lottie backhanded Doc's shoulder and said, "It's just been over two days."

Doc moved around to the opposite side of Caleb's bed and said, "I bet that makes you feel better, doesn't it? You see? It's all a matter of perspective."

Although he meant to laugh, Caleb let out

something that was more like a grunt that had been forced up from the bottom of his gut. "Can I have some more water?"

"Sure," Lottie said. "I'll go get it."

After watching her leave the room, Caleb shifted so he could get a look at Doc. The slender Georgian was sitting on a small padded chair against the wall. The room had a soft glow to it, thanks to the tinted lantern covers, the dark color of the furnishings, and the expensive carpet on the floor. There were a few tables set up here and there, each of which had flowers set on it in a different size of vase.

Doc sat in his chair with one arm draped over the back. Once Lottie was well out of earshot, he said, "I think she's sweet on you."

"Too bad I had to get stabbed to bring that out of her."

"Shot," Doc corrected. "You were shot."

Pressing his palms against his eyes, Caleb took a deep breath and let it out slowly. It hurt, but not as much as when he'd tried to sit up a few moments ago. "Oh . . . yeah." Suddenly, all the memories snapped back into focus, and Caleb tried to get out of bed one more time. "What happened after I was shot? Where's Taylor?"

"He had more men waiting outside. Since

nobody else but me and Owen were in any condition to chase after him, it seemed prudent to let him go. I must give him a bit of credit, though. He was man enough to leave his money behind."

"After all that, you still figure on getting out of that game a winner."

"And why not? I earned it."

"Earned it? You cheated, Doc. We cheated. If that kind of thing had happened in my saloon, I would have chased us out of there and run us out of town."

"That's why a professional must know how to keep his moves quick and quiet. You did a fine job. Actually, we all did."

Caleb opened his eyes and saw Doc truly basking in the moment.

When he saw he was being watched, Doc shrugged and said, "It could have been a whole lot worse, you know. None of us wound up dead."

"Close," Caleb grunted.

"Close only counts in horseshoes, and it sure as hell doesn't count in poker."

"I don't even think I'm remembering how that last hand went."

"Beautifully." Doc beamed. "It was absolutely beautiful."

"The way I recall, I had two of the cards you wound up showing before all the shooting started."

"You did have those cards. And, thanks to Mike putting the deadwood pile closer to me, you tossed those cards my way when you folded."

"I thought that part was a little obvious," Lottie said as she came back into the room with Caleb's water. "But it went over pretty well. Taylor must have been fixing the deal, so he knew who was getting what cards. I'm amazed he left that much to chance."

"You're not a card mechanic, are you?" Doc asked.

Lottie shrugged. "It's not one of my strengths. At least, not in poker."

"It's hard enough to deal the cards you want to one or even two people, but dealing them to everyone at the table either requires a deck that you've already stacked or cards that have been rigged some other way. He dealt his own cards and my cards. The rest were just random trash."

"So I just happened to get the cards you needed?" Caleb asked.

Grinning, Doc said, "That's right. I did mention that I had to wait the better part of a day for those pieces to come together. You showed them to me perfectly, by the way."

Lottie looked down at Caleb and asked, "You showed Doc your cards?"

"We've been practicing."

"Very nice," she said with genuine admiration. "Still, it was a risky play."

Doc waved that off with one hand. "It was everyone working together. Mike shifted the discard pile, Caleb fed me the cards, and you distracted Taylor so he wouldn't see any of it coming. I don't see why everyone's so surprised. After all, we were going into this as a team. Despite a few injuries, we all came out of it fairly well. Which reminds me . . ."

As Doc's voice trailed off, he fished two bundles of money from inside his jacket. "Donnelly was kind enough to cash me out even after all the commotion. We had to pay for the damage to his place, but all of us came out ahead."

Caleb took his money even though it hurt to move. Lottie, on the other hand, looked down at the cash as if it were a snake coiled in Doc's hand.

"What's the matter?" Doc asked.

Letting out a sigh, Lottie replied, "I shouldn't take that money."

"Why not?"

"Because I'm the one who brought Taylor to that game. Because of me, two men are dead, Mike and Caleb were hurt, and the rest of us could have been killed as well."

"First of all," Doc said, "we all take a certain amount of risk when we do a job like this. It's what makes the payoff that much sweeter. Secondly, you bringing Taylor to that game is what resulted in us getting his money."

"And third," Caleb added, "the men that were killed were working for Taylor."

Doc nodded. "And, if I may add, they were trying their damnedest to kill us at the time. Don't forget that."

When she looked at Caleb, Lottie got a nod in return. That was enough for her to reach out to take the money Doc was offering. When she tried to take that money from Doc, however, she wasn't able to pry it from his grasp.

Staring her dead in the eyes, Doc asked, "Did you know Taylor was connected to the Tiger?"

"No," she said. "I didn't. All I knew was that he was rich and looking for a game of high-stakes poker. Boyer's always been the man to collect the taxes around here."

"Did you look into who he was at all?"

"A bit, but I should have looked a whole lot deeper. That's why I was going to refuse this money."

After chewing on that for a while, Doc slowly started to nod. He let go of the money and put a smile on his face. "Consider this a lesson learned . . . for all of us."

"Yeah, Doc," Caleb grunted. "You start learning to drive people crazy and I'll start learning how to dodge bullets."

"I'm already doing just fine in that regard," Doc said.

"Yes," Lottie said as she tucked her money away and patted Doc on the cheek, "you most certainly are. Take all the time you need here, Caleb. I've got some errands to run. Will you be at your faro table tonight, Doc?"

"Yes, ma'am."

"Good. There are some players coming in from Denver and they're looking for a game. Since I'll be occupied tonight, I'll steer them your way."

"Much appreciated."

Lottie stepped over to Caleb and leaned down so she could kiss him on the forehead. After pausing to look into his eyes for a moment, she leaned down again so she could place a distinctly less nurturing kiss on his lips. Before backing away, she drew Caleb's bottom lip into her mouth and gave it a quick nibble. "Feel better soon," she said. "I want you able to move around again."

Unable to hide the stunned expression on his face, Caleb said, "Yes, ma'am."

Lottie turned on her heel and headed for the door with a bounce in her step that held a special spot in every man's dreams. Doc was still looking in that direction when Caleb let out the breath he'd been holding.

"Now, that's what I call a good person to have on our side," Caleb said.

"Indeed, she would be. Except for one thing."

"What's that?"

"Remember what she said about not knowing who Taylor was?" Doc asked.

"Yeah."

"She was lying."

18

Just over a week passed, and Caleb had heard nothing more about the Tiger, the game that had exploded into a war inside the Beehive, or much of anything else that took place outside his room. Once he made his way out of Lottie's place, Caleb slept through most of every day and made several agonizing attempts to get back on his feet.

His most recent attempt had proved to be the most agonizing and resulted in Caleb sitting backward in a chair for close to an hour without ever leaving his room. As another jolt of pain stabbed through him, Caleb grabbed on to the chair so tightly he nearly ripped it to pieces.

"Son of a . . . bitch!" Caleb snarled.

Another man sat in a chair next to Caleb. Actually, he looked more like a grizzled old bird perched on the edge of the chair. His shoulder-length gray hair hung in unkempt waves, and his wrinkled face was clean-shaven except for a patch of black and gray hair sprouting from his chin. With one hand, the old man inserted a probe into the bloody wound in Caleb's back. His other hand manipulated a pair of pliers within that hole.

"Sit still, Caleb," the old man said through gritted teeth.

"Fuck that!" Caleb grunted. "I think you're pulling out a goddamn bone! How come we couldn't do this before? Like when I was dead to the world."

"You were losing too much blood," the old man said as he kept digging. "And it's not good to put you under this much stress while you're not even strong enough to stay awake. Besides, the bullet managed to miss everything vital, so it was best to let it set until you were strong enough to bear through this procedure."

"Real good policy," Caleb snarled. "Real fucking good."

The old man shook his head and kept working. "You've been strong enough for days, but you wouldn't bother calling me. I had to wait until Dr. Holliday mentioned it." When the muffled sound of metal crunching against metal could be heard, his eyes widened and Caleb tightened his grip even more around the back of the chair.

"I think I got it," the old man said.

Caleb tried to speak, but only got out a series of vicious snarls.

Finally, the old man removed the pliers and eased out a hunk of twisted lead.

"You get the bullet out?" Caleb asked.

"Yep. That is, unless you're growing these things in your shoulder."

Caleb didn't even try to laugh. When he let out a haggard breath, he practically wilted against the chair. "Lord, that feels better."

"Told you it would. It would have been better a lot sooner if you would have come to see me again like I asked."

"I know. It's just —"

"Save it," the old man interrupted. He then wrapped Caleb's shoulder in bandages and tied them off with a sturdy knot.

"Thanks, Doctor," Caleb said while carefully testing his arm as well as the bandages. "How much do I owe you?"

"I'm also here to visit John Henry. He said he'd settle up with me all at once. Now, if you'll excuse me . . ." The old man gathered up his equipment and tipped his hat. Before leaving the room, he asked, "You need anything for the pain?"

"Since I'm feeling good enough to walk to a saloon, I'll be able to find plenty there to ease my pain."

Grumbling under his breath, the old man stepped out of Caleb's room and headed to the room directly beside it. He tipped his hat once more to the woman who watched the hallway like a nervous hawk. Ever since the trouble at the Beehive, the owner of the boardinghouse had started paying especially close attention to the boarders who'd been recommended by Owen Donnelly.

As soon as he got into the other room, the old man immediately set down his bag and fished out another set of instruments.

"Afternoon, Dr. Sanderson," Doc said cordially. "I take it by the screams coming from the next room that my associate is feeling better?"

"He will after a bit more rest. How's your condition been treating you?"

Doc was sitting on a narrow bed with a cigarette case resting beside him. He wore a pair of black trousers with the suspenders gathered at his waist. A white undershirt could be seen beneath the more formal shirt that was unbuttoned all the way down to the waist. His skin was the same color as his undershirt and an almost skeletal frame could be detected through his clothing.

"I've never felt better," Doc answered.

Sanderson fit the earpieces of a stethoscope in place and pressed the round end against Doc's chest. While listening, Sanderson shook his head slightly and grumbled to himself. "Your friend in there got shot and I see him the same amount of times as I've seen you. I don't know which one of you that makes me madder at."

"The air has been doing wonders for my condition," Doc recited. "And I have been watching my diet whenever possible."

"I've heard all about you, John. The only time you get fresh air is when you're stumbling in or out of a saloon. Your diet consists of whatever slop those bartenders throw at you and all that smoking doesn't help matters either."

"Some of those bartenders are excellent cooks."

"They're not to blame," Sanderson snapped. "You are. For Christ's sake, would it kill you to keep normal hours or eat healthier?"

Rather than put together any sort of answer, Doc took a cigarette from the case and lifted it to his mouth. By the time he found and struck a match, he seemed close to passing out from exertion.

"I can't be the first doctor to tell you this," Sanderson said.

Doc shook his head and expelled a smoky breath.

"Then why won't you listen to anyone?"

"And what if I do listen?" Doc asked. "What good will that do? Will it keep me alive?"

"Yes, it just might."

"For how long? Another couple of months? A year?"

"You're only twenty-three, so time might not have as much of an impact as it does on a man closer to my age, but there's no reason why you shouldn't try to get every bit out of it that you're entitled to."

"My concept of time is just fine," Doc said. "In fact, I feel every second slap me in the face. Now, why the hell would I want to fight for any more?"

"You can get better if you try. Your condition has been known to improve."

"You and every other doctor out there would have me eat like a bird and take a morning constitutional and all sorts of other nonsense just to make yourselves feel better."

"It will help," Sanderson insisted. "Just give it a chance."

"A life following the orders I've been given is hardly a life."

"You'd prefer spending your days in a

smoky saloon playing cards and getting shot at?"

"Wouldn't anyone?"

Sanderson pulled in a deep breath and let it out slowly. "So why the hell am I wasting my time with you?"

"Contrary to what you might believe, I do like to know where I stand."

"You're standing on the edge of a cliff, John. How about that for an answer?"

Doc grinned and took another puff of his cigarette. "I was hoping for something a bit more technical."

"Have you had any bad spells lately?" Sanderson asked. "Any time in particular where your condition acted up?"

"There's been some weariness lately. I've been tiring out somewhat quicker than normal and it's been harder to relieve my cough."

"Hacked up any blood?"

Slowly, Doc nodded.

After digging a few more things out of his black bag, Sanderson examined Doc a bit more before saying, "You're doing better than one might expect, but that's not saying a whole lot. Near as I can tell, your situation is remaining stagnant rather than swinging one way or another. Since you won't listen to everything I have to say,

205

perhaps you could cut back on the smoking or try to trim back your late nights. At this point, every little bit helps."

"I can do that."

"After you have a bad fit, you might want to stay off your feet for a while. If you must move around, you might consider using a cane to help you."

"A cane?" Doc asked in disbelief.

"Some find them to be very fashionable," Sanderson retorted. "Considering your fancy clothes and expensive tastes, I dare say carrying a cane wouldn't be too out of place. Hell, you could hollow it out and fill it full of whiskey."

Doc shook his head as if to clear his ears and then started laughing. The physician wasn't too far behind, although his laughter seemed more of a guilty pleasure.

"I'll see about a cane," Doc conceded. "What about a different location? Would that help add some time onto the end of my sentence on this mortal coil?"

Sanderson nodded and genuinely seemed to lighten up a bit as he did so. "It might. Anyplace with clearer air would help. Preferably somewhere near the mountains."

"You mean like Denver?"

"Good Lord, John. If I didn't know any better, I'd say you were actually starting to care whether or not you lived or died. Denver would be splendid for your condition. In fact, there are several different clinics that I would highly recommend."

"Make a list and I'll look into them, but I won't make any promises."

Squaring his shoulders, Sanderson placed a strong hand on Doc's shoulder and said, "The fact that you're able to do . . . what you do . . . is amazing. I may not approve, but I must say it gives me some hope."

"How much hope?" Doc asked.

After something of a pause, Sanderson said, "My guess is that you've probably got another year or two. Perhaps double that, if you started cracking down and following my orders."

"That's all I needed to hear. Thank you very much."

"I just hope you heard everything, John. At least think about what I said, won't you?"

Doc took a wad of folded bills from his pocket and peeled off a few from the top.

When he saw the money he'd been given, Sanderson immediately shook his head and handed some of it back. "I don't mind the occasional gratuity, John, but this is too much."

"Keep it. You can earn the rest by forgetting about the particulars of your appointments with myself and my friend in the next room."

"Particulars?"

"As in, everything. If anyone asks, you don't know our names and you don't know what condition we're in. Understand?"

Sanderson nodded, but kept his hand with the leftover money extended toward Doc. "I understand just fine. You think whoever shot up Caleb might come around to finish the job?"

"Something like that."

"Then it's my duty as a physician to keep that information to myself," Sanderson said while setting the remaining money on the edge of the bed. "That sort of thing falls under keeping the two of you healthy, even if you are infrequent patients of mine."

"At least take some of it," Doc said. "It's not much, but you've earned every bit of it."

After a few nervous glances toward the money, Sanderson took a few of the extra bills that Doc had offered. "There is some new equipment coming in from California that I've had my eye on."

"Have at it," Doc said as he lifted the flask that he'd fished from the jacket hanging on the back of a nearby chair.

As soon as the door to Doc's room was

shut, there came another knock and the door was opened once more. Caleb stuck his head inside and nodded a quick greeting. "What did the doctor say?" he asked.

"It seems I have a condition that affects my lungs," Doc reported dryly.

"Well, if you feel like stretching your legs, we can head down to the Beehive. I'm buying."

"Maybe some other time."

"Will you be there to deal your game?"

"You can set your clock by me."

"All right. I'll look for you." With that, Caleb winced and grabbed onto the door frame for support. Even that wasn't enough to cause his anxious grin to fade.

"Are you certain you're in a condition to walk all that way?" Doc asked.

"Coming from a man who deals faro while looking like death warmed over, that's downright touching."

Doc shrugged and stubbed out his cigarette against the bedside table.

"You, there," came a familiarly grating voice from the hall.

Caleb didn't have to look at the old lady running the boardinghouse to know it was her. "I'm going, I'm going," he said over his shoulder.

"Just make sure you're going to the Beehive and that you're going quick. Mr. Donnelly told me to tell you there's trouble."

"What kind of trouble?" Caleb asked as he turned toward the old woman.

"The kind that makes Sheriff Jacobs angry enough to threaten closing that saloon down for good."

19

Caleb and Doc practically exploded from their rooms, despite the variety of ailments that were plaguing them at the time. They were a pair that attracted plenty of looks from folks they passed, but not a single word to catch their attention. Just seeing the pair charge toward the Beehive got rumors flying about another fight brewing in the saloon. Doc and Caleb ignored all of the suspicious looks and pushed past the few people who were too slow to get out of their way. They had business to attend to and would tolerate no obstruction.

By the time he arrived at the Beehive, Caleb was looking through a red haze that had filtered in behind his eyes. The pain had stopped by now after being washed away by a throbbing numbness that started beneath the freshly wrapped bandages and crept all the way out to the tips of his fingers.

Doc's eyes were a bit more hooded than

normal, but that wasn't as big of a difference for him as were the clothes that he wore when walking into his current place of employment. Some of the people that looked toward the front door when it opened didn't even seem to recognize the house's faro dealer. Sheriff Jacobs was not one of those people.

"We were just talking about you two," Jacobs said as two of his deputies stepped up on either side of him. "Seems your game caused quite a stir."

"Owen knew where to find us," Caleb said. "Anytime you wanted to have a word, all you had to do was ask."

"I thought I'd wait until you were feeling better. Truth is, I heard you hadn't even paid a proper visit to Dr. Sanderson yet, so I thought it would be a while. Glad to see you up and around."

"So you can drag me into jail?"

Sheriff Jacobs lowered his head and stepped closer to where Caleb and Doc were standing. Compared to the fairly amiable voice he'd been using before, the one he switched to was a fierce growl. "You want to spend some time behind bars, then that's the way to go about it."

Owen Donnelly rushed up to the growing group at the front door and placed a friendly hand on both Caleb and Doc's shoulders. "Why don't you two come in and have a seat? It's important for a saloon to have folks be able to come and go as they please. You and your men are free to join us, of course, Sheriff."

The moment he got some distance between himself and the lawmen, Donnelly spoke to Doc and Caleb in a quick whisper. "I didn't tell them the whole story about what went on in here, but I think he's heard about it from some of the others that saw what happened."

"You mean he doesn't know about the men that were killed?" Caleb asked.

"He knows about that. He just doesn't know exactly how they wound up that way. Since that rich fella didn't stick around to give his account, it wasn't too hard to pass off the story."

"Where is Taylor?"

"Haven't seen him for a while and I ain't about to go looking." By now, Donnelly had taken them to the farthest table he could find from the door. He turned and saw the lawmen taking their time in joining them. By the looks of it, Jacobs and his deputies were swapping some last-minute words among themselves.

"I saw most of what happened and I know

you both a hell of a lot better than I knew Taylor," Donnelly said in a fast ramble. "You and I go back a ways, Doc, so I figured you'd want to know that Jacobs and his boys were coming around looking for you and they meant business. That said, I don't want any more trouble in here. I can justify cleaning up after some asshole that steps out of line or some dispute over gambling debts, but I ain't about to be a part of lawmen getting gunned down in my place, Caleb, and I won't see those same lawmen kill a friend of mine in front of me. Don't put me in that position, Doc. I'm beggin' ya."

"Why does the sheriff want to speak to us?" Doc asked.

"He —" Although Donnelly started to throw out a quick answer to that question, he stopped short when he heard the sound of approaching footsteps.

The lawmen surrounded the table. "Have a seat, Doc," Sheriff Jacobs said. "You too, Caleb. Owen, you can get back to your business."

Since there was obviously no reason or use in questioning the orders they'd been given, the three of them carried them out. Caleb eased himself into a chair with a painful wince and Doc reluctantly did the same. Shrugging his apologies, Donnelly turned and headed back toward the bar.

"You two look like shit," Jacobs said.

"Feel like it, too," Caleb replied. "What's the problem?"

"The problem is that you've been holding questionable games in my town and you've been doing it right out in the open."

Doc waited for a few seconds, but the lawman didn't say anything else. "That's it? Sheriff, every game played in any place is questionable."

"Gambling in a place where liquor is sold is against state and county laws," Jacobs reported. "There are plenty of witnesses around who can testify to you men doing just that."

"This is a joke, right?" Caleb asked. Looking around, he said, "Everyone in here's gambling. Why don't you arrest them?"

"As far as I know, they're engaging in friendly games of chance."

"And what are the chips for?"

"Tokens to represent the score. Being a gambler yourself, you shouldn't need to ask these questions."

Doc laughed and fished his cigarette case from his pocket. The moment his hand drifted under his jacket, every deputy positioned around the table went for his gun. Despite the sudden flare of temper,

Doc retrieved his cigarettes after the slightest of pauses. He even removed one, lit it, and started smoking, as if he were on his own front porch.

"This is a load of bullshit," Doc said.

Oddly enough, Caleb was a bit surprised to hear that kind of language coming from Doc. Judging by the look on Sheriff Jacobs's face, he was, too.

"Would you rather I hauled you in for murder?" Jacobs asked.

Doc stared a hole through the lawman as the cigarette in his mouth flared up. "If you could do that, you wouldn't be wasting your time with this nonsense."

"I can do that, Doc, don't doubt it. After all the blood that was spilled in here during your little game, we could toss both of you in a cell and then go after your friend Mike Lynch." Picking up on something in Doc's eyes, Jacobs added, "We already spoke to Lynch. He was smart enough to take his charge without a fuss. Even so, I doubt he'll show up for his court date."

"And that suits you just fine, doesn't it?" Doc asked.

"Just so long as I don't have to look at his face anymore."

Caleb laughed under his breath and repositioned himself in his chair so he could sit without aggravating his wound. "I guess I see where some of those taxes go."

"No secret there," Jacobs said. "We're servants of the governing bodies of Fort Griffin."

"Not those taxes. The taxes collected by the asshole who stomped out of this place when the smoke was still in the air. The asshole who probably still had blood on the bottom of his boots when he told you to run us out of town."

"That's a hell of an accusation. You'd better be able to back it up."

"Why would he want to do that?" Doc asked. "So you'd be justified in shooting us while we were committing some other sort of trumped-up charge?"

"The charge is real. You can look it up in any law book there is."

"Sure it is, Sheriff," Caleb sneered. "But it's only enforced when it suits your purpose. Otherwise, none of the saloons in town would be open and Fort Griffin wouldn't be such a popular place for local gamblers."

Jacobs listened to all of this with a blank stare. Finally, he crossed one leg over the other and started drumming his fingers on top of his knee. "If I were you, I'd take this little bit of harassment with a smile. Plenty more before you weren't so lucky."

"And why's the Tiger being so generous with us?" Doc asked.

Without blinking at the mention of that moniker, Sheriff Jacobs said, "It's not their call to make. You owned a saloon back in Dallas, right, Caleb?"

Caleb nodded.

"From what I've heard, it was as good a place as any." Narrowing his eyes, Jacobs asked, "Did every bit of your income come from selling liquor? Of course it didn't. Like every good businessman, you did some fast dealing of your own and you were also forced to feed from the same trough as a whole lot of dirty sons of bitches. You can like it or hate it, but it's a necessary part of the business. Am I right?"

As much as he wanted to disagree with the sheriff, Caleb would have had an easier time debating that rain wasn't really wet. Still, he decided to keep quiet rather than agree with the sheriff.

Jacobs didn't need to hear the words to know what was going on inside Caleb's head. He nodded and kept talking as if he'd already gotten what he wanted just by looking at Caleb's face. "I like to think I'm making this as easy as it can be for everyone involved. You two can go along with it and try your luck somewhere else. Hell, you might even try your luck here again someday after things cool down."

"We don't get a day in court?" Doc asked with a straight face.

"Sure you do, Holliday. And you'll get to hear a preponderance of evidence that shows how much of a bad influence you are on this town and the good people that live in it. Now, if you'll excuse me," Jacobs said as he got to his feet. "I have other matters to attend to. When you see Lottie, be sure to send my regards."

With that, Jacobs turned his back to the table and walked away. One of his deputies walked along with him, leaving the rest to stay behind and make sure nobody was going to get any bad ideas when the sheriff wasn't looking. Once they saw that Caleb and Doc had no such notions, the remaining deputies left the saloon.

"Goddamn," Caleb grunted. "I should not have rushed down here like that. I feel like I've been gored by a bull."

"Here you go," Donnelly said. He stepped up to the table as if to fill the spot that Sheriff Jacobs had left. "On the house."

Normally, Caleb left the whiskey drinking to Doc. Although he preferred beer any day of the week, Caleb also didn't normally get a taste of Donnelly's specially brewed whiskey. It was a concoction that Doc raved about the way a poet would praise a sunrise, and it did a real good job of taking some of the bite out of the pain that throbbed in his wounded back. Caleb barely even realized he'd tossed back all of the whiskey until he was setting the empty glass back onto the table.

Donnelly was right there to refill it. "I guess that wasn't too bad after all, huh?" he asked while pouring. He seemed more than a little surprised to find Doc's glass still full.

Rolling his cigarette between his fingers, Doc hardly seemed to notice that the whiskey was in front of him. "We were arrested for gambling," he mused. "Isn't that a pip?"

"Hold on, let me see if I can remember." Donnelly closed his eyes as a wistful smile drifted onto his face. Without opening his eyes, he recited, "Playing a game of cards in a house where spirituous liquors are sold."

"Pretty much," Caleb said.

"I haven't heard that one in a long time." Shrugging, Donnelly left the bottle of whiskey and headed back to where a group of customers had gathered at the bar.

"I've heard it before," Caleb said reluctantly. "The sheriff was right. It is a real law and it is statewide. I can't speak for the county, but it's in the Texas books."

Doc wrapped his fingers around the whiskey glass, but didn't lift it from the table. "It was nothing," he said, "but a polite way to ask us to leave town."

"Polite?" Caleb grunted. "Is that what you call it?"

"Most certainly."

Doc stared down at his glass while swirling the amber liquid inside. He eventually lifted it to his mouth and sipped just enough of it to feel the burn on his lips. After savoring that for a bit, he poured a bit more into himself and let out a breath as the firewater made its way into his stomach. "I'm sure going to miss this stuff."

"What?" Caleb asked in disbelief. "You actually want to leave town because that badge-wearing asshole told us to?"

"Don't sound so put out, Caleb. We're not running away."

"Then what would you call it?"

"Moving on to greener pastures. Running a game here will be too difficult for a while, so there's no reason to stay when there's a whole circuit out there waiting to be explored. Besides, my doctor told me that I don't have much time left to enjoy."

Caleb rolled his eyes and groaned. "Don't

even try to put on the sickly act with me, Doc."

"He said the climate in Denver would suit my delicate constitution much better."

"Denver, huh?" Caleb asked with a gleam in his eye.

Doc nodded. "I owe some back taxes that I'd prefer to pay in person."

20

"You're leaving?" Lottie asked as she stood in her sitting room with her arms folded. "Caleb, stand still for a second and answer me."

Gathering up his belongings didn't take very long. Caleb normally lived with his things packed up and ready to go. Without the lead in his wound to slow him down, it was much less of an ordeal to throw his stuff together now than when he'd left Lottie's. After stuffing the last of his shirts into his bag, Caleb took a breath and looked over at her.

Lottie stood with her eyes fixed on him. A grim expression shrouded her face. "When did you decide this?" she asked.

"About an hour ago," Caleb replied. "Mike's already gone. I wouldn't be too surprised if you got a visit from the sheriff next."

"Will you come back?"

"Probably, but not for a while." Forcing himself to truly look into her eyes, Caleb stopped what he was doing and walked over to her. When he placed his hands on her shoulders, he felt Lottie draw closer to him rather than pull away. "I don't even think a real warrant was issued for any of us. Doc was right. This is just a way to shove us out of town. It's also a way for Taylor to flex his muscles without sticking his nose out from wherever he's hiding."

"It could be Taylor or it might have come from higher up," Lottie pointed out.

Caleb let out a grunt of a laugh, which sent a painful twinge through his back. "Straight from the Tiger's mouth, huh? Every time I hear that name, I can't get over how fucking ridiculous it is."

"Whatever name they go by, they're known all over the circuit. Boyer always said they had the law on their side. I guess this serves to remind everyone about that very thing."

"Which also means they'll spread the word about how we got run out of Fort Griffin," Caleb said. "I might as well go back to Dallas and sweep the floors at my old saloon. We won't be given a real game anywhere that's heard about this. We'll be pegged as suckers or weak enough to step on whenever it suits someone's purpose."

"Apart from bruising your pride, that's not a bad arrangement. You and Doc make a hell of a pair. You took Taylor for all he had and he was ready for you. I'm not the only one that's impressed with that." She leaned forward while slipping her arms around him and being careful not to touch Caleb's bandaged wound. "Anyone else who still thinks you're easy pickings," she whispered into his ear, "will play accordingly. I'm not the only cardplayer who would kill for that sort of attention."

"There are some possibilities," Caleb admitted.

When she nodded, Lottie brushed her lips against Caleb's earlobe. "I never thought anyone would be able to humble Taylor like you two did."

"Doc did most of the work on that one."

She shook her head, causing some of her red locks to tickle Caleb's neck. "You set them up and fed Doc the cards he needed. The only reason I caught you doing it was because I couldn't take my eyes off you that whole night. It was a work of art, Caleb."

"You think so?" Caleb asked as he settled his hands on the sloping curves of her hips.

Lottie's reply was an intoxicating touch of warm breath against Caleb's skin. "Mmm hmmm. When do you plan on leaving?"

"Tomorrow morning after me and Doc get up and eat. So that makes it closer to tomorrow afternoon."

"Then let's enjoy what's left of our time together."

As Caleb moved his hand along the top of Lottie's blouse, she shrugged her shoulders so the material slipped down. Her hands were busy as well, slowly peeling off his shirt while still minding the bandages underneath.

"You're leaving?" Trish asked in a voice that rose sharply to an ear-splitting pitch.

Doc was once again in bed, but there were two major differences from the last time he'd been stretched out and savoring a cigarette: he wasn't thinking about his health and it wasn't his own bed.

"It's only going to be for a while," Doc said. "There's some business that needs to be taken care of."

Trish wore a pout on her face as she moved across the floor toward the bed. Apart from the pout and a silk slip, she wasn't wearing anything else. "But I just got used to having you here."

"That's sweet, but there's nothing I can do about it." At just the right moment, Doc winced. He put just enough drama into it to get Trish rushing over to him and climbing onto the bed.

"Are you feeling all right?" she asked. "Did you see the doctor?"

"He told me that all I needed was to get some rest and have someone care for me. Since I'm traveling, I don't see how I'll fill either of those bills."

Straddling his waist, Trish straightened her back and looked down at him with a glimmer in her eyes. "I can make you feel better," she said.

"I don't know. It may be too much to ask."

Slowly, Trish gathered up her slip and peeled it up and over her head. When she tossed it to one corner, she leaned forward to make sure Doc got a good look at her trim body.

"Actually," Doc said, "you may just be up to the challenge."

She smiled and slipped under the covers with him. "I think I can manage."

Doc and Caleb left Fort Griffin quietly the next afternoon. There was a fine that was supposed to have been paid, but neither of them felt like contributing one more penny to the very thing that had pushed them out of town in the first place. One of Jacobs's deputies was at the platform where the stage to Denver was being loaded. He watched the men climb on board and stayed there to make certain they were truly intent on leaving.

Doc tossed a friendly wave toward the deputy as the driver snapped his reins and got the stagecoach moving.

The next several days were filled with the growing heat of a quickly approaching summer. That, compounded by being cooped up in yet another cramped carriage, made the trip much less easier for Doc to bear than the one that had originally brought him into town. To make matters worse, the stage didn't travel directly to Denver. In fact, there was some backtracking to be done as the stage needed to cross paths with another stage in Jacksboro.

Caleb leaned his head back so he could rest his eyes and allow a smug little grin to creep onto his face.

Doc sat next to a bald preacher, who was the only other passenger in the carriage. He gazed out the window until the scenery failed to strike his fancy and then he turned his attention to Caleb. "You look unusually chipper," he said.

Without opening his eyes, Caleb said, "Just relishing the moment."

"I know the inside of this coach smells like ambrosia, but I highly doubt it's worth relishing. You must be dwelling on the image of a certain redhead."

"And what if I am?"

"Then, by all means, share that image with your friend and partner."

Caleb gave Doc a quick look from one partially opened eye. Making certain to add a bit more to his smile, he said, "We're not partners in everything, Doc. Besides, it looked to me like that blonde kept you busy."

"Trish was pretty," Doc said. "She has her talents. But she's just . . . I don't even know how to say it."

"Just a sip of water when you had your hopes set on wine?" Caleb offered.

Doc snapped his head back with blatant surprise. "That's it, exactly!"

"I've had a few women like that. Still, Trish had some awfully fine talents."

"She did, indeed."

Sitting up a bit, Caleb glanced over to the preacher sitting next to Doc. The bald man was snoring loudly and slumped to one side, just as he'd been for most of the ride. "By the way, you were right about Lottie."

"How so?"

"She was lying about not knowing who

Taylor truly was. I don't know for certain how much she knew, but it was definitely more than she was letting on."

"That's a shame."

"Not really," Caleb said. "Because she let a few more things slip throughout the night."

"You two had a conversation?"

"Just bits and pieces where the Tiger was concerned, but I could put them together."

Doc grinned and nodded approvingly. "You sly devil. Proceed."

"Even though people pay those taxes, none of them are happy about it. I think it's something that's done more as a convenience than anything else."

"They must get something out of it."

"Oh, they do. For one thing, they get steered toward games by whoever is dropping the Tiger's name at the moment. Targets are set up and picked off and the profits are taxed."

"Not a bad idea," Doc said.

"Also, the law is kept happy enough to let the gamblers do what they want even when some of the more respected members of a community are fleeced. That's a tough feat for anyone to pull off."

"True."

"But the biggest thing is that the law

doesn't actually work in league with the Tiger. In some places, the law doesn't even know about them."

"Now that's what I call a bluff. I'm a little jealous. You did a whole lot of talking last night, Caleb. How disappointing. Do you think she can be trusted since she lied to us before?"

"Lottie's been working with the Tiger here and there as a way to cover herself. That's all."

Narrowing his eyes, Doc asked, "Can you be sure about that?"

"Not completely, but my gut tells me that's the case. She mentioned it was the only way some professionals could operate and stay alive. Since she was running a game on her own and has been known to do the same in plenty of other towns, it stands to reason that she's been getting her protection from somewhere."

"It may be a fairly new arrangement, since Boyer killed the man who was acting as her protection before we arrived," Doc pointed out.

"Exactly. She could have turned on us a dozen times during that game and she didn't. She stuck to her part of the plan and even protected Mike when the lead started to fly."

"I saw the look in her eyes when she was with Mike in those last few moments. If she did have an arrangement with Taylor, I don't think Mike almost getting killed was part of it. Did you find out anything else?"

Caleb grinned and started to nod. "I sure did."

"Saving the best for last?"

"Once someone has proven to be a good little earner and keeps up on their taxes, they're able to find the Tiger wherever they go and don't have to wait around for an introduction."

"Was she good enough to share who we might look for in Denver once some of these recent troubles simmer down?"

Caleb nodded.

"Then we are most definitely still in business."

21

Jacksboro was the sort of town that everyone knew about just because it was on the way to somewhere else. Stagecoaches stopped over or passed through on a regular schedule, and cowboys would sometimes spend a night or two in one of the hotels simply because they were too tired to move along to Dallas or Fort Griffin.

Doc's first instinct was to stop just long enough to refill his flask and then try to persuade the driver to keep right on going. Caleb, on the other hand, felt something nagging at him that made him want to stay for a bit longer.

"Why on earth would you rather stay here than move along to Denver?" Doc asked. "There should be a stage passing through here that's heading into Colorado within a few hours."

"A few hours?" Caleb asked.

"Well, I didn't check the schedule."

They climbed down from the stage, leaving the preacher to sleep or wake up on his own time. When Doc's boots hit the dirt, he pulled in a deep breath and let it out easily. When Caleb tentatively set a foot down, he winced and sucked in a breath through gritted teeth.

"I don't care what the schedule is," Caleb said. "I can't take being shaken up in that damned box for much longer."

Doc put a hand on Caleb's shoulder and turned him around. Sure enough, the back of his shirt was starting to soak through with blood in a spot the size of a silver dollar. "You need to get these bandages changed. Are you feeling dizzy?"

"A bit."

"Come on, then. Let's get you looked at."

The doctor in Jacksboro operated from a small storefront office not far from a drugstore, which sold mostly powders and scented oils that had dropped off the backs of wagons and were never reclaimed.

"You stay here as long as you need," Doc said. "I'll arrange for a few rooms."

"You think it's serious?" Caleb asked.

"No, just a little blood loss. I've seen it plenty of times in my own practice."

"Actually, I'm already feeling better."

"Just go see what the doctor says and I'll

be at that place we passed along the way."

"You mean the poker hall?"

"I believe that was it."

Caleb nodded. "I get it. Thanks for all the concern, Doc."

"I'm concerned," Doc said defensively. "But there's no reason one of us can't earn while the other rests."

"Sure, Doc."

"If you had a problem with your teeth, I'd help you out. If I had a supply of spare bandages in my pocket, I'd do the same. Would you like me to hold your hand and lead you to the doctor's table?"

"No."

Doc straightened his jacket and checked his watch. "Good. Now stop your whining and get some fresh dressings. After that, I'll buy you a drink and we can get to work on seeing how much of an impression we can make in this place."

"You're all heart, Doc. It's no wonder most folks would rather have their teeth rot than see a dentist."

"That's just the blood loss talking. Crying about it won't make you feel any better. Here we are," Doc said cheerily as he stopped in front of the doctor's office. "If I don't see you in a few hours, I'll assume you died from your grievous wounds. By the way, I am your sole beneficiary as far as your personal finances go, right?"

"I bequeath one of my boots to be delivered straight up your ass. You want it now?"

Doc chuckled and patted Caleb on the shoulder before turning around and heading back up the street.

Caleb was in too much pain to think about Doc's needling. As the stagecoach ride had progressed, the wound in his back had felt like a nail being slowly tapped into his shoulder. By the time he walked into what passed for the doctor's office in Jacksboro, that nail felt more like a railroad spike.

"What can I do fer ya?" asked a small man in his late forties with a receding hairline and a bulbous nose.

"I need to see a doctor," Caleb replied.

"That's me. Pull up a chair and sit in it. You look like hell."

That much could also be said about the doctor's office. It was so small that Caleb barely even realized he was inside of it until he sat down. There was a counter along one side that looked like it belonged in a general store. Rather than candy or watches displayed within the counter's glass case, there were a few bottles of tablets and some fairly clean medical instruments.

"Them pills ain't fer sale unless I prescribe

'em," the doctor grunted. "If that's what yer after, then you can just turn 'round and head right back out."

Caleb did turn around, but only after he'd settled into the creaking chair the doctor had offered. "I'm here for this," he said while hooking a thumb over his shoulder.

Squinting and mumbling to himself, the doctor balanced a set of spectacles upon the bridge of his nose and started peeling off Caleb's shirt. "What happened here?" he asked.

"I got shot."

After a brief pause, the doctor made some more noises and then stripped off the bandages. "Eh," he said after cleaning up the wound and having a closer look. "Could've been worse. Bullet still in there?"

"No."

"Can you move yer arm?"

"Yes."

"Does it hurt?"

"Yes," Caleb said emphatically.

"Then you might get some of them drugs after all."

"I'm not after drugs. I just want to make sure the doctor in Fort Griffin didn't do more harm than good."

"You may need stitches, but that's about it."

"What?"

"You were hoping for worse news?"

"No," Caleb said. "I just thought that it was something worse. I mean, I did get shot."

"Nicked is more like it. Appears that all the damage was in the meat of the shoulder. Otherwise, you wouldn't be able to move around half as much as you do. All you need is some time to heal and a good batch of clean bandages. I got plenty of them on sale right here."

"That's it?"

"Oh. And stitches. You need to do that or you'll keep losing blood as that wound reopens. Your other doctor probably would have gotten around to it. If you like, I can do that right now, but it might sting."

"Go on," Caleb sighed.

22

The front door to the Beehive swung open, allowing a tall man with wide shoulders to step through. He wore a pleasant expression on his face, along with a waxed mustache that looked like it had been clipped directly from an advertisement. He surveyed the room with mild interest as he made his way to the bar.

"What can I get for you?" Owen Donnelly asked as he approached the new customer.

"I'd like to have a game at Dr. Holliday's table," the man replied. "I hear he runs one hell of a game."

"Doc's not in town anymore. Left just a few days ago. If you want a game, there's plenty of seats at Lottie's table."

"Lottie Deno? She's working here?"

Donnelly nodded. "Took over Doc's spot and I haven't had one complaint yet."

Glancing toward the table that Donnelly had pointed out, the well-dressed man immediately picked out the redhead dealing cards. "I don't see anything to complain about. By the way, did you happen to hear where Doc went?"

After scratching his chin, Donnelly shrugged. "Not certain."

"Thanks anyway. I believe I'll have a game along with some gin."

Donnelly turned around and took a dusty bottle from the shelf behind the bar. After pouring a splash of clear liquor into a glass, he slid the drink toward the man who'd ordered it "Enjoy."

The man nodded once and paid for his drink before sliding through the few people milling about the saloon at that time of day. There were only two seats taken at Lottie's table, but she smiled and laughed as if she were entertaining a full room.

She acknowledged the well-dressed man with a wink and said, "Hello there, stranger. Looking to buck the tiger?"

"Actually," the man said, "I wanted to have a word with you on that very subject."

"You want to know how to play the game?"

"No, I'd like to talk about the Tiger."

Lottie paused for a heartbeat, which felt a hell of a lot longer. She recovered gracefully, however, by dealing her next hand while making a show of explaining the rules of faro to the newest player. After that hand, she gathered up her cards and politely shut down her table. There were a few groans from the other players, but they were appeased by a quick kiss on the cheek from Lottie and a promise that she'd be back real soon.

As the well-dressed man went to a table closer to the stage at the back of the saloon, Lottie went to the bar.

"You know that fella?" Donnelly asked.

Lottie smiled, but couldn't keep from looking uncomfortable about it. "He's an associate of someone else I knew."

"One of those, huh?"

"Yes," she said, not really knowing exactly what Donnelly meant. "One of those. Can I have something to drink?"

"Some wine?"

"Whiskey."

Donnelly raised his eyebrows at that, but poured it just the same. "Little stronger than usual, Lottie. You sure everything's all right?"

"It should be fine, but I would appreciate it if you kept an eye on us."

"Will do," Donnelly said with a nod. "You need anything, just give me a holler."

Sensing the intent glare coming from the

well-dressed man at the back of the room, Lottie patted Donnelly's hand and turned away from the bar. She walked straight over to the table, where the man was waiting with his drink in hand and a steely confidence in his eyes.

"I made my payments already," Lottie said. "Just ask any of the other thugs that have come around looking for a handout."

"This isn't about the tax," the man said.

"Really? The only time anyone comes around mentioning the Tiger is when they're after their filthy money."

The man's eyes narrowed as a chilling smile crept onto his face. "That Tiger business is nothing but dramatics. My name's Stakely."

Lottie shook the hand that Stakely offered, which caused a shiver to roll beneath her skin. The man's grip had strength, but he was careful not to squeeze her hand too tightly. Instead, his fingers wrapped around her the way a noose wrapped around a man's neck — resting easily in place with no intention of letting go.

"All right, Mr. Stakely," Lottie said. "If this isn't about money, then what is it about?"

"Taylor was right about you. He said you were every bit as sweet as you looked. He also mentioned that you were smart and one hell of a cardplayer."

"That's nice."

"Even if all that's true, any reputation can be soiled by the company you keep." Stakely paused so he could watch Lottie's face. His eyes brushed up and down over her like an unsolicited touch. "You know who I'm talking about."

"The only problems I've had was when I was in a game with Mr. Taylor."

"I'm talking about that lunger Doc Holliday and the half-Injun he works with. Those pieces of shit came in here like they owned Fort Griffin and didn't pay me a dime."

"They paid their dues," Lottie insisted. "They ran their games here with Donnelly's blessing."

"And that helps Donnelly pay what he owes. You know damn well that each fucking cardplayer who wants to stay healthy pays his own taxes or it'll catch up to him in a rush. Holliday and his accomplice are headed for one hell of a catch-up and they won't like it one bit. That is, unless you can tell me where to find them," Stakely added in a softer tone that wouldn't have fooled anybody. "Maybe if I got a chance to sit down with them, we could straighten this whole thing out."

"If you want to find Doc, you can track him down yourself. I'm not his keeper."

Stakely let out a measured breath and leaned back in his chair. He glanced toward the bar and held up his empty glass. Almost immediately, Donnelly walked over to give him another portion of gin. The bartender tossed Lottie a friendly nod and then made his way back to the bar.

Once Donnelly was gone, Stakely parted his lips and licked them with the tip of his tongue before speaking. "I could have that barkeep choking on his own blood before you thought twice about asking him for help."

Since Lottie couldn't keep herself from pulling in a quick breath, she filled her lungs until she was able to gather the strength to sit up straight and look Stakely in the eye. "I told you, I don't know where to find Doc and Caleb."

"Is that the Injun's name?"

"And you've got a hell of a lot of nerve coming here and threatening me. If Taylor would have stuck to our plan, things wouldn't have gone so badly."

"The plan was to take Holliday down a notch without having to put a gun to his head. You ask me, Taylor was overly senti-mental since that lunger obviously isn't long for this world."

"It's not my fault Taylor was outmatched," Lottie said.

"Outmatched or outmaneuvered?"

"Is there a difference?"

Stakely remained still as a slab of rock, allowing his mouth to move only when it was necessary to form his words. "One involves skill and the other involves getting stabbed in the back by a lying cunt who was supposed to be on your side."

Lottie's hand flashed up and smacked Stakely in the face before she even knew she was going to do it. The slap was more a reflex than anything else, and though she looked surprised that it happened, she wouldn't have taken it back for the world.

For a moment, Stakely didn't move. Eventually, he lifted one hand to rub his face and then nodded slowly. "I had that coming," he said. "But you've got some things coming as well and you know exactly what I'm talking about."

"I told Taylor at the start that I wouldn't have a part in cheating Doc or Caleb. I wouldn't have cheated Mike, either, for that matter. I was to keep the game under control and get Taylor in. That's it. You may have your own code, but the rest of us do, too."

"Honor among thieves? Don't try to get that shit past me."

Staring at Stakely with undisguised contempt, Lottie said, "I did what I could during that game. To be perfectly honest with you, if I hadn't been there, your man Taylor would have been fleeced in half the time."

"All right, so tell me where to find them."

"Doc didn't say where . . ." Lottie's voice trailed off when she felt the cold touch of iron against her thigh. She froze and felt her breath catch in her throat as she shifted her legs to feel what was pressed against her.

There was no mistaking the shape of the gun barrel that had somehow been eased under a few layers of her skirts.

Stakely grinned and rubbed the gun up and down along her leg. "You like word games, Lottie? I sure don't. I've dealt with enough gamblers to know when you're trying to play your little games, so don't even try them on me. Since you didn't say anything to Doc, then you must have said something to the Injun.

"Didn't he get under these skirts as well?" Stakely whispered as he moved his pistol even higher against Lottie's thigh. "Didn't he get right up in there? He must have been real good if you're so ready to get shot right now just to protect him."

Watching her carefully, Stakely asked, "You're thinking of him right now, aren't you? Try to imagine what lengths he'd go to in order to protect you. I wonder if that Injun's got a code like you do?"

Sitting up straight, Lottie reached down and wrapped her fingers around the barrel of the gun that was being forced between her legs. She moved it up and away until it knocked against the bottom of the table. "I'm not protecting anyone," she snarled. "I'd just rather pull my own hair out before doing anything to help a piece of shit like you."

When Stakely tried to take his gun back, he had to pull three times before it would come loose from Lottie's grip. Without pausing for a moment, he brought the gun up and slammed it onto the table. It was a weathered Colt that carried more than a few scars to show it was no stranger to its owner's hand. The barrel and handle were engraved with the same design that had adorned Taylor's knife. This Tiger, however, was etched in gold and had two small diamonds for eyes.

There were also a few large streaks of rust discoloring the end of the barrel.

"You surprised me," he said. "I didn't think you'd have this much fire in you. Of course, I would have thought that you'd be smarter than your friend Mike Lynch."

Stakely uttered those last two words with an unmistakable finality.

When she looked down at the barrel of the gun, Lottie saw that those dark red streaks might not be rust after all.

"What happened to Mike?" she asked.

Easing back from the table, Stakely got up and slipped his gun back into its holster. He ignored the fact that Donnelly was coming around the bar with his shotgun in hand.

"You'd better be more concerned with the ones that are still alive," Stakely said. With that, he turned and stepped around Donnelly as if the barkeep wasn't even there.

23

A year ago, Caleb would have begged for a chance to get out of his little office in the back of his saloon and try his hand at gambling for a living. Now, after spending the last few weeks in Jacksboro nursing a gunshot wound while Doc nursed a winning streak, Caleb thought back fondly to those days when his biggest worries were fixing a leaky roof or dealing with another liquor salesman.

The doctor had stitched up Caleb's shoulder and sent him on his way with a full bottle of tablets that he'd ground up himself. After that, Caleb got real comfortable in his rented room and slept in for the next few days. When he woke up, Doc was still playing cards at the same table. Only the different color of Doc's suit told Caleb that the former dentist had gotten up from that spot since the last time he'd checked.

It was late afternoon when Caleb decided

to pay another visit to the Jackrabbit Saloon, and the summer sun was blazing down on his shoulders with a vengeance. Sweat pushed out from his scalp and trickled down his face. There was plenty of shade to be had inside the saloon, so Caleb stomped through the doors and let out a discontented growl.

"How about some raw meat for my friend?" Doc shouted from his normal table along the edge of the room.

Nobody but a drunk or two even responded to that, but Doc laughed enough to make up for the mild reaction. He sat at a table that had clearly once been a larger dining table but had been sawed in half. A shredded tablecloth was spread over the weathered surface and was stained with more colors than the side of a desert rock.

"Say hello to my friend, Admiral."

The man sitting adjacent to Doc looked over at him with slack-jawed aggression. "Admirals run ships," he said while slapping his hand against the insignias pinned to his rumpled blue shirt. "Do I look like a goddamn sailor?"

Doc leaned over and squinted at the man's uniform until he finally shook his head. "My apologies, sir. I haven't seen a military uniform up close since my youth."

"Probably one of those sorry-ass Rebel suits by the sound of you."

"Indeed. Look here, Caleb," Doc said. "Now this is how a man brings respect to his ship."

Although Doc's joking wasn't particularly harsh, Caleb saw right away why the jokes kept coming. The man in uniform wore his colors as if they'd been dragged behind a horse and then beaten against a rock, but he bristled every time Doc mentioned anything to do with them.

"I don't serve on no ship," the man growled.

As he walked past the table, Caleb extended a hand. "I'm Caleb Wayfinder. What's your proper title?"

The man in uniform gaped at Caleb and took a few noisy breaths. "You're an Injun?"

"Partly."

"I'm Corporal Jesse Butler, Sixth Cavalry Regiment, United States Army."

Caleb held up his hands and said, "No need to circle your wagons. I'm just here for a drink."

There were a few more laughs, but most of the others inside the saloon were more interested in their own business. The Jackrabbit had only two solid walls and part of a roof overhead. The rest was tacked together using spare planks and some large sheets of canvas. Even the front door was there mostly as a formality, since folks could come and go through any number of slits cut in the flimsier sections of the saloon's walls.

"I got plenty of friends that got killed by Injuns," Corporal Butler said. "You think that's funny?"

Caleb shook his head and kept walking until he reached the bar. Only when he leaned against it did he realize the bar was actually a couple of stacks of old crates with a tarp thrown on top of them.

"My friend meant nothing by it, Admiral," Doc chimed in. "Shall we continue our game?"

Butler managed to peel his eyes off Caleb before saying, "I got some money in my bedroll. Save my seat while I get it."

Since Butler didn't bother checking to see if anyone would actually follow his command, he didn't notice when one of the other players at the table reached out to swipe a few of his chips. Doc saw the theft, but ignored it as he got up from his chair. That simple action was accompanied by a labored wince and a few long, wheezing breaths.

"You feeling any better, Doc?" Caleb asked.

"I was just about to ask you the same."

Caleb knew better than to press it if Doc didn't feel like talking about his health. Besides, the Georgian was sounding better by the time he walked over to the bar.

"I'm all stitched up and ready to go," Caleb said. "There's a stage to Denver leaving tomorrow at two."

"Then, by all means, you should be on it."

"Just me, Doc? I thought you were itching to get to Denver. That place has got a whole lot more possibilities than this hole of a town."

"Perhaps, but my military friend has plenty of money left and he's dying to hand it over. He's mentioned a few others from Fort Richardson that will be joining him and I can only figure they're in his same league."

"You also figure they can pay off more than a big game in Denver?"

Doc shrugged and said, "They're easy pickings and they'll be here in another day or two. After wringing them dry, I'll have more than enough for a stake in Denver. I may even have enough to loan out to get you started."

"We'll see if I need it," Caleb said.

"If you want to recuperate for a while longer, you can —"

Caleb cut him off with a swiftly raised hand. "I'm more than ready to get the hell out of Texas for a while. All that talk of fresh mountain air has got me itching to get a move on and take a taste for myself."

"Just try to leave some for me."

Nodding, Caleb shook Doc's hand and said, "The plan's still the same. I haven't forgotten about that. Soon as I get situated, I'll see if I can find if there are any tigers prowling in those mountains."

"Actually, I have no doubt that such local wildlife will not only be easy to spot, but will seek you out."

"God help 'em."

Still shaking Caleb's hand, Doc slapped the man's shoulder and took a step back. "I'll be there before too long. I'm sure my business here in town won't keep me here for very long."

"Just try not to get on the army's bad side, Doc. There's only so much one accomplice can do."

"I'll try to keep that in mind."

Just then, Butler stomped into the saloon and made his way to the table as if he intended on pounding holes in the floor with every step. He slapped a bundle onto the dirty tablecloth and sat down roughly. "Let's play some cards," he grunted.

Doc smirked and headed back to his chair. "My sentiments exactly, Admiral."

Caleb had to turn his back on the table and leave before he busted out laughing at how easily Doc got under Butler's skin. As soon as he was outside, he took a look around and pulled in a lungful of Jacksboro atmosphere. The place smelled like a healthy mix of horseflesh and sweaty armpits. Soldiers from the nearby fort walked in small packs up and down the streets, ogling whores who looked as if they were sitting down merely because they'd been worked too hard to stand on their own.

It was a perfect place to lay low and heal up, since there was no reason on earth why anyone would bother trying to cut in on the gambling action there. If anyone claiming to represent the Tiger even knew about Jacksboro, it was as a stopover on the way back onto the gambler's circuit.

Caleb wasn't feeling great, but he was feeling a whole lot better. By the time he crossed the street and made his way to a tent that had been pitched on a nearby corner, he barely even felt the stitches in his back.

The tent Caleb approached might have been large enough to fit a few people rather comfortably under its canvas cover. Because it was stretched to more than double its intended height, the tent only had two and a half sides to go along with its tattered top. A sign stuck in the dirt in front of it read: HORSES FOR SALE.

"Are these the only ones you've got?" Caleb asked the short man sitting on the ground with a shotgun across his lap.

The man inside the tent had deep pockmarks in his face and teeth that were nearly the same color as the Texas soil. He reflexively tightened his grip on his shotgun as he sized up Caleb with a quick glance. "These are all fine for whatever you need."

"How about a ride to Denver?"

"Whatever you need."

"Mind if I take a look?"

The man shrugged and nodded toward the selection, which consisted of two somewhat likely prospects and three more nags that barely looked healthy enough to cross the street without falling over.

Settling on a gray mare, Caleb knew better than to ask if the horse would make it. The man with the pockmarked face didn't exactly strike him as the sort who would be honest when it came to selling his animals.

Fortunately, Caleb had enough experience under his own belt to make a decision.

"I'll pay fifty for this one," Caleb said to the seller.

"A hundred and not a dime less."

"Seventy-five."

"Ninety-five."

Glaring down at the seller, Caleb shifted on his feet so his hand just so happened to come to rest on the barrel of his holstered pistol. "Eighty-five and that better include the saddle. If this horse makes it all the way to Denver, I'll come back and pay you the rest."

"All right, all right. Hand it over."

After paying for the horse and buckling a beat-up saddle over its back, Caleb rode out of Jacksboro and headed toward Colorado. He was sick of hiding.

It was time to do some seeking.

24

Compared to all the other camps, dirty towns, and forts that Caleb had gone through on his ride, Denver was more than just a jolt to his senses. The sounds and sights had an even bigger impact on him due to the fact that he'd spent more than a few nights along the way sleeping under the stars in a bedroll he'd won off a miner whose left eye ticked every time he was dealt anything better than two pair.

Caleb wasn't the only one to benefit from that little stopover. The gray mare he'd bought in Jacksboro now sported a newer saddle as well as a fresh set of shoes. Caleb figured it was more important to keep her in good condition instead of padding his own pockets with the specks of gold dust that the miner had to offer. It had worked out pretty well, since he'd made it in far less time than he'd figured.

Denver sprawled in every direction like

the mountains themselves. On his way through town, Caleb passed at least three churches and even found himself traveling down a few streets that were paved by wooden planks. The boardwalks were crowded, but not with the rowdy sort he'd grown accustomed to. These were normal folks, as well as a good supply of families, who looked at Caleb without hiding their discomfort.

After traveling through Indian country, Caleb had become very aware of his own appearance. Thanks to spending more time in the sun than he had in a long time, his normally dark coloring had become even darker, until he looked closer to a full-blooded Indian rather than the mix that his family tree would actually show. His coal-black hair had grown out a bit since the last time he'd cut it in Fort Griffin, adding even more of a savageness to his appearance.

But Caleb soon realized it wasn't the color of his skin or hair that put the locals on edge. Their eyes drifted more to the guns around his waist and the rifle that was strapped to his horse's side. The wound in his back still gnawed at him every now and then, reminding him to never again be caught without a weapon at the ready. He'd picked up a few pistols as a result of his growing prowess at cards and a close call with a drunk cavalry scout who didn't know the difference between bluffing and cheating.

Caleb took to wearing the guns on his person — two bolstered around his waist, one stuck under the back of his belt, and another wedged in his left boot. There were plenty of men who wore more guns or displayed them with more flair, but no men like that were to be seen on the street at the moment. As such, Caleb felt more and more like a wild dog that had wandered into the middle of a flock of sheep.

"Afternoon, sir," Caleb said to a balding man with a thick gray beard hanging down long enough to completely cover his neck. "Wonder if you could direct me to a clean room and a bath?"

"Try one of the saloons," the older man replied as if he were wading in the muck to do so. He pointed toward the end of a row of brick buildings, adding, "There's plenty of them that way."

"Much obliged, sir." With that, Caleb pointed his horse's nose in the direction he'd been shown and flicked the reins.

Soon, he spotted a row of saloons and poker halls, which called to him like a chorus of muses. As he rode down that street, he got fewer suspicious glares thrown his way and saw more sights that were familiar to his weary eyes. Although the places may have been bigger and better maintained, they were still saloons, and even the smell of them made Caleb feel more at home.

He tied his horse in front of a small barbershop and stepped inside.

"Help you?" asked a man in his forties wearing a clean apron while sweeping the floor in front of a shiny barber's chair.

"How much for a bath and shave?"

"Dollar fifty." The man looked Caleb up and down as if counting the dirty smudges on his face and clothes. "Make it two dollars."

Caleb paid the money, cleaned up, and got a recommendation for a place to rent a room, as well as the closest stable for his horse. In under an hour's time, he was walking the streets of Denver in a fresh set of clothes, with a smile on his face. Never before had he felt so far from where he'd started. The Busted Flush seemed like a distant memory, even though he'd owned the saloon less than a year ago.

Now, as he walked along by the saloons outside the door of his hotel, Caleb pulled in a breath of clean air and let it out slowly.

There was no Texas dust catching in his throat and no cowboys screaming in the distance. Denver truly felt like foreign soil, and Caleb was more than happy to do some exploring.

Every time he caught sight of a piece of mountainous scenery, it nearly took Caleb's breath away. For the rest of that night, he wandered around, until he found himself in the Chinese district and among folks who made him feel even more out of sorts.

Caleb had met plenty of Chinese, but it was on their streets that Caleb got a subtle reminder of why he'd come to Denver in the first place. Hanging in one window, there was a white banner with a picture of a red tiger painted upon it. Caleb stepped up to the picture and quickly saw that it wasn't the same picture that had been carved on Taylor's blade. Even so, Caleb walked a little more carefully after seeing that painting. He made his way back to the saloon district with his arms hanging at his sides so he could always feel the touch of his guns holstered in his newly acquired double rig.

Despite the darkness that accompanied thoughts of the Tiger, Caleb couldn't stay under that cloud for long. There was something about Denver that energized him. Until now, he'd always just thought of "a breath of fresh air" as just another phrase. Indeed, he could see why Colorado was recommended for people with health conditions. As he stepped into a saloon called the Mint, Caleb was feeling almost as good as he had before catching lead back in Fort Griffin.

The Mint had a definite Southern air about it. Although the building fit in with the others on its portion of Blake Street, the inside was done up like a plantation he'd visited once as a child. The tables were round and covered with nicer than average cloths. The banisters were polished and not too chipped. Near the door was a man with a banjo playing music that was lazy as a Louisiana summer.

Caleb stepped up to the bar and placed his foot on a polished brass rail. He took quick stock of the liquor supply shelved in front of an expensive mirror behind the bar and nodded his approval.

"Good evening, sir," said a man in a drawl that reminded Caleb of Doc's. "I don't believe I've seen you around here."

"I just got into Denver."

"That explains it," the barkeep said. "The name's Charley Ward."

"Caleb Wayfinder."

"Ah. A savage from the wilds, eh?" The

good-natured way in which Charley spoke made it impossible for any of his words to cause offense. The brimming smile on his face took a few more steps in that direction. "Can I interest you in a drink?"

"If you'd offered me a peace pipe," Caleb said in a manner that was almost as good-natured as Charley's, "I would've had to knock out a few teeth."

Charley was a burly fellow with a thick beard that made him look like one of the men coming in from the mountains. He had thick, meaty hands covered in calluses and a bit of a belly protruding over the top of his belt.

"I suppose I had that coming," Charley admitted. "How's about I buy the first round and we can be square?"

"Sounds good."

When Charley turned and poured a drink for him, Caleb expected to find either beer or whiskey in the glass. What he saw was neither of those. Staring down at the glass, Caleb asked, "What is that?"

"A mint julep. Don't tell me you've never had one."

"Not in a place this far north."

"Aw, just drink it. It's the specialty of the house."

"I guess that explains the sign out front."

264

"Sure enough."

Caleb lifted the glass to his lips, shrugged, and took a sip. It trickled down his throat like his first taste of cold water. "Damn! If I could mix a drink like that, I'd name a place after it, too."

"Glad you like it. There's plenty more where that came from."

"Actually, I was looking for a game."

"What's your flavor?" Charley asked. "We've got everything that's worth playing."

"I see a few poker games going on," Caleb said while surveying the main room. "What about faro?"

"Bucking the tiger, eh? There's a few tables in the next room."

"Actually, I was thinking about having a word with a man named Morris. Can you help me on that end?"

Charley's eyes narrowed a bit and his smile lost a bit of its humor. "I see you're more than just a casual player."

"You might say that."

"So you'd be looking to deal faro rather than play?"

Caleb nodded. "I'd be happy to stick to poker for a while if there's no other openings yet."

"What'd you say your name was?" This time when he asked, Charley squinted as if he were studying the fine print of a contract.

"Caleb Wayfinder."

"And where're you from?"

"Formerly from Dallas. I owned a place there called the Busted Flush, but more recently I've been in Fort Griffin."

Charley's eyes widened and he nodded quickly. "The Busted Flush? I've heard of that place. Survived a bunch of fires a while back didn't it?"

"Yeah," Caleb answered. "I didn't know news like that would make it this far."

Letting out a rumbling belly laugh, Charley said, "A man's gotta listen to the gamblers to know what's going on. They've been talking about your place since it made it onto the circuit."

"I handed over controlling interest to my partner. Since then, I've been doing some traveling."

Charley kept nodding. "I guess there were a bunch of fires that put a lot of other saloons around there out of business. Since your place survived, folks started saying it was lucky. That, along with a few big games held there, made plenty of cardsharps mighty anxious to see if some of that luck would rub off on them."

Thinking back to the Flush made Caleb smile. "I'll be damned."

"Will you be around here for long?" Charley asked.

"If I can sit in on a few games."

"Good. I'll see about getting a word with the Tiger and point him in your direction."

"Perfect. And one more thing. I'll need another one of these juleps."

25

A few hours later, Caleb was still in the Mint and still feeling good about being there. After working a few kinks from his neck, he pulled up the tops of his cards so he could take another quick glance at them. After that, he took his time looking around at the other faces gathered at the table.

He'd picked out one or two that might be professionals, but he was fairly certain they hadn't picked him out. Either that or they just didn't consider him any sort of threat.

"Raise . . . um . . . three dollars," Caleb said without much gusto behind it.

"Make it five," came the immediate response from the man on his left.

The next one in line folded, allowing the one after him to declare, "Raise it to twenty."

Caleb started to act surprised and then took it back before fully committing to it. That way, anyone who could read a man would see just enough to get the point. "All right, then," Caleb said. "I'll call."

There was a quick glance between the two players who'd raised, which gave Caleb a sliver of hope. Of course, there was only one way for him to be certain he was right.

On the last round of betting, Caleb took a breath and made sure not to look at the others when he pushed in a good portion of his chips. "Fifty," he said.

After another pause, the next man in line asked, "How many more chips do you have?"

It was all Caleb could do to keep from grinning.

The last show of the evening started at just past midnight. Caleb sat at a small table alongside the narrow stage, where a pretty brunette from San Juan was singing something in her native tongue. Caleb understood bits and pieces of it, but was only listening to the sweet tone of her voice while counting his winnings.

He caught sight of someone approaching his table, and his hand drifted toward the gun on his left hip. Keeping his eyes more or less trained on the stage, he watched the approaching figure from the outer edge of his field of vision. Not until the figure stopped at his table did Caleb turn to look.

"There you are," the figure said. "It took you long enough to get here."

Caleb stood up so quickly that he knocked over his chair behind him. "Lottie? Is that really you?"

The redhead was dressed in a simple brown skirt with a blouse that was baggy enough to conceal her impressive figure. She opened her arms and put on a smile that was like the first rays of a sunrise. "Of course it's me," she said. "Who else would follow you all the way from Fort Griffin?"

Caleb pulled out a chair for her and then righted his own. "You followed me?"

"Well, not exactly. I did come up here looking for you, though. Where have you been hiding? I hadn't even heard you were in town until earlier tonight."

"I just arrived. You've got some real good ears if you knew I was here already."

"Those two men you fleeced a little while ago weren't just some local players, you know."

"They also weren't that great at bluffing me out of my money," Caleb replied. "Were they friends of yours?"

"More like acquaintances. We've run a few games together, but I'm not too surprised that they got cleaned out. They always were suckers for new faces. I am impressed you were able to do it alone, though."

"Should I be offended by that?"

"Not at all," Lottie said. "I meant it as a compliment. You and Doc make a hell of a team, but you seem to be doing just fine on your own. Everyone on the circuit will be keeping their eyes on you. Where have you been and where's Doc?"

"We spent a little time in Jacksboro. Doc found a few soldiers who were overly eager to bet their wages while I was getting stitched up."

Gritting her teeth and pulling in a breath, Lottie reached out to place a tentative hand on Caleb's shoulder. "I almost forgot about that. How are you feeling?"

"Much better. The bullet just sort of got stuck in there without doing a whole lot of damage."

"Thank goodness."

"What about you?" Caleb asked. "Why did you come all the way to Denver? It must have been important."

Lottie's face darkened a bit as she nodded. "It is important, actually. There's been some talk going around about you and Doc."

"Seems like there always is."

"First of all . . ." Lowering her head,

271

Lottie let out a breath as if she just didn't have the strength to look Caleb in the eye. "I've got to tell you that I wasn't completely in the dark about who Taylor was."

Without missing a beat, Caleb replied, "I figured as much."

Lottie's head snapped up again. "You did?"

"For you to vouch for someone like that would have made you either stupid or a terrible judge of character. The first was already ruled out, and you couldn't be the latter while also lasting more than a day in our line of work, so that doesn't leave many choices."

"You've got to know that I didn't want things to turn out the way they did." As she spoke, Lottie reached out to place her hand on top of Caleb's. Although he didn't take his own hand away, he didn't exactly warm to her touch.

"It could have been worse."

She winced at the sound of that and then shifted her eyes once more away from Caleb. "Then you haven't heard about Mike?"

"Only that he got the hell out of Fort Griffin before me and Doc."

"He's dead."

"What?"

She nodded. "I heard about it and then

got proof when his body was found a few miles outside of Fort Griffin."

Gritting his teeth, Caleb asked, "Was it Taylor?"

"I don't know for certain, but I doubt it. That's not his line of work."

"But it does have something to do with the Tiger?"

Reflexively glancing around, Lottie nodded again.

Caleb took his hand out from under Lottie's, balled it into a fist, and slammed it on the table. "Son of a bitch!"

A few people from nearby tables looked over at Caleb, but quickly got back to their own business. Although Caleb didn't seem too concerned about those glances, Lottie was very much aware of them.

Once he'd collected himself, Caleb was unable to take his eyes off Lottie. Unlike the previous times he'd found himself in that predicament, this time wasn't because of her red hair or beaming smile. "Why'd they kill Mike?" he asked. "And don't tell me you don't know. If those assholes wanted to kill us, why'd they bother running us out of town?"

"Because . . . running you out of town was my idea," Lottie said.

Slowly, Caleb's eyes narrowed and his

hand drifted toward the gun at his side. "What did you just say?"

She didn't seem to mind keeping her eyes trained on Caleb's gun hand. At the moment, that was a much more appealing alternative than looking him in the eye. "I had some pull with Taylor, and since he had the most influence with the Tiger in Fort Griffin, I convinced him to let the three of you leave town rather than . . . anything worse."

"Which is eventually what happened anyway."

"I told you that wasn't Taylor's doing."

"Oh," Caleb grunted. "Isn't he just a fucking saint? I suppose you can just take his word as gospel."

Still shaking her head, Lottie explained, "He's not the one with the most say in Fort Griffin anymore. At least, he wasn't when it was decided that Mike was to be killed."

"Different ranks among the tigers?"

"Something like that. There was one man in town who seemed to outrank all the others. He strutted into Fort Griffin and sat down with the law and gamblers alike as if he was the mayor."

"What's his name?" Caleb asked.

"Stakely. He's the one who had Mike killed and he almost killed me."

"Why didn't he?"

"Because I ran," Lottie snapped before looking up at him defiantly. "I ran because I felt like I owed you another visit after what I did."

"But you were forced into it," Caleb said sarcastically.

"I could have refused, but I didn't. I may have been in on both sides of the same game, but don't you dare tell me that you and Doc haven't made some good money doing the same damn thing!"

"All right, so you said your piece. Mike's dead and you're on the run. I guess you should keep running before you're spotted with me. I've got a meeting set up with Morris. That is, unless you were lying to me about that, too."

"I wasn't," Lottie said. "And I know about the meeting. You can't go through with it."

"Why not?"

"Because Mike wasn't the only one set up to be killed. Stakely's put a price on your and Doc's heads for what you did at that card game."

"Is that why you wanted to know where he's at so badly?" Caleb asked with a vicious tone in his voice. "So you could report it back to the Tiger and garner some favor from that group of assholes?"

"No. Stakely and his men are looking for him over you simply because they've heard more about him. Last I heard, they were sniffing around Denison and even back as far as Dallas. There's plenty of men around here as well and they'll be more than happy to take you when they can get you."

"Doc isn't exactly the sort to lay low and keep quiet for very long," Caleb said. "I'm sure you could have found him just like you found me."

"I didn't want to find him first, Caleb. I wanted to find you."

"So tell me," Caleb said, "how much work have you done for the Tiger? How many men have you handed over or set up?"

"Anyone on the circuit has worked for the Tiger whether they know it or not. Take a look at the newspapers right here in Denver, Caleb. There's corruption in the government and crooked dealings with the law that are reported every day, but nobody cares. Those same men in the government or behind those badges also do a lot of good. It's not one or the other. When you ran your saloon, you must have made payments to men that weren't officials of any sort. The same thing happens with business owners and ranchers."

"All of that may be fine and good," Caleb

said. "But there's one big difference between us and the rest of those folks you mentioned. We don't have to pretend that what we do is right or even fair. Everybody cheats. The main difference is who gets caught." As he spoke, Caleb felt his anger at Lottie fade away.

Lottie put on a thin smile and said, "You have learned a lot, and it took you a lot less time than it took me."

"Even so, there's a limit to what anyone should be able to get away with, but there's no limit on what anyone will try. Whoever these assholes are, they will keep pushing until someone pushes back."

"It's been tried, Caleb."

"Then it should be tried again. You're not the one with a price on your head, so you don't have to get mixed up in this anymore. You gave your warning, so you can leave with a clear conscience."

"I came because I wanted to help," Lottie said.

"You really want to help?"

"Yes," she replied without hesitation. "I've done some things that I'm not very proud of, but I'm not about to be made into a traitor by the likes of Taylor and Stakely. Whatever you need me to do, I'll do it. It's too late for me to start worrying about what will happen because of it."

"Bucking the Tiger, huh?" Caleb asked with a smirk. "Doc might call this ironic."

26

For the first time in the last several days, Corporal Butler wasn't the only man in uniform at the card table with Doc. Two others slouched in their chairs, wearing standard-issue blues that barely looked official due to their poor upkeep. All three of the military men looked just as grizzled as the cowboy also sitting in on the game. What few medals those soldiers had didn't look half as polished as the slender dentist sitting at their table.

Doc had been in Jacksboro for just under two weeks, which was more than enough time for him to stake out his territory within the Jackrabbit Saloon. He sat in his normal chair at his regular table and played his normal game. The servers there knew Doc on sight and kept his whiskey glass full.

"What's the matter, Holliday?" Butler asked. "You ain't so talkative now that you're losing."

"What can I say to that?" Doc asked dryly. "You are an excellent judge of character."

"You hear that, Coop?" Butler asked while looking over to the man on his left. "I won Doc's respect along with most of his money."

Coop wore the insignia of a lieutenant and seemed to be the most professional of the three soldiers. That only meant his clothes were half as rumpled and he was half as drunk as the other two. His stack of chips was also half as big. "Don't count your chicks before they're hatched, Corporal. I'm still in this game."

The third soldier's uniform was devoid of everything but the barest of essentials to mark him as a member of the United States Army.

"What about you, Jorgens?" Coop asked as he shoved in enough money to cover the current bet. "Are you still in with me?"

"Yeah," the youngest of the soldiers said in a crackling voice. "I suppose." The cowboy sitting between him and the lieutenant had already folded, leaving Doc as the only one who had yet to answer the bet.

Doc pulled in a deep breath and held up his cards so he could get another look at what he'd drawn. "I raise," he said while tossing in a few more chips. As Butler grunted and mumbled to himself, Doc winced and reached for the handkerchief that was never too far from his grasp.

With his head bowed and his shoulders shaking with each cough, he took a few quick glances at the men around him. None of the soldiers were paying him any mind, but Butler and the lower-ranked soldier seemed to be staring each other down. When Doc cleared his throat at the end of his coughing fit the two soldiers quickly shifted their eyes away from each other.

"I'll call," Butler said confidently.

Although he wasn't quite so confident, Coop nodded and tossed in enough to cover the raise. Jorgens folded.

Doc shrugged and laid down his cards. "I went for the straight, but all I got was another five."

Coop's eyes brightened and he slapped his cards down faceup. "I may only have fours, but I got three of 'em!"

"Well played, sir," Doc said amiably. "I only had you pegged for a pair."

Chuckling while reaching for the pot, Coop said, "You had me pegged as usual, Doc, but I lucked out on the draw."

"Before you two start kissing and holding hands," Butler sneered, "maybe you ought to take a look at these." Saying that, Butler laid down his cards to show three jacks flanked by a seven of hearts and the ten of diamonds. "Them three are my favorites," he added, while touching the jacks and showing Doc a shit-eating grin.

Coop took his hands away from the middle of the table as if he'd accidentally stuck them into a fire. He then let out a breath through gritted teeth, collected what remained of his chips, and said, "That about does it for me. I've got a wife and two daughters to feed."

Doc nodded and extended his hand across the table. "It's been a pleasure, Lieutenant."

Butler let out a few grunting laughs as he raked in his chips. "Yeah, yeah. Anytime you want to hand over some more money to me, you just let me know, Coop."

The lieutenant shot a quick glance over to Butler and then shook his head at Doc. "You all behave, now."

The next round of cards were dealt by the cowboy who'd practically been asleep for the entire last hand.

"You're still awfully quiet, Doc," Butler said. "Doesn't feel too good to lose every now and then, does it?"

"As my grandmother used to say, it ebbs and flows."

Snorting to himself while examining his

cards, Butler said, "I'll bet your grandma could play better poker than you. Raising with a pair of threes? That's just stupid."

"Stupid as hell," Jorgans said.

"Then I suppose this is just as stupid," Doc said as he threw in a raise.

Butler was quick to call and grunted, "You ain't nothing but a half-assed, broken-down drunk that got lucky a few times, Holliday. I can see right through you."

"And it only took you this long?" Doc asked. "That's impressive."

"Impressive enough to beat the hell out of you."

Even though he'd done his share of bragging throughout the game, the cowboy sitting between the two soldiers knew enough to keep his mouth shut and just deal out the second round.

After a glance to Butler, Jorgens knocked the table and leaned back.

"Check to me?" Doc asked. "I guess it's time for a raise."

Butler shook his head. "Yeah, nobody saw that one coming. Raise it again."

The cowboy covered the raises and looked to the man beside him.

"Too much for me," Jorgens said as he folded his cards. "I think I'll just watch."

"A wise decision," Doc said. "Since that's

what you seem to be best at."

"What's that supposed to mean?" Jorgens asked.

Butler leaned forward with both forearms resting against the table. "Yeah, Doc. What's that supposed to mean?"

"Just that he's been watching my cards all night long," Doc replied. "I just pray to God our country's security doesn't rest on his skills as a scout."

The cowboy snickered under his hand, but wasn't joined by anyone else at that table. Butler glared across at Doc while Jorgens shifted nervously in his chair.

"I don't —"

"Shut up, Jorgens," Butler snapped. "This asshole must be getting dizzy on account of all that blood he's coughed up. Otherwise, I would've thought he just accused you of cheating."

"Not at all," Doc said. "I accused both of you of cheating."

"Yeah? Maybe you should prove it."

"All right, then." Gripping his cards in a tight fist, Doc glanced down at them for less than a fraction of a second before looking up again. "This is the first time for the last few hands that I've looked at my cards without your partner next to me getting a chance at them as well. Let's see if you play

284

this hand half as well as the last few."

Twitching at the corner of one eye, Butler said, "It's your own fault if you can't keep your cards from being seen."

"And it's your fault if you have someone watching my cards and then passing bits and pieces of that information to you," Doc retorted.

While gnawing on his lip, Butler leaned back and forced a look of calm upon his face. "You'd know all about cheating. We're just a couple of soldiers."

"Which explains why this is the best you two could come up with. My bet is that you won't even be able to keep that arrogant smirk on your face without getting the nod from this little pisser next to me," Doc said while nodding over at Jorgens. Once he saw his words inflict their damage on Butler, Doc eased in a few more chips. "I raise."

Butler's eyes darted back and forth between Doc and Jorgens.

"Don't look at him," Doc snapped. "Look at me. Or, better yet, look at your own damn cards."

Puffing out his chest, Butler said, "I call."

The cowboy shoved in his chips as well.

Without taking his eyes from Butler, Doc flipped over his cards. "Two pair. Kings and nines."

"Son of a bitch," Butler said as he pitched his cards away like they were stinging his fingers. "You knew you could beat me, Holliday! If that ain't a cheat I don't know what is!"

"These are the only cards I touched," Doc pointed out. "I didn't even deal them."

"But you knew you could beat me!"

Before Doc could respond, the cowboy's voice drifted across the table. "What I'd like to know," he said, "is if you can beat these." With that, the cowboy laid down his cards to show a pair of fours along with three deuces to boot.

Doc started laughing as he got up to give the cowboy a short round of applause.

"What the hell was that?" Butler asked with shock etched into every last one of his features.

"That," Doc replied, "is what poker is all about."

When he saw the cowboy tentatively reaching for the rest of his money, Butler slammed one hand on the last few dollars that had previously belonged to him. "I heard you were working with the Injun, Doc. You also start up something with this asshole as well?"

Doc situated himself back in his seat and

took a drink of whiskey. "Who told you that?"

"Never mind that. Just deal the next hand."

"Maybe we should get back to —" Jorgens started to say before he was cut off by Butler's booming voice.

"I said deal the fucking cards!"

Jorgens did as he was told while the cowboy next to him stacked his chips and Butler stewed to himself. Doc, on the other hand, seemed more interested in folding his handkerchief. He didn't even look at his cards before shoving some of his chips into the pot.

"What the hell is that, Holliday?" Butler asked.

Doc blinked and took a look for himself. "Looks like a raise, Admiral."

"Without even looking at what you got?"

"I'm betting that, whatever it is, it'll beat you."

Through gritted teeth, Butler snarled, "I call."

The cowboy folded his cards and gathered up his chips. "That does it for me. I suppose I'll cash these in."

"The fuck you will."

"If the man wants to leave, that's his right," Doc said.

Butler's voice trembled as if his temper was literally bubbling up to hit the back of his throat. "He can't just win all that money and leave."

"It's smarter than anything you'd be likely to do."

"That's awfully strange talk coming from a dead man, Holliday. Maybe you should just shut the hell up before I put you out of your goddamn misery."

The man who stepped up to refill Doc's glass was slightly bigger than Butler, but carried most of that weight around his middle. "If you can't play a civil game, then take it somewheres else."

"You stay out of this," Butler said to the barkeep. "I got all the elbow room I need where that lunger's concerned."

"Then call the bet," Doc said.

Butler did just that and tossed two cards toward Jorgens.

Looking toward Doc, Jorgens waited until he got a casual shake of the head from the gambler.

"You . . . haven't looked at your —"

"Shut yer hole, Jorgens," Butler interrupted. "If the lunger's feeling lucky, then let him."

"I appreciate that," Doc said. "I'll bet a hundred."

Butler grunted and rearranged his hand. "Hell, Doc, why stop there?"

"Indeed. Make it six hundred."

Butler's eyes snapped up as his hand tightened around his cards. "I call."

The barkeep let out a weary sigh. "You don't even have that many chips on the table."

"I'm good for it," Butler snarled. "With the money that's being offered for this skinny little rat, I'll be good for everything else I owe you on top of this bet."

"What money is being offered?" Doc asked. "That wouldn't have come from Fort Griffin, would it?" After a slight pause, Doc grinned and nodded. "Ah, I see that it did."

"You don't know a goddamn thing, Holliday."

"And you're not holding a goddamn thing. That's the only thing I needed to know to take every cent you have."

"Your bet's been called," Butler said.

Doc glanced over at the barkeep, since that was the man who supposedly was speaking for the remainder of money needed to square the pot. The barkeep threw up his hands and walked away.

"Looks like you're out of your league," Doc said. "But I suppose you're fairly familiar with that predicament. I'll let your

289

bet stand if you tell me how much of a bounty is being offered for me and who else knows about it."

"I know about it," Butler said in a voice that trembled with rage. "That's the only thing that matters."

Blinking calmly, Doc asked, "Are you heeled, Admiral?"

"You're damn right I am." With that, Butler started to get up, and his hand dropped toward the holster buckled around his waist.

Doc's arm flickered with a motion that was so quick it barely attracted any attention. His Colt cleared leather and barked once.

For a moment, Butler stood his ground and blinked in disbelief.

Soon, he had to let his own gun drop so he could brace himself against the table.

When he looked up again, Butler didn't even have the strength to let out the obscenities that were on the tip of his tongue. The soldier flopped forward and then slid from the table onto the floor.

Doc calmly looked around and holstered his gun when he saw nobody else was interested in jumping to Butler's aid. Even Jorgens merely leaned back and held both arms out to show he had no intention of making another move.

Turning over Butler's cards. Doc counted up three eights and then went to his own cards to find three kings. "I guess this is mine," he said while gathering up his chips. "I'll need to cash out."

27

"So that's the man himself, huh?" Caleb asked as he sat in one of the darker corners of the Mint.

Lottie sat beside him, wearing a dark dress that went well with what the other ladies in the place were wearing, but didn't make her stand out from them. Her hair was gathered into a simple braid and was slung over one shoulder. "That's the one," she confirmed.

"He doesn't look like much." Shifting his eyes to other tables scattered throughout the place, Caleb nodded to a few and said, "But they do."

Lottie craned her neck to get a look at what he was talking about.

It was early evening, and the small floor show inside the Mint was going along at full steam. Most of the lights in the place were focused on the long, narrow stage, where a pair of singers wound their way through a row of chorus girls. Although

Caleb admired more than a few of those chorus girls, his eyes were continually drawn back to the line of Lottie's dress, which was pulled down around her shoulders to expose an enticing slope of smooth, pale skin. If he looked closely enough, he could see wisps of red hair that had come loose from her braid to brush against the nape of her neck.

"Who are you talking about?" she asked.

Before it became painfully obvious that he was staring at her, Caleb moved his eyes away and subtly pointed to a couple of tables. "That one," he said, indicating a table in the shadows to the left of the stage. "And that one," he said, pointing to another table less than ten feet from the first.

Once she saw the men sitting at those tables, Lottie nodded. "They look like rough fellows," she said. "But are you sure they're looking for you?"

"They're not looking at the stage," Caleb pointed out. "Haven't even glanced at it. That, combined with the fact that their hands haven't strayed more than a few inches from their guns, tells me an awful lot."

Turning away from the rough-looking men just as they were starting to glance in her direction, Lottie smiled and rested her chin on the back of her hand. "That's pretty good."

"Running a saloon is a real good way to practice spotting troublemakers."

"And I thought I had a good eye."

"Actually, you've got two very good eyes." She was quiet for a moment and maintained her smile.

"Jesus Christ," Caleb muttered. "I can't believe I just said that."

Lottie started laughing and said, "I'll just chalk it up to you being tired."

"And shot," Caleb added. "Don't forget that I was shot, too."

"Oh, that's right. That explains why you've started talking like a drunk who thinks he can get up under my skirts. Have you already forgotten why we're here?"

Just talking and laughing with Lottie was almost enough to make him forget about everything else and just enjoy the night in Denver. Forcing himself to take another look around the room, Caleb stopped when he picked out another table even farther away from the stage.

"There's another one," he said.

Lottie seemed reluctant to take her eyes away from him, but eventually she picked out the large man sitting with his hat resting on the table in front of him. "I think he's got a shotgun on his lap."

"Really?"

She nodded. "He's sitting too close to the table. His back's too straight and that hat is there to keep everyone else from seeing."

"I'll take your word for it."

"You have your experience running a saloon and I have mine running a faro table. Trust me, that's how a man sits when he's got a shotgun in his lap."

"Either that, or he really likes the looks of those chorus girls."

It took her a moment, but Lottie caught Caleb's joke and started laughing. "Are we just going to sit back here or are you going to that meeting?"

"I don't know. I haven't decided yet."

Caleb studied the man that Lottie had pointed out to him a few moments ago. Unlike the bulkier men who were clearly acting as lookouts or guards, the man nearer the stage might not have even been armed. He was a tall fellow who sat like a proper gentleman, with his hands folded neatly one over the other. An expensive bowler hat rested on the table in front of him. In the time since he'd arrived, the man had been watching the crowd while also sneaking a few glances at the stage. Dark hair was plastered to his scalp and a mustache crossed his upper lip as if it had been drawn there by a pencil.

"So he's the Tiger here in Denver?" Caleb asked.

"The one that I know about."

"Judging by all these hired guns he brought with him, I'm starting to think that sitting at that table might not be such a good idea."

"It's not going to get any better later," she said. "Morris always travels with a pack of dogs like that. Most of the men like him in the larger stops along the circuit do. You should see the man who works in San Francisco. He's practically got his own army."

"And would they have any problem shooting someone in plain sight?"

Lottie chewed on her lower lip and thought that over. Before she could say anything, Caleb was standing up.

"That tells me more than enough," he said.

"And you're still heading over there?"

"It's only a matter of time before we're either spotted or someone picks us out of this crowd. I'd rather take my chances right by the stage than in a dark corner."

"We could always leave."

"Too late for that," Caleb told her as he

straightened the lapels of his dark brown suit jacket.

As he walked between the tables around the stage, Caleb didn't even glance at the guards he passed along the way. He could feel their eyes boring into him, however, until the back of his head felt as if it were resting against a branding iron. To put on a face that was a little anxious, while also being a bit nervous, Caleb imagined he was holding a straight while going against a possible flush, and then sat down at Morris's table.

"You're late," Morris said in a voice that reminded Caleb of a fork scraping against a porcelain plate.

"Sorry about that. I'm —"

"I know who you are, Mr. Wayfinder. I also know that, after your performance in Fort Griffin, you're either very bold or very stupid to seek me out like this."

"Maybe a little of both."

Morris sat perfectly still before conceding the point with a slight nod.

"I'll be honest with you," Caleb said. "All I want to do is work."

"You could have done that in Fort Griffin. Instead, you and your partner decided to turn a card game into a shooting war."

"Sometimes that happens during card

games," Caleb said with a straight face. "Especially when one of the people at the table was trying to cheat his way into stealing everyone's money."

"It's become common knowledge that your partner isn't above such a thing, and I daresay you were in on that particular scheme as well."

"You daresay, huh?" After letting those words hang in the air for a moment, Caleb snapped his head forward like a snake. He stopped several inches short of Morris, which was still close enough to get the tall man in the tailored suit to jump back a foot or two.

"The cheater I was talking about wasn't me and it wasn't Doc," Caleb snarled. "It was Taylor, who I know damn well works in the same line of work as you do."

By now, two of the guards that had been posted at other tables had made their way behind Caleb and were pulling him away from Morris. They slammed Caleb into his seat and loomed over him.

"I'd suggest you rethink your current situation," Morris said in a voice that reeked of the sprawling cities on the opposite end of the country.

"And I'd suggest you think twice before spreading the word about who's cheating and who wasn't. You weren't there."

After a few tense moments, Morris glanced to either side and made a quick waving gesture. The two guards stepped back far enough for the people at other tables to get back to watching the stage show.

"You're right, Mr. Wayfinder. I wasn't there. But word travels quickly in our circles. Since I and my associates control those words, you might find it difficult to get any meaningful work in any saloons of this caliber."

"Which is exactly why I came to ask for your permission."

"You'll need to pay your taxes," Morris said. "Doubly so, to make up for the trouble you've caused."

"Just let me know where to make the payments and you'll get them as soon as I start earning some money."

"I'll find you," Morris said. "That's how this works."

"Fine." Without another word, Caleb got up from his seat and headed through the crowd in the opposite direction from which he'd arrived. The fact that he could hear Morris trying to catch his attention in a grating, annoyed shout only brought a smirk to Caleb's face.

Lottie was at the bar, and Caleb passed her without so much as a nod. Instead, he kept right on going until he was out of the Mint and across the street.

From there, Caleb broke into a run and headed straight into an alley. His eyes darted back and forth so quickly that he started to get a little dizzy, but he kept up the frantic search to make sure he wasn't running into another batch of armed vultures like the ones that had descended upon him at Morris's table.

So far, Caleb only saw shadows and a few drunks sleeping against the back of another building. There was only a sliver of moon in the sky, which made the shadows that much deeper. Fortunately, Denver was alive and kicking at the late hour, and Caleb was able to circle around the building without drawing any attention.

When the Mint was once again in his sight, Caleb slowed his breathing and listened to the night around him. For a few seconds, only the pounding of his own heart filled his ears. Then, the sounds of laughter and wild music drifted toward him. That was soon followed by a familiar, grating voice.

"That man thinks he can waltz into my town and talk to me like that?" Morris griped. "He's probably too stupid to even realize how close he was to getting killed right there in that room."

"He's got to be around here somewhere," one of the gunmen said. "I can probably drag him back here without much trouble."

Morris stopped and planted his feet on the boardwalk outside the Mint.

Reflexively, Caleb backed a bit farther into the shadow that wrapped around him like a cool, dark shroud.

Twisting on the balls of his feet to look over his shoulder, Morris glanced back through the saloon's front door and then turned around to face the street. "No," he said, finally. "There's too many people."

"So?"

"When I want someone to move against that man, I'll let you know. Now is not that time. Go back in there and make the necessary arrangements with Mr. Ward. Be sure to tell him to keep this one on a short leash or he'll find himself in a very uncomfortable position."

The gunman nodded and walked back into the Mint, leaving Morris with only four more men to stand around him.

Morris spoke to his men as he walked away, but Caleb wasn't able to pick up any specific words. Once the procession turned a corner, Caleb crossed the street and pulled open the saloon's front door. The moment it came open, he saw Morris's gunman turn around to face him. Caleb managed to step to one side before being spotted.

The gunman walked by without giving Caleb so much as a glance.

Lottie was the next one to walk out, so Caleb took her by the elbow and led her in the opposite direction Morris had gone.

"Had enough excitement for one day?" she asked.

"You have," Caleb replied. "Go back to your room and stay there until I get back."

"What are you doing?"

"Just go back and wait for me."

She let out a sigh, shook free of his grasp, and walked down the street. "Just try not to get in front of any more bullets."

"I'll do my best."

28

After leaving Lottie behind, it took Caleb less than two minutes to pick up Morris's trail. The well-dressed man strutted down the street like he owned it and preferred to keep his hired guns surrounding him like a royal entourage.

Following the group through town was so easy that Caleb started to get anxious, as he was certain he was being led into some sort of trap. But Morris led him all the way to the Cedarwood Hotel, leaving one man outside as the rest marched in through the front door.

From there, all Caleb needed to do was circle around the place until he found a side door. It opened into the kitchen, putting Caleb face-to-face with a couple of startled young women who were cleaning up the place.

"This the lobby?" Caleb asked with a bit of a drunken slur in his voice.

One of the women started laughing as the other one showed Caleb into the dining room and pointed him in the right direction. He tipped his hat to them and stumbled along until he heard the kitchen door shut behind him.

The Cedarwood was one of those places that smelled as if it had just been built. Every tabletop was clean enough to sparkle, and the rugs looked almost too fancy to walk on. Caleb made his way to the front desk slowly enough to keep from bumping into Morris or any of his men, while moving quickly enough to avoid drawing any more glances from the few people who were having a late meal in the dining room.

After Morris and his men had left the lobby, Caleb thought of a few different lies he could tell to whoever was working at the front desk so he could find out which room Morris was using. But all Caleb needed to do was follow the sound of stomping footsteps as they climbed the front staircase.

He didn't have to sneak behind them for very long, however, before he got what he was after. Once he saw which door Morris was unlocking, Caleb grinned to himself and then headed back down the stairs.

The bespectacled man behind the front desk watched with mild curiosity. After a quick wave from Caleb, however, he nodded halfheartedly, unfolded his newspaper, and got back to more interesting matters.

When Caleb got back to Lottie's room, he found it empty.

For a few seconds, he stood there as if expecting her to jump out from where she was hiding and surprise him. Before long, he knew she wasn't there. Normally, he wouldn't have thought twice about her stepping out like that. Considering everything that had been going on, however, Caleb felt an uncomfortable knot twist into the middle of his stomach.

He turned on the balls of his feet and sped back out of the hotel. As much as he wanted to run down the street to find Lottie, Caleb didn't have any particular direction in mind. With his heart slamming against the inside of his ribs and the blood rushing through his veins in a hot torrent, he stood on the boardwalk with his hands resting on his holstered guns.

The streets were mostly empty.

When he closed his eyes and concentrated, he could only hear the sounds drifting through the air from various saloons, consisting of loud music, laughter, and working girls plying their trade.

Something festered at the bottom of Caleb's gut, like a single bubble working its way up through swamp water. It left his innards cold and filthy as it got to the back of his throat.

"God damn!" he cursed as he turned and slammed his fist against the front of the hotel.

Responding to that commotion, the squat man who worked at the hotel's front desk walked outside and took a look around. "What the hell was all that?"

"Did you see where Miss Deno went?"

"Lottie? Sure I did."

Caleb wheeled around so he could look directly into the shorter man's eyes. "What happened to her?"

"I don't know if anything happened, but she left a bit before you got here."

"Was she alone?"

"No. There were some other fellas with her."

"What others?" Caleb asked while trying not to lose too much more of his patience. "Did you know them?"

The clerk thought it over while rubbing his chin. "Don't believe I seen 'em before."

"What did they look like?"

"Aw, the hell if I know," the clerk replied as he quickly reached the limit of his own patience and turned to walk back into the hotel. "I've got work to do."

Following the man inside, Caleb asked, "Was one of them tall with a fancy suit?"

"No," the clerk replied quickly.

"Are you sure?"

"Yeah."

"Are you just saying that, or are you really sure?"

"Jesus Christ, if I knew you'd be all riled up like this, I wouldn't have said a damn word. Whatever she's doing with those fellas, I'm sure she'll be back before too long. She seems like a good woman, so I wouldn't worry too much."

By this time, the man had settled in behind his desk and found a drink that was kept out of plain sight. After taking a quick sip, he looked up and seemed surprised that Caleb was still there. It wasn't the good kind of surprised, either.

"I'm worried that she might be in trouble," Caleb said. "Did it look like those men were taking her somewhere she didn't want to go?"

"Not hardly," the clerk grumbled.

"What's that mean?"

"Just what I said. She wasn't smiles and laughs, but she wasn't kicking and scream-ing, either. If she was, I'd have fetched the law and told them about it rather than poke my nose outside just to tell some lunatic pounding against the front of my hotel. What kind of man do you take me for, anyway?"

Caleb leaned with both hands flat against the top of the desk. He took a few seconds to breathe deeply before asking, "Think you could tell me where they went?"

"Ain't my business." Suddenly, the clerk's eyes shot open and he straightened up as if something had bitten his toe. "I almost forgot!"

"What?"

"There's a message for you."

"Is it from Lottie?"

"No, no," the clerk replied with a dismissive wave as he turned and dug through a small pile of papers behind him. "Someone's been coming around looking for you."

Caleb's eyes narrowed as he asked, "Who was it?"

Muttering under his breath until he found one particular slip of paper, the clerk held it up, stared at it, and shook his head. "Name he left was . . . Tom Mackey."

"Tom Mackey?"

"Don't you know him?"

Shaking his head, Caleb asked, "What did he want?"

"See for yourself." With that, the clerk flipped the paper across the top of the counter so it could fly right into Caleb's chest. "And don't bother me anymore with what Miss Deno's doing and *don't* pound yer fists against my walls like some goddamn animal. This ain't some whorehouse and Denver ain't some cow town like you're probably used to, you Texan son of a bitch."

Although Caleb had been pushed way past frustration with the squat man behind the counter, anger wasn't exactly his next stop. Under normal circumstances, the mix of whining and wheezing in the other man's voice might have been funny. What he'd seen and heard, however, just made Caleb feel as if he'd been picked up, spun around, shaken up, and set back down again. He was so flustered that it took a moment or two for him to focus on the slip of paper in his hand.

Sure enough, printed there in handwriting that was much too florid to have been done by the squat man himself, the name Tom Mackey was written plain as day. Beneath that were the words, "Theatre Comique" in somewhat smaller letters.

"When did he come looking for me?" Caleb asked.

The clerk shrugged. "It was there when I

got here at five."

Caleb didn't have to think much at all to recall where he was at that time. He'd been at the Mint playing five-card draw. In fact, Caleb had been there nearly every waking moment since his arrival in Denver.

"So you didn't see this Mackey person?" Caleb asked.

The clerk shook his head.

"What about this theater? Do you know where that is?"

Grudgingly, the clerk leaned forward so he could take another look at the paper. After examining it for a good, long time, he shook his head again. "Nah."

"Thanks a lot. You've been a big help."

29

Since he didn't have any better ideas of where to go and he was too tired to head back to his own room, Caleb started asking around about the Theatre Comique. Finding the place wasn't all that difficult once he asked someone other than the clerk at his hotel. The Theatre was an ornate brick building in a good section of town.

There was plenty of liquor being poured, cards being dealt, and women being groped, but it was done with a more respectable quality. The music wafting through the air was played on pianos that were actually in tune, and accompanied by violins rather than fiddles. It was a subtle difference, but one that hit Caleb square in the face. He was just walking up to the wide double doors of the Theatre when he was stopped by a firm grip upon his shoulder.

"Excuse me," came a calm yet insistent voice from behind him. "I'm afraid you can't go in there."

Caleb's first instinct was to turn around and glare at whoever had stopped him. Luckily, he spotted the badge on the man's chest before he did anything too stupid. "Why not?" he asked in the most civil tone he could manage.

The man was in his twenties, but had the smooth face of someone even younger. A well-trimmed mustache complemented rounded features, as well as the expensive cut of his suit. "Are you new to Denver?" he asked. "I don't believe I've seen you around here."

"I've been here awhile."

"From Texas?"

"Yeah. How'd you know?"

"Your accent gave you away. Also, you bow up like a Texan the moment someone tries to keep you from your whiskey."

Caleb didn't know quite what to say to that. At least, he didn't know quite what to say that wouldn't end up with him being tossed into a cell for misconduct. Fortunately, he only had to wait a few seconds before the lawman started to chuckle.

"No offense meant," the lawman said. "Just testing the waters, is all. Most rowdies or drunks would have slipped up by now. Better out here on the street than inside where ladies are present."

"Oh. I see."

"I've been to Texas. It's some beautiful country."

Caleb nodded slowly and waited. Once he saw that the lawman was perfectly content to stand and enjoy the night air, he asked, "Was there a reason you stopped me?"

"Like I said, you must be new in town. Otherwise, you wouldn't be wearing those in public." When he spoke, the lawman pointed toward the guns strapped around Caleb's waist.

"Is there an ordinance or something against being heeled?" Caleb asked. While doing so, Caleb reached for the guns to tap their handles. His hands froze when he saw the lawman flick open his jacket and place a hand on the pistol holstered there.

"I'd appreciate it if you didn't do that," the lawman said in a voice that was suddenly devoid of all the friendliness that had been there only moments ago. "You'll need to hand those over."

"If you tell me where your office is, I can run them over —"

"Hand them over, mister. Right now."

Caleb stood his ground without moving a muscle. His and the lawman's eyes were locked in a quiet standoff that had plenty of potential to turn ugly at any moment. A few folks on their way into the Theatre had even stopped to watch the show just outside the front door.

Only after Caleb eased his arms away from his guns did the lawman follow suit. The smile that came back on the lawman's face seemed as relieved as it was amicable.

"I apologize for the display," the lawman said. "But there's been too many problems with guns in this area."

Caleb eased his holster from around his waist and handed it over. "I just hope I'm not the only one to be disarmed around here."

"Take a look around and point out another man who's sporting pistols, and I'll go have a word with him."

Just to be difficult, Caleb took a look around so he could point to the closest armed man he could see and watch what the lawman did about it. When he didn't find anyone carrying a gun, he took another look. The second try was as successful as the first, prompting Caleb to look back to the lawman. With nothing else left to do, Caleb shrugged.

"You can pick these back up at the office down the street," the lawman said. "Or, if you plan on staying in Denver for a while, you can leave them with us and we'll keep them safe."

"I guess if you're thorough enough, there shouldn't be much cause for worry."

"That's the idea." With that, the lawman tipped his hat and slung Caleb's holster over his shoulder. "You have a good night."

Caleb watched his guns be carried away, wondering what the hell had just happened. Although he wasn't completely helpless, he knew that walking around without his guns was akin to crawling past a bear's den while covered in honey. Or, more likely, a tiger's den.

Pulling his jacket closed to cover the spot where his holster was normally buckled, Caleb walked into the Theatre Comique and put on his most convincing confident face.

The Theatre was pretty much what he'd expected from the name. It was a large, open room with a second-floor balcony wrapped around nearly all of its perimeter. Most of the main floor was dominated by the large stage, which came complete with dark velvet curtains and a fairly elaborate backdrop, which currently displayed a nicely painted ocean scene. The stage was lit by a row of hooded lanterns at the feet of a large group of singers composed of men and women dressed in what appeared to be long underwear.

A small orchestra accompanied the singers as they went through their finely choreographed motions while gazing back at the brightly painted sun. Caleb wasn't much for dance troupes, but he found himself watching them long enough to be nudged to one side to clear the doorway.

A long bar was built against the wall closest to the door and opposite the stage. There were a few tables scattered where Caleb was standing, but most of the real action was taking place farther inside the Theatre. While walking through the place, Caleb spotted at least half a dozen promising poker games being played, some faro tables, and even a couple backgammon tables. Although he couldn't see the roulette wheels, he could hear at least two of them rattling somewhere in the room.

Upstairs, things appeared to be a little quieter. There were a few sections of seats looking down on the stage, but most of that second-floor space was occupied by finely dressed ladies and the men talking to them. Those people leaned against the rail to look down on the rest of the Theatre, and behind them were a few smaller doors that led to private rooms.

Although he could have spent a good

amount of time just standing where he was and admiring the sights, Caleb forced himself back to the business that had brought him into the Theatre in the first place. He had his sights set on the bartender when he started walking across the room. Perhaps, that's why the well-dressed man who stopped him nearly got up to him without being noticed.

At the last second. Caleb pivoted on his heel and faced the man.

"Whoa, there," the man said as he raised his hands a bit and put on a wary smile. "Didn't mean to startle you. I just wanted to welcome you to the Theatre Comique."

"Thanks."

"I see you got harassed by the law outside. I felt like I was walking with my pants around my ankles the first couple days I went without my gun, but that's because I spent the last few years in some rough towns in Old Mexico. Where you hail from?"

"Dallas."

"Ah, seems like we've been getting a good amount of new faces around here. My name's Andrew Corday."

"Do you run this place?" Caleb asked.

"I'm part owner."

"Do you know anyone named Tom Mackey?"

Corday cocked his head to one side and put on a sly grin. "Perhaps, but I don't discuss such matters with strangers."

For a moment, Caleb felt the muscles in his jaw clench. Then, he looked down to see Corday offering an outstretched hand. He shook it and said, "Caleb Wayfinder."

"Wayfinder? Is that Indian?"

"Partly."

"Well, it's a pleasure to meet you, Caleb. Now that we're no longer strangers, I can tell you the man you're looking for is right over there."

When he looked in the direction Corday was pointing, Caleb spotted another row of faro tables that he'd overlooked earlier.

"Which one is Mackey?" Caleb asked.

"I'd say he's the one in the dark suit, but that doesn't exactly narrow down your choices. Why are you looking for him?"

"Actually, I heard he's been looking for me."

"Does this have anything to do with Morris?"

Caleb shifted his eyes back to Corday and asked, "What do you know about that?"

Corday shrugged. "Anyone in my line of work tends to hear a lot about whatever that asshole does."

"I'd imagine there's no admirer of his that

owns a piece of any saloon. There's enough hard work to do without having another prick strut around to collect some bullshit taxes."

"Sounds like you know something about it. Most folks think owning a saloon is like running a candy store."

Caleb laughed and shook his head. "I owned a place myself."

"Really? How'd you like it?"

"Let's just say it's less of a gamble bucking the tiger than it is trying to turn a profit off a bunch of rowdy drunks."

Corday laughed and slapped Caleb on the shoulder. "I'd heard you might be trouble, but I can see that was just a lot of smoke."

"Where'd you hear that?"

"Your friend Morris. When they're not taking our money, he and his men do their best to talk folks up or down. He's not too fond of you, by the way."

"I know."

"I figured as much. Those tax collectors aren't exactly subtle." Keeping his hand on Caleb's shoulder, Corday turned him so he was facing the faro tables once again. "Mackey is at the table closest to the wall over there. Watch yourself, my friend. I've heard some troubling things about that fellow."

"Thanks."

When Caleb started to walk away, he realized that Corday wasn't so quick to let go of his shoulder. In fact, he tightened his grip and lowered his voice to a fierce whisper.

"I know you got more guns on you than what the law took away," Corday said. "But I got plenty of guns myself, and if you spill blood in my place after I've been so civil to you, I'll make sure you see more guns than you'll like."

Caleb nodded as if he were listening to a recipe for blueberry cobbler. "You've got a real nice place here. I won't mess it up."

Shifting back to his neighborly smile, Corday patted Caleb's shoulder and let him go. "That's good to hear. You're a real gentleman." After that, Corday found someone else in the vicinity to welcome and moved along to do just that.

As he walked through the milling crowd of people in the Theatre, Caleb checked to make sure that everything was in place. He could still feel the small revolver in his boot as well as the one kept at the small of his back. Drawing either of them would take slightly longer than pulling one from his holster, but Caleb figured it was only a matter of a second or so difference.

Caleb made it to the faro table closest to

the wall without spotting one familiar face. He had a few ideas as to what to look for and how to react once Mackey showed himself. But none of that preparation was enough to keep him from being surprised once he got a good look at who was sitting at that table between two gamblers and doing a bad job of protecting decent-sized stacks of chips.

"Doc? What the hell are you doing here?"

"Ah," Doc said with only a hint of mild interest in his voice. "I see you got my message."

30

It took more than a little prodding, but Doc was finally convinced to get up from his seat. After saying his farewells to the other gamblers, he took hold of a polished black cane that had been propped against the table and leaned on its silver handle as he walked. When he got to the bar, Doc produced a pair of twenty-dollar chips in his right hand before making them disappear again with a slight flourish. "I've been helping myself to these all night," Doc said. "Those two on either side of me were playing so badly they never even noticed."

"What's with the cane?" Caleb asked.

Doc shrugged and then postured like an aristocrat in an old painting. "I find it makes me look distinguished." After seeing that Caleb wasn't impressed, he added, "It also makes things a bit easier on my rough days."

Caleb knew better than to press Doc on

matters regarding his health. Since Doc was clear-eyed and speaking without coughing, he knew the slender Georgian was doing as well as could be expected. "How long have you been in town?"

"Just a few days. I must say, I'm feeling a whole lot better since I've arrived. This mountain air does wonders."

"Who's Tom Mackey?"

"I am," Doc replied with a smirk. "I thought you would have deduced that by now."

"You took a new name?"

"It seemed prudent, especially after the way I left Fort Griffin." All Doc had to do was nod at the barkeep for him to get a fresh glass of whiskey set in front of him. After taking a sip, Doc added, "It was a bit of a mess."

"That sounds about how things have turned out around here."

"Oh really? I take it you've crossed paths with the Tiger?"

"Yeah," Caleb said. "His name's Morris. Did you know there's a price on our heads?"

Doc nodded. "I heard about that before I got here."

"It made it back to Fort Griffin already?"

Doc nodded again. "I imagine so."

"Jesus. This has got to stop. Otherwise, we

won't be able to play a game of solitaire anywhere near the circuit. Hell, we'll be forced to run like outlaws once enough money-hungry cowboys get word of this."

"Say what you want about the Tiger, but they certainly do have an efficient system in place."

"Fine," Caleb grunted. "We can just pay our taxes like everyone else and then get on with our business."

"That's fine talk from you. First you get shot by these animals and now you want to pay them for it."

"And what the hell have you done, Doc? Besides drink a lot of whiskey and spout off at them, I mean."

"I walked out of Jacksboro after someone tried to cash in on that bounty you mentioned. I'll be damned if I'll slink off somewhere and hope some group of extortionists forget about me. I've got a life to lead and don't have that kind of time to waste in doing it."

"You had some trouble in Jacksboro?" Caleb asked.

Doc nodded casually, but kept his mouth shut as the barkeep approached him. The big man had a friendly face, but arms thicker than tree trunks. Somehow, the burly man managed to clean off a glass without crushing it between his thick fingers.

"You still owe for that whiskey you've been drinking, Mr. Mackey," the barkeep said.

"Oh, how forgetful of me," Doc said, replying to his new alias without missing a beat. He produced one of his stolen chips and set it on the bar. "I believe that should cover it."

"And then some. I'll get your change."

"Keep it. Just keep the drinks coming."

The big man grinned and nodded. "Thanks, Mr. Mackey."

"Please, call me Tom." After the barkeep had moved on, Doc looked to Caleb and said, "That's the sort of fellow I'd rather have on my side."

"What happened in Fort Griffin?"

"You seem particularly nervous, Caleb. I'd like to know what happened here."

Realizing that he wasn't going to get any information out of Doc if he didn't want it known, Caleb sighed and said, "Morris made it clear that the Tiger is through making threats and promises. They're starting to play rough, and now Lottie's nowhere to be found."

"Lottie's here?"

"She was. I went to her room and she was

missing. Apparently, she was taken right from her hotel by a couple of men."

Suddenly, all the humor that was such a natural part of Doc's face was gone. "She's been kidnapped?"

Caleb's gut reaction was to say she had been. Before he could get the words out, however, he stopped himself and stared down at the bar. "From what I heard, a few men came to get her and she left with them. I've been tearing through town expecting to find a door that needed to be kicked down so I could charge in with guns blazing."

"To save the fair damsel in distress," Doc said as if to complete Caleb's line of thought. "I never had you figured for the noble sort."

"What about the stupid sort? That's what I feel like right about now. For all I know, she's got another game set up somewhere."

"Or she's having a word with the Tiger herself. She did, after all, know who to look for around here."

Reluctantly, Caleb nodded.

"You must not have taken the Tiger's threat too seriously," Doc pointed out. "Otherwise, you wouldn't have decided to come here and take in this fine establishment."

"I got the message from you, Doc. That's

why I'm here."

"Oh, that's right. If it makes you feel any better, I haven't heard a thing about Lottie or any terrible fate that might have befallen her. Still," he added while swirling the whiskey around in his glass, "she has been known to partake in rather dubious company. We being the exceptions of course."

"She's been helping me," Caleb said.

"Are you sure of that?"

"What's that supposed to mean?"

Doc shrugged and sipped his drink. "She's been looking after her own interests for quite a while. She certainly didn't have our well-being in mind at that game in Fort Griffin. I'm sure Mike would agree on that."

"We've already been through that."

"Fine, fine," Doc grumbled. "She's never been too hard to find before, so I doubt she will be now. There's a few people we can ask about her whereabouts. That sure beats running up and down the streets hoping to catch a glimpse of red hair."

Suddenly, Doc froze while lifting his glass to his mouth. The look of surprise on his face was something Caleb had rarely ever seen before. "Then again," Doc said, "perhaps waiting for a glimpse of her was all we needed to do."

Turning to see what had caught Doc's attention, Caleb spotted Lottie at the front door of the Theatre. Caleb headed for the front door in a heartbeat, and the moment he got to her, he wrapped his arms around her and buried his face in her fragrant red hair.

"Where the hell have you been?" he asked.

"I just needed to talk to some friends."

"Friends? I thought you were dragged out of that hotel."

"The man at the desk said you were upset when I wasn't there," she replied. "He also said I could find you here."

"Who were the men you left with?" Caleb asked. "What friends did you have to see?"

Rather than answer any of those questions, Lottie was staring back toward the bar. The sound of a cane knocking against the floor announced Doc's approach seconds before he spoke up.

"Hello, Lottie," Doc said. "Good to see you again."

"Likewise, Doc. I didn't know you were in Denver."

Taking hold of her and forcing her to look directly at him, Caleb said, "You two can catch up later. I want you to answer my questions."

"Why are you being so rough with me?" Lottie asked.

"Because Doc and I are being hunted down and you decide to disappear in the middle of it all. Who came to get you at the hotel?"

"He's just an acquaintance of mine."

"He's still outside, isn't he?" Even though he didn't get a spoken answer to that question, Caleb could tell that he'd hit a nerve. Moving her toward the bar, Caleb told Lottie to stay put as he stomped out of the Theatre.

That left her and Doc facing each other. Although Doc wasn't imposing himself in any way, the intensity in his eyes made Lottie feel as if they were the only two people in the room. She shifted on her feet, but couldn't quite get herself to leave.

"Caleb's not going to find anyone outside, is he?" Doc asked.

"I'm in here with you, Doc. How would I know what he'll find?"

"Fair enough. Then let me ask you another question. Whose side are you on?"

Letting out a breath, Lottie straightened her back and looked Doc dead in the eyes. "I'm on my side. And if you try to come off like you're any different, then you're a damn liar."

"I prefer to think of myself as a bluffer. A damn good one. The only problem is that you're a damn good one yourself. Something else I know for certain about you is that you're not the sort of woman who needs frequent rescuing. So where have you been that's gotten Caleb so worked up?"

She paused for a moment and then took a quick glance over her shoulder toward the door. When she saw nobody coming in, she looked back to Doc and spoke in a more hurried voice. "I've had a little talk with Morris. He found me because I checked in with him to see where you and Caleb stood. Things are bad and they're about to get worse."

"What happened to you while you were there?"

"Nothing. We just talked."

As Doc studied her, he could hear the front door opening and a set of angry footsteps stomping toward the bar.

"It's too late for me to get out of this," Lottie said quickly. "I know it's too late for you. It's not too late for Caleb. He can still set up another saloon somewhere instead of scraping out his living under the heels of men like Morris and Stakely."

"Who's Stakely?"

"He's the one that intends on bringing all of this to an end so bloody that nobody will try to cross him or anyone else collecting

330

his taxes ever again."

As the steps came closer, Doc looked again, to see Caleb eyeing everyone in the Theatre as he made his way to Lottie's side.

"Where did Stakely take you?" Doc asked in a rush.

"Babbitt's."

"There's nobody out there," Caleb said as he stepped up to the bar. "At least, nobody who doesn't belong."

"Why don't you take her somewhere she can rest?" Doc asked. "Perhaps one of the rooms upstairs would be better than a hotel. I believe the management here is somewhat sympathetic to our situation."

When she saw Doc looking at her, Lottie gave a quick, appreciative nod.

"I'll check in with you later," Doc said. "I have an appointment elsewhere."

31

Babbitt's was a respectable little gaming hall that catered to men who didn't care about a stage show. Although there was always a bit of music being played and a few dancers around, most of the noise inside the main room was the murmurs of gamblers poring over their cards and the occasional pounding of an angry fist against the top of a table.

The main floor was dark and taken up by card tables and roulette wheels. The bar was only as big as it needed to be to keep the gamblers drunk, and the rooms in the back weren't much more than a place for someone to rest his eyes between big games.

One room, in particular, was bigger than the rest. Normally, it was used as an office for the owner, but it was sometimes lent out to special guests for their own purposes. Stakely was such a guest in any saloon he visited, whether the saloon owners liked it or not.

Walking around the desk like a vulture circling a fresh corpse, Stakely reached out with one hand to slap Morris's feet from where they'd been propped up. Morris reflexively bolted upright with fire shining in his eyes.

"What?" Stakely snarled as he squared his shoulders to the man. "You want to say something to me about my behavior? You want to put me back into line so you can kick back and relax some more?"

Finally, Morris shook his head and situated his legs under the desk.

"You hear about what happened to that soldier in Jacksboro?" Stakely asked.

"Holliday killed him."

"That's right. And you know what's being done about it?"

Morris didn't bother responding to the question, since he knew hell would be coming no matter what he did.

"Nothing!" Stakely growled. "The fucking army isn't even looking into it, because it's being written off as one of their men stepping out of line and getting into a scrape that he shouldn't have been in." Leaning forward to press both hands flat on the top of the desk, Stakely glared directly into Morris's eyes and added, "That man was going after the bounty we offered and now nobody in Texas is even *asking* about the money on Holliday's skinny ass. Most folks act like they don't even know about the other one."

"Caleb Wayfinder," Morris said.

"I don't give a shit if his name is Benjamin Fucking Franklin! If someone is doing work that's paid by me, he's one of my men, and nobody guns down one of my men in one of the towns under my control!"

"Jacksboro isn't —"

"No, but this town is, and *you're* the man that's supposed to be controlling it! I want Holliday and that Wayfinder asshole *dead!* You hear me? Not warned. Not chased out of town. Not threatened. Dead. I've already seen saloon owners around here acting like they don't need to pay our taxes, and I can't allow that. If we're gonna whip everyone back into line, blood needs to be spilled. Either that blood comes from one of those two that's stirring this shit up, or it comes from you. Those are the only two choices on the table. Understand?"

"Ye—"

"Good," Stakely growled. With that, Stakely pounded his knuckles against the desk once more before turning and storming toward the door. One of the men that had been doing his best to remain in the background during Stakely's rampage opened the door for him and followed him out.

That left two other men in there with Morris, and judging by the looks on their faces, they were not happy about being there.

Morris put his head in his hands and let out a slow, exasperated breath. "Where's Lottie Deno?"

"Budd said she was headed for that theater down on Blake Street."

"Go there and find her. She's probably with Wayfinder, and if she's not, I want you to take her and use her to draw him out."

The big man wore a large, Navy model Colt tucked under his belt and a hunting knife at his hip. Despite those fearsome weapons on his person, he cringed when he was given that order. "But . . . she and Stakely just got through —"

"I don't give a shit what she's been through," Morris interrupted. "Didn't you hear what just happened? Do you think I'm the only one that will be replaced if Stakely decides to make changes around here?"

"No, sir."

"Then just go and do what you're told. If you catch sight of Wayfinder, kill him. I don't care where he is or what he's doing.

Kill him, and we'll deal with the consequences later."

While the big man was nodding, someone knocked on the door.

Morris looked up and said, "That's probably the food. Bring it in."

The big guard opened the door a crack and looked outside. Turning to glance over his shoulder, he said, "It's Budd Ryan."

Morris flapped his hand impatiently to get the other man to open the door. Standing in the hall was a solidly built man with a prominent gut hanging just over his belt buckle. "What is it?" Morris asked.

Budd's mouth hung open, so he licked his lips and forced it shut. His labored breathing made it sound as if he'd run all the way from the Rocky Mountains rather than his usual poker table in the next room. "There's . . . uhh . . . something you should see."

"Come in and tell me about it or show me. Just be quick about it."

The gunman stepped aside and opened the door the rest of the way so Budd could step inside. Although he wasn't as big as the gunman at the door, Budd filled out a good portion of the doorway. He was most certainly bigger than the skinny, pale figure that came in directly behind him.

Doc stepped in while staying directly behind Budd, surveying the room with quickly darting eyes.

"What the hell?" Morris shouted as he jumped to his feet.

Before Morris or any of his men could make another move, Budd held out both hands and said, "Don't! He's got a gun to my back."

Doc smirked and laughed under his breath. "Oh, I must apologize about that. The law around here is quite strict about such things." With that, he shoved Budd forward to reveal the end of his cane protruding from his fist. Doc loosened his fingers and allowed the cane to slide through them until the handle fell into his grasp and the tip knocked against the floor.

"But Budd was nice enough to remedy the problem," Doc added as he lifted his other hand to show the pistol he held in it, "by lending me the firearm from his own pocket. Wasn't that thoughtful?"

Morris looked around at his men, both of whom were glancing right back at him, waiting for orders. "You're Doc Holliday?"

"Correct."

"Why are you here? I would have gladly sat down with you to discus—"

"Discuss what? The price on my head? Or

would you prefer to discuss what you did to Lottie Deno?"

"That wasn't me. It was Stakely."

"And where's Stakely?"

Suddenly, the fear that was in Morris's eyes evaporated. Just hearing Stakely's name repeated a few times was like a splash of cold water in his face. He lowered his hand to his desk to open the drawer and check that his gun was still where he'd left it. A quick look to either side was enough to see that his two gunmen were in prime positions on either side of the door.

"You and your friend had your chances to pay us off," Morris said. "You even had a chance to run away, but you insisted on staying where you're not wanted."

"I like it here," Doc said in his smooth, Southern drawl. "The mountain air is good for my condition."

"Well, I'll be sure to bury you in a nice spot in the Rockies." To his men, Morris said, "Kill him."

Doc's eyes were the first things to move. He looked toward the first trace of motion he saw and found the gunman to his right lifting his pistol to sight along its barrel. Doc shifted his weight from one foot to the other, brought his left arm across his body, and fired. Since he was using his off-hand,

Doc fired once more just to be certain.

The gunman lurched back and stumbled toward the wall with both arms splayed out to either side.

The other gunman fired a shot as quickly as he could while snarling an obscenity through gritted teeth.

That bullet hissed through the air near Doc's head, without causing so much as a twitch from Doc in response.

While looking toward the second gunman, Doc saw Morris bringing up his gun as well. Relying on his memory, Doc kept his eyes on Morris while quickly aiming at the man that was just out of his field of vision. Doc pulled his trigger once and then shifted into a duelist's stance, which lined up his shoulders to Morris so he presented a narrower target.

Morris fired once by anxiously jerking his finger around his trigger, which sent his bullet into the wall to Doc's right. He took another quick shot while praying desperately for one of his men to finish Doc off.

Rather than think about the bullets flying around him, Doc focused on the blind panic in Morris's eyes. That, alone, was enough to convince him that he could take his time with his next shot to make sure it was done properly. His ears rang from the gunfire, making the dry wheezing in the back of his own throat the only thing Doc could hear with any clarity.

The pistol bucked against Doc's palm once more, punching a hole directly through the center of Morris's face. Morris dropped back into his chair and then fell into a heap on the floor. The impact of his body against the boards was covered by the sound of Doc's pistol as it sent another round into the second gunman.

Just then, Doc realized he'd been holding his breath. He let it out and took a step toward the second gunman to make sure the man was down for good. Sure enough, there were two holes in that one's chest. Doc figured the shot that was off-center and in the man's stomach was the shot he'd taken without looking.

When he pulled in a breath, the acrid smoke lanced like a set of talons straight down the back of Doc's throat. He coughed once, which lit a burning pain in his lungs as the taste of blood spattered against the back of his tongue.

The ringing in Doc's ears faded just enough for him to hear the pounding of footsteps approaching the door. At any moment, he knew someone would work up the courage to open the door or just shoot through it with the biggest gun they could find.

"I got you now!" Budd shouted as he charged Doc with both hands balled into fists.

Doc's first reaction was to pull away from the man while also bringing his arm up to fire the pistol he'd taken. But the Colt's long barrel weighed heavily in his grasp and the gun began feeling like a cannon at the end of his arm.

Too rattled to be afraid of the gun, Budd grabbed hold of Doc's wrist and wrenched it to one side. Just as he was thinking he might have broken Doc's arm, Budd felt the Georgian regain his composure and fight to take back control of the weapon.

Doc snapped up his right hand, which was still wrapped around the handle of his cane. His silver knob caught Budd solidly in the gut. Although he felt the dull thud of the cane's impact, Budd hauled another breath into his lungs to replace the wind that had just been knocked out of him. His next breath came a lot easier once he felt the gun come loose from Doc's hand.

Budd grinned triumphantly as he lifted the gun. One moment, he was sighting down its barrel, and the next found him staring straight up at the ceiling as Doc's cane caught him solidly under the jaw. Feeling as if the floor were being tilted under his feet, Budd staggered back until his shoulders hit the door behind him and slammed it shut just as it was being tentatively pushed open.

Letting out a haggard breath, Doc swung his cane with all the strength he could manage. After landing the previous two blows with the makeshift weapon, his blood was burning through his veins like wildfire. When his cane smashed into Budd's arm, Doc felt the impact all the way up to his shoulder.

Budd let out the cry of a wounded animal as his finger reflexively tightened around his trigger. The gunshot punched a hole through the floor, while also shearing off the smallest toe on Budd's right foot.

Although he was relieved to see Budd crumple over and lean against the wall, Doc knew it hadn't been any of his blows that had put him there. When he saw the bloody mess on the side of Budd's foot, he couldn't help but laugh.

"What's so . . . god . . . damn . . . funny?" Budd gasped.

"All the tough talk you spout off when you're playing cards," Doc said with a wheeze just beneath his voice, "and you wind up shooting yourself in the foot when everything boils over. I guess . . . that proves what men like you are made of."

Budd gritted his teeth and forced his eyes open. Focusing on Doc's pale, sweating face, he said, "You're crazy, Holliday."

"I want you to tell the Tiger to come find me. I believe Stakely is his name."

Budd lifted his gun and shoved the barrel into Doc's chest. The only move Doc made was to lean against it with all of his weight.

When Budd pulled his trigger, all he got for his trouble was the hollow slap of a hammer against empty brass.

"Looks like this moment's just not your best." Doc taunted him. "For a man that's so good with numbers, I would have thought you'd at least be able to count down from six."

Budd pushed himself up against the wall, but pressed a little too hard against his bloody foot. With a loud groan, his legs slipped out from under him and he landed on his backside with a thump against the floor.

Since Budd was sitting against a good portion of the door, Doc allowed himself a moment to catch his breath. He reached into his pocket and found his flask. After taking a sip of whiskey, he offered it to Budd. When the wounded man shook his head, Doc shrugged. "Are you sure about that? This helps the pain go away. Trust me on that much, if nothing else."

"Choke on it, Holliday."

"Tell me who's the Tiger at the top of the heap. Is it Stakely?"

"Hell yes, it's Stakely. He came to Denver just to bury you and your Injun friend personally, and that's just what he'll do."

"Where can I find him?"

"He knows that Injun was at the theater. He's probably gutting him right about now."

"And once he hears about this and sees his partner over there, I figure he'll be mad enough to shoot the first man he can find." Doc straightened up and tucked his flask away. "Too bad you can't run so well any longer."

Budd shook his head as he reached down to grab his wounded foot. His hand stopped short, however, and reached into his boot to pull out a revolver that was slightly smaller than the one Doc had taken from him.

As Budd lifted his small backup pistol and his thumb was pulling back the hammer, Doc's hand flashed over his right shoulder as if he were scratching the back of his neck. When his arm snapped back again, Doc was holding a small knife with a T-shaped handle and a short blade that extended from his clenched fist.

Doc's first slash caught Budd across the face to open his cheek and slice through his chin. After pushing Budd's gun hand away, Doc took a second backhanded slash that cut through Budd's throat all the way down to the bone.

Doc stood hunched over with his knuckles turning white around the handle of his knife. As much as he wanted to, he simply couldn't take his eyes off Budd's face. In a matter of seconds, Budd's face turned pale and the entire front of his shirt was stained almost black.

Straightening up, Doc started to wipe his blade on his shirt, but found it was soaked as well. He used Budd's pant leg to quickly clean off his knife and then stood up to take a look around.

Doc's eyes were narrow and his breath was still coming in labored gusts. Covering his mouth as a hacking fit nearly doubled him over, Doc used up a good deal of his strength to open the door enough for him to step into the hall. When he let the door go, Budd's body thumped back into place behind it. He found a set of stairs leading into the kitchen before encountering a single person brave enough to take a step anywhere near the room he'd left behind.

32

The rooms for rent inside the Theatre Comique immediately struck Caleb as too expensive. The furniture was too new and the bed was too comfortable for him to normally afford. Price wasn't exactly as important, however, as the strength of the locks on the doors.

When he heard the knock, Caleb drew the gun that resided at the small of his back and stood against the wall next to the door.

"It's me," Doc said from the hallway.

Caleb unlocked the door and opened it without lowering his gun. As Doc walked in, Caleb took a glance outside and then closed the door and locked it.

"Did you find those assholes?" Caleb asked.

Doc's dark jacket was buttoned to cover his shirt. He nodded and took a sip of whiskey. "I sure did."

Suddenly noticing the dark smudges of

gunpowder on Doc's face, Caleb asked, "Are you all right?"

"Morris is dead."

"Are you sure?"

"Very much so."

Studying the grim look on Doc's face, Caleb asked, "You got to him?"

"I'm not the only one. A Mr. Stakely was there just before I was. Apparently, he's the one who set Morris and his men on edge."

"How many men?"

"Three."

"I'll go back there with you and we can clean them out."

"No need for that. It's already done."

Lottie had been sitting on the edge of the bed with her hands folded in her lap. When she heard that, her head snapped up and her eyes fixed on Doc. "You killed Morris and three of his men while you were gone?"

"I thought I might get one of them to tell me where Stakely was, but when I heard that Morris was already there and Stakely was close by, I couldn't resist paying them a visit."

"Jesus," Caleb muttered. "It's all gone to hell now. First there was the problem of getting out from under the price on our heads and now God only knows what else is about to be thrown at us."

Doc laughed to himself and took a drink. "You talk as if everything's been a field of daisies up until a few days ago."

"What's that supposed to mean?"

"It means that I'm sick to death of hearing about this fucking Tiger and all the other animals that go along with him," Doc sneered. "And I consider myself something of an expert as far as being sick to death is concerned."

"Everyone is fed up with this goddamn Tiger," Caleb said. "There's nothing to do about it, though."

Doc jabbed a finger at him and said, "You see? Right there is what I'm talking about and it's also where these extortionists are slipping up. It's been hard to see while in the middle of it all, but this whole thing strikes me as a bigger con than anything we ever thought of pulling off."

"Say what you want, Doc, but the Tiger is real. Funny name or not, they're out there."

"Of course he is . . . they are . . . whatever . . . and under any other circumstances, these same men would be called a gang and they'd be hunted down like one. But they're not. They're the Big Bad Tiger and everyone's scared because they show up everywhere like some kind of nightmare."

As Doc went on, he grasped the top of his cane in one hand. His voice became like a beam of light focused through a spyglass as he tapped the cane against the floor to emphasize certain words here and there. "It's bullshit," Doc said. "All of it is. This is nothing more than another gang of thieves who just happened to come up with an angle that allowed them to fleece an even bigger group of thieves."

"The system works well enough for them to collect taxes and put a price on our heads that gets spread across at least two states."

"It works because most people would rather go along with that system and complain about it than go through the trouble of bucking it."

"And going against these men is more trouble than it's worth, anyway," Caleb added.

Doc nodded once and tapped the floor with his cane as if he were applauding the dancing troupe on stage. "Exactly. They've got fear going along with the bullshit they've been pitching to all the saloon owners and lawmen. Whatever service the Tiger provides is minuscule at best. A crooked lawman will take money from anyone and an honest one won't. No Tiger in the jungle will change that."

Caleb's brow furrowed as he thought that over.

"Rumors are spread about certain gamblers, saloons, or games with or without a middleman," Doc went on to say. "If Stakely is the man who put this Tiger thing into motion, I'd like to shake his hand because he is a damn genius."

"So you don't think that price on our heads means anything?"

"Oh, it means something," Doc said. "But any idiot can offer a reward to have someone caught or killed. That doesn't make him anything more than someone with money in his pockets. I'll also grant the fact that they have some amount of leverage as far as polishing or tarnishing another gambler's reputation."

Caleb rolled his eyes and muttered, "Jesus, here we go again with the reputation talk."

"You know what I had to pay to get permission to deal a faro game here?" Doc asked.

"The normal taxes plus the percentage?"

"Try no taxes and a quarter less of the percentage we've been getting."

"How'd you manage that?"

"By the reputation that I built for myself. At the start, the Tiger might have provided a service that was worth paying for. I imagine you would have liked getting all your information on transients like us from one reliable source when you owned the Busted Flush."

"I suppose."

"Those days are over," Doc said. "The Tiger's worn out what little welcome he had and folks are tired of getting gouged by these ridiculous taxes and watching these idiots strut around like they own these towns. The only thing still working in the Tiger's favor is that most folks are too scared or too lazy to go against them. As soon as folks look into what's left of Morris's office, they'll see that the Tiger is just a bunch of flesh-and-blood men sharing a silly name."

Caleb nodded. "Now I see where this is headed."

"So do I," Lottie said. "And I don't like it one bit. You don't know about the blood these men spilled, Doc. Going against a few of them is fine, but there's plenty more where those came from."

Doc stepped over to the bed and leaned against his cane as he knelt down to look her directly in the eyes. "I know about pain and I don't have to ask what those godless bastards did to you when they had you alone."

A response started to come out of Lottie's mouth like a reflexive twitch from her muscles, but it stopped before she let out much more than a squeak. Although she kept her eyes on Doc, she couldn't hold in the tears that began trickling down her cheeks.

"What did they do to you?" Caleb asked.

After steeling herself, Lottie said, "They came and took me from my room. They hauled me off so quickly that I didn't even know where we were going. All I knew is that there were at least two guns digging into me the entire way and that they would shoot if I made one wrong move."

Her eyes drifted away from Caleb and Doc to focus on the back of her hand. "They . . . tried to hurt me. Stakely . . . he . . . did things and told me to tell you all about it so you'd face him down. He wants you to be off balance and sloppy." Shaking her head, she added, "It's the oldest trick there is, but I knew it would work if I told you. You would have charged after them, Caleb. I know you would have and then you would have been killed because they were just waiting for you."

"So you kept this to yourself?" Caleb asked.

She nodded. "The damage was done.

353

Nothing you did would have made it better. The only thing I could do was keep you from playing right into Stakely's hands."

"I'm not about to disgrace myself by saying I'm a saint," Doc told her quietly. "And I won't deny killing Morris and those men he hired, because every last one of them got what they deserved. What I did may not have been right, but seeing the pain they put into you only makes me wish I could breathe some life into them so I could kill them all over again."

"You keep this fight going, and you'll be set up for trouble from more than just the Tiger," Lottie said. "The law won't care about your reasons. And those dead men will have friends who'll be out for blood. If you do this —"

"Too late," Doc interrupted. "It's already done."

Lottie sat there with the rest of what she'd meant to say perched on the tip of her tongue. She looked at Doc and saw a fierceness in his sunken eyes that defied the very forces of nature that were tearing him apart. In the presence of that, she simply couldn't muster up the will to continue what she was saying.

Instead, Lottie wrapped her arms around Doc's neck and gave him a hug. "Thank you," she whispered.

Straightening up, Doc cleared his throat and tightened his grip around the handle of his cane. "That's the problem with loud-mouthed assholes like these," he said. "Someone brings the fight to them sooner or later. The funny thing is that they never see it coming."

After patting Doc on the shoulder, Caleb moved to Lottie's side and asked, "Is Stakely the top of the heap as far as these extortionists go?"

She nodded. "He's the one behind the Tiger."

"And he's still in town?"

"I was supposed to tell you he was at the Mint, but that was just so he could set you up. I know Morris's office is at Babbitt's. Once Stakely hears about what happened to Morris, he'll be tearing Denver apart to find you two. He already wanted blood and now he'll just want more."

"Then I don't see any reason why he should be disappointed."

Doc grinned and tapped his cane once against the floor. "If word about the money being offered for us can spread so fast, imagine how quickly it would spread if the Tiger were to stop collecting those taxes."

"A whole lot of folks would become very

grateful."

"I like the way you think." Opening his jacket, Doc revealed a pair of mismatched guns that were stuck under his belt, as well as a newly restocked shoulder holster. "Before I freshened up, I relieved Morris of some pistols to save us a trip down to the sheriff's office."

Caleb took two of Doc's spare guns and tucked them under his jacket. "I wouldn't mind taking these assholes on myself, Doc. You've already done more than your share."

"I beg to differ," Doc said. "This is just my game."

33

"Those sons of bitches are going to pay for this," Stakely growled. Looking up to the side of the Theatre Comique that faced the street, he shouted, "You all hear that? Nobody spits in my face and gets away with it! If anyone's hiding Holliday or that accomplice of his, you'll earn a pretty penny by handing them over right now! Otherwise, stay out of our way and watch what happens to cowardly killers like them!"

Drinking in the silence that had fallen onto the street, Stakely looked around at the men surrounding him. There were seven of them, not counting Stakely himself, and every last man was armed to the teeth. They stood in the middle of Blake Street, tightening their fists around their weapons.

"I can't allow this," huffed the same dapper lawman who'd disarmed Caleb earlier that night.

Stakely shot half a glance toward the lawman before shifting his eyes back toward the Theatre. "You're paid to allow whatever I want, so that's just what you'll do."

But the lawman stood his ground and rested his hand on his holstered pistol. "You and your men will have to move on."

"Have you been to Babbitt's?" Stakely asked.

"Yes, and the sheriff himself is doing all he can to find whoever killed those men."

"I know damn well who killed them, but Holliday's still roaming free."

"There hasn't been anyone to back that story up. A few even said they shot each other during some sort of an argument."

Wheeling around to face the lawman, Stakely started to snarl something, but was cut short at the sound of horses thundering from a nearby alley and veering onto Blake Street. Stakely only managed to catch a fleeting glimpse of who was riding those horses, but that was all he needed. "That's them! They're making a run for it!"

The lawman was pushed aside as Stakely and the rest of his men dashed for the horses that they'd tied up only a few moments ago. As the group tore down the street after the two riders, the lawman fumed to himself and watched them leave. He then ran across the street and charged into the Theatre.

"Where's Holliday?" the lawman asked the bartender.

"If he's not dealing faro at his table during his shift, it ain't my business."

"What about his accomplice?"

Even though the lawman didn't know exactly who Stakely had been referring to, throwing out that term was a gamble that paid off with a nod from the barkeep.

"If you mean the one who Doc was expecting earlier, he rented a room a while ago and took Lottie Deno up there. It's up the stairs and all the way down the hall, but you might want to stay out of there if you know what I mean."

"Just give me the key."

Doing his best to ignore the lurid chuckle coming from the barkeep, the lawman took the spare key, bolted up the stairs, and headed for the room. Rapping on the door, he asked, "Miss Deno? Are you in there?"

The lawman fitted the key in the door and opened it. He found Lottie alone in the room with a Smith & Wesson in her hand.

"Put the gun down, ma'am, I just —"

Before he could finish, the lawman saw a plume of fire erupt from the barrel of Lottie's gun. Thunder filled the room as he reflexively dropped to the floor. When he was finally able to open his eyes, he saw Lottie still in her spot with the smoking gun in her hands.

Since he wasn't hit, the lawman went for his own pistol. That's about the time he heard the heavy thump of something hitting the floor behind him. The lawman swiveled around and saw a large man slumped against the railing of the balcony overlooking the main floor.

The dead man was one of the hired guns who routinely made collections at the Theatre and delivered more than a few payments to sworn deputies.

"I think it'd be safer for you to hand over that gun and come with me," the lawman said.

Lottie lowered the pistol and calmly stepped forward. "Yes," she said while placing the gun in the lawman's hand. "I believe you're right."

There were times in Caleb's life when he felt like he was running in the dark without knowing if he was heading for a stretch of open road or the edge of a cliff. Lately, he'd felt more like he was charging through the dark on the back of a wild horse toward what might just be a rock wall.

Oddly enough, now that he actually was

on the back of a horse and charging through the night, he felt more in control of things than ever.

There was always something special about being on the back of a horse running full-out with the wind in his face. It was something that normal folks simply didn't do, which made doing it all the more satisfying. Given the fact that the men who'd put the price on his head were following him like a good bunch of doggies doubled that sense of satisfaction.

The well-kept Denver streets had disappeared from under his horse's hooves and the lively fronts of the saloons and gambling halls were behind him. After that was a good stretch of darker stores that were closed for the night, followed by clusters of houses on the outskirts of town. Caleb's horse was going so fast that the tents pitched around Denver's city limits fluttered past him like dirty laundry hanging from a line.

Now that the trail was opening up in front of him, he could make out the distinct pounding of several sets of hooves riding up on his tail. Caleb took another look over his shoulder and saw the riders tearing after him like wolves chasing down fresh meat.

With more riders coming after him, that left fewer men to go after Lottie. But now wasn't the time to worry about her. She could take care of herself, leaving Caleb to take care of his own business.

Now that his eyes had had a chance to adjust to the utter darkness outside of town, Caleb could see the looming shapes of the rock formations around him. One in particular caught his eye and when he passed it, Caleb shifted in his saddle to watch the trail behind him.

Sure enough, after the other riders passed that rock formation, another shadow swung in from the side of the trail and sent a few shots into the larger group. There was some shouting back and forth between the other men, and some of them peeled off from the main group to chase the solitary figure that now rode back into the shadows.

Caleb shook his head and grinned as he looked back toward the trail ahead. "Punctual as ever, Doc," he said to himself. "Now let's see if I can hold up my end."

As soon as he picked out a safe spot to break away from the trail, Caleb steered his horse into a thick group of shadows being cast by a tall bunch of rocks. Stopping just short of those rocks, he pulled back on his reins and swung down from the saddle. Caleb's boots hit the dirt before his horse had even come to a stop. While drawing a rifle from the scabbard on the side of the saddle, he smacked the horse's rump and stepped back.

The smack, combined with the thunder of approaching riders, was all Caleb's horse needed to send him galloping around the rocks.

Caleb dropped to one knee, pressed the rifle to his shoulder, and sighted along the top of the barrel. He was able to take two full breaths before the riders stampeded into his sights and veered to avoid the rocks while chasing the fleeing horse. His first shot blazed through the air in front of one of the riders. Although that bullet didn't draw any blood, it came close enough to one horse's ear to stop it dead in its tracks and make it rear up nervously. With that rider perched up high, Caleb sent a round into the man's skull.

One of the three riders was too far ahead and kept charging after Caleb's horse. The other two brought their horses around and started firing the instant they were facing in the direction from which those rifle shots had come.

Caleb pulled his rifle in close to his body and backed into the shadows until his shoulder bumped against the rock. Sparks flew over his head and bullets ricocheted noisily all around him. Forcing himself to ignore all the noise and chaos drawing closer to him, Caleb aimed and fired at the nearest rider.

That man hollered in pain and fell awkwardly from his saddle. He hit the ground hard enough for Caleb to hear the wet snap of a breaking bone.

"Goddammit!" the rider howled. "My leg's busted!"

"I see him," the other rider said as he aimed his pistol in Caleb's general direction. "He's right there!"

Since both men were now looking directly at him, Caleb got both feet dug into the dirt and lunged straight for them. His first shot was rushed and thrown off by his sudden movement, so the bullet hissed through empty air.

Quickly levering in a fresh round, Caleb fired again and got close enough to force the rider to hunker down over his horse's back. With the scent of fresh blood in his nostrils, Caleb reloaded and fired as quickly as he could while rushing toward the riders.

The echo of gunfire was still rattling in his brain as Caleb pulled his trigger a few times without any more fire coming from his barrel. Fortunately, the riders were so thrown off by Caleb's suicidal move that they noticed his current predicament a heartbeat after he did. By that time, Caleb had wrapped his fist around the rifle's barrel and swung its stock toward the closest rider's chin.

Heat from the barrel seared into Caleb's flesh. Since he wasn't about to let go of the weapon, he gritted his teeth and followed through until he felt the satisfying crack of the rifle's stock against flesh and bone.

The rider's head snapped back, throwing a streak of bloody spit into the air. He kept right on going until he dropped off the other side of his horse to land with a thump.

Suddenly, another shot blasted through the air. Caleb instinctively dropped to the ground as the incoming bullet whipped past the side of his neck and slapped into the horse directly in front of him. The animal let out a pained groan and started bucking and kicking wildly.

Although Caleb meant to draw his pistol, he found it difficult to drop the rifle since his fingers were partially stuck to the hot barrel. The iron wasn't exactly seared onto him, but it stuck just long enough to throw off his draw. The rifle finally dropped away and knocked against his legs before hitting the dirt.

By that time, the man with the broken leg

had sucked in a breath to steady his hand and take aim. Before he could pull his trigger, he let out a surprised scream and rolled to one side as the wounded horse thrashed straight toward him and slammed both hooves into the dirt less than a foot away from him.

Caleb was still taking in that sight when he felt an iron grip clamp around his shoulder. The next thing he felt was a fist slam into his freshly stitched back, followed by a wave of pain that brought the bile up from the pit of his stomach.

"You like that?" the man behind him snarled.

As much as Caleb wanted to answer that punch with something of his own, his body wasn't obeying a single one of his commands. Instead, his knees were becoming wobbly under him and a wave of dizziness rolled through the inside of his head.

Laughter drifted through the air as the man tightened his grip on Caleb's shoulder. "Let's see if you like this any better."

When the second punch landed in the same spot, Caleb heard it more than he felt it. The sound was a dull thump resembling the stomping of the wild horse nearby, mixed with the crunch of bones grinding together. Although there was another wave of burning pain, it was quickly followed by a numbness that engulfed most of Caleb's body.

Without being weighed down by such things as pain or common sense for the moment, Caleb twisted out of the other man's grasp and drove his elbow into his attacker's gut. Caleb saw the man double over and even draw his gun, but he didn't pay either of those things too much attention.

All Caleb wanted was to get his hands around the man's throat, which was exactly what he did. As the numbness subsided and the pain came back, Caleb locked his left hand around the other man's neck and squeezed with everything he had.

The man tried to peel away Caleb's fingers, but they wouldn't come loose from his throat. He then started to bring up his gun, which was about the time he heard a loud thump and felt a quick, intense pain in his chest. Soon, smoke drifted up from the pistol in Caleb's hand.

Caleb held on to the man's throat for a few seconds, until he was certain the man was finished. After the life drained from the man's eyes, Caleb let go of him and turned to check on the one with the broken leg. All he found was a bloody mess that had been stomped into pulp by the wounded horse.

Caleb put the animal out of its misery and chased down his own horse for the ride back.

34

When Caleb got back into Denver, he was surprised to find someone already waiting for him at the agreed spot.

"Back so soon, Doc?" Caleb asked.

Doc sat with one hand draped casually on one knee and the other holding his horse's reins. His horse was still breathing heavily and shifting nervously. With a cigarette clenched between his teeth, Doc replied, "Those fellows should have been more careful when charging into the dark like that. Those trails outside of town can be awfully treacherous."

"You managed to shake free of them?"

"And took two of them out for good. I take it you fared just as well?"

"Burned my hands and reopened my stitches, but I made it."

Doc nodded and took another pull from his cigarette. "With all this stagecoach riding, I'd nearly forgotten the feel of riding on your own. It's quite exhilarating."

"Yeah, well we can reflect on it later. Was Stakely one of the men you took out?"

Doc shook his head. "I checked."

"All right then," Caleb said. "We should head back to the Theatre, since Lottie is still there."

"Agreed."

Nothing else needed to be said before both men snapped their reins and rode toward the Theatre Comique.

After scuffling with those riders, Caleb could still feel his blood burning through his veins. That fire was stoked even more by the throbbing in his shoulder and the sharp pain coming from the burns on his hands. That pain was like the pain a man felt when he was pulling an arrow out of himself. It was bad now and was going to get worse, but there was no way in hell Caleb was about to give in until the arrow was out.

Looking over at Doc, Caleb expected to see the same intensity on his face that he, himself, was feeling. Doc, on the other hand, looked as if he was thoroughly enjoying himself. His eyes were alight with an excited glint and he rode his horse as if he owned the streets of Denver.

There was something more than a little disconcerting about that glint in Doc's eye.

Before Caleb had a chance to think it over, they were arriving at the Theatre and climbing down from their horses. Just as their boots hit the street, the door to the Theatre swung open and two men stomped outside.

"If you're looking for the redheaded bitch, she's not in there!" Stakely roared. "Where is she hiding?"

"Even if I knew where she was, I wouldn't tell you," Caleb said. "Besides, she's the least of your worries."

"I suppose you also don't know about the man she killed," Stakely said.

Doc's eyes narrowed as if he were looking at Stakely under a magnifying glass. "What man did she kill?"

"One of my boys! That bitch shot him dead and there's a witness to the crime, so don't play dumb with me, Holliday. You two already owe me for the blood you spilled and now she owes me, too."

"Take it out of the taxes you've been collecting," Caleb said, "because nobody owes you a damn thing anymore."

Stakely wore a wild, twisted smile as he nodded slowly to himself. The man next to him was one of the gunmen that was always at Stakely's side, and he shifted on his feet while waiting to see what his boss would say next. The crowd that had formed around

371

the front of the Theatre also waited.

Dropping his voice to a low whisper, Stakely asked, "You think you can just put me out of business?"

"It's already done," Caleb replied. "Those men you sent after us won't be coming back."

"And neither will your man Morris," Doc added.

Stakely fumed and shifted on his feet while his eyes darted to glance at the people gathering along the street. "You men made a big mistake in starting this."

Suddenly, Doc stepped forward. Holding his arms out as if to address everyone within earshot as well as Stakely, he said, "Really? If it's such a big mistake, then where's the divine retribution? Where's the punishment from on high?"

Stakely straightened up and stared at Doc as if he couldn't believe what he was seeing. "Do you know who I am? Do you know how easy it would be for me to —"

"I know who you are! Unfortunately for you, I just don't give a damn!"

Even though the fire was still burning inside of him, Caleb wished he could reach out and pull Doc back a few steps. Since that wouldn't have done any good, Caleb let Doc walk right up to place one foot on the bottommost of the steps leading to the Theatre's front door. Stakely stood at the top of those steps with his hired gun standing next to him.

"Plenty of these people don't have the first clue who you are," Doc said while looking directly into Stakely's eyes. "And the ones who do wish they could do exactly what I'm about to do."

Those words hung in the air, and everyone who heard them fell silent.

While Stakely did his best to stare a set of holes through Doc's head, Doc's only response was a smug grin and a subtle nod.

After that, there wasn't anything else to be done except let the fire burn.

Stakely's gunman was the first to reach for his weapon, but Stakely was only a heartbeat behind him. Both men had their sights set on Doc, who'd already conceded the lower ground by remaining with one foot perched on that bottom step.

Things happened too quickly for Caleb to even think about them. As he watched the men at the top of the steps draw their weapons, Caleb pulled his gun from its spot at his side.

Doc stood perfectly still until the last possible moment. When the time came, he snapped the pistol from where it had been tucked under his belt and hefted the weapon up while thumbing the hammer back. It was a slightly older model and almost caught on his belt as he drew it. For a fraction of a second, Caleb wondered if that old pistol would slow Doc down long enough to catch a bullet from Stakely's gunman.

It didn't.

Doc drew, aimed, and fired in a set of motions that was almost as finely honed as the way he handled his cards. At that same time, Caleb sent a round into the chest of Stakely's gunman, knocking him solidly against the front of the Theatre.

As he slid down the wall, the gunman's finger tightened around his trigger and sent a bullet into the boardwalk.

When the gun bucked against his palm, the first thing Doc noticed was the surprised look on Stakely's face as hot lead drilled through his skull. Stakely gritted his teeth while still trying to take his shot. Doc fired again and dropped Stakely into a heap at the top of the steps.

Only then did Doc look over to see that Stakely's gunman was down. Nodding, Doc looked at Caleb and said, "That poor Tiger. Still trying to bite even after his fangs have been pulled."

Caleb stood his ground and didn't allow

himself to think about what Doc was saying. His eyes were darting back and forth among the faces in the crowd, waiting for one or more of them to step forward and take a shot at him. He looked to the upper windows of the Theatre as well as the other windows overlooking Blake Street, but saw nothing more than several frightened eyes staring back at him.

When he finally heard the sound of footsteps stomping toward him, Caleb spun on the balls of his feet and turned to face them.

Three lawmen approached the Theatre with their guns drawn. One of them was the man who'd disarmed Caleb and Doc. The other two were fresh faces.

"You men throw down your weapons!" the oldest of the lawmen said. He looked to be in his late forties or early fifties with a clean-shaven face and streaks of gray in his hair. Even after Caleb and Doc complied with the order, the lawman kept his gun trained on them. "What the hell went on here?"

Doc blinked and looked at the lawmen before looking at Caleb. "We heard the commotion and thought we could be of some help."

"What?"

"That's right," Caleb said. "I came to check on Lottie Deno after hearing some men were after her."

"You expect me to believe that line of crap?"

Next, the younger lawman who normally patrolled that part of town spoke up. "It's true, Dean. I have Miss Deno in protective custody."

"So who shot these men?" Dean asked.

"More than likely, they shot each other," Doc offered. "Much in the same vein as those fellows at Babbitt's. It truly is disgraceful how animals like these insist on gnawing at each other."

Shrugging, Caleb added, "Better that they kill each other than anyone else."

As Dean was soaking that up, Andrew Corday stepped out of the Theatre and approached the lawmen. "I saw everything, Dean. These men got into a squabble and started shooting. I was lucky to push them out the door before things got too bad."

"Do you know who they are?" Dean asked.

"Here. Take a look for yourself." With that, Corday put the toe of his boot against Stakely's shoulder and rolled him onto his back. The body flopped over so Stakely's dead eyes stared up at the Theatre's front awning.

Dean, as well as the other lawmen, stared down at the corpse just a bit too long before glancing nervously at one another.

"I think this is a simple matter of things resolving themselves," the familiar lawman said. "That is, unless you think we should look into who these men were . . . as well as what their business was here in Denver."

Dean looked over at the third deputy, who had yet to say a word and didn't seem too interested in breaking his silence now.

"You'll produce witnesses to verify that story?" Dean asked.

Corday nodded immediately. "Some of my dealers saw what happened earlier, and my partner was inside by the front window the whole time."

"Well," Dean muttered, "I guess that's the end of it."

The look of relief on the quiet lawman's face was as unmistakable as the relief in Dean's voice.

"Excuse me," said a man from the crowd that had gathered a little farther along the boardwalk. "But I saw what happened, and it wasn't —"

"I said that's the end of it!" Dean barked.

After that show of support from the local law, the bystander shrugged and walked away.

Turning to Doc and Caleb, Dean said, "Hand over those guns and you can collect them on the way out of town. And if I were you, I'd be collecting them real soon." With that, Dean and the silent lawman left the Theatre to round up someone to clean up the mess on the boardwalk.

When the younger lawman came by to take his guns, Caleb smiled and said, "Disarming me seems to be your biggest job."

"Yeah, well, after we clean up this mess, we should be able to get back to more important matters. By the way, Miss Deno is asking about you. She's at a little place just down the street."

"Is she all right?"

The lawman nodded. "That hotel doesn't serve liquor and doesn't have any card tables, so it's not known to anyone associated with the likes of Morris or his men. Even though nobody's sad to see these men go," he added while glancing toward the two bodies in front of the Theatre, "I'd still recommend that you take the marshal's advice and find somewhere else to be. At least, for a little while."

"I'll do that." Caleb extended his hand and said, "I never did get your name."

"And you don't need it," the lawman said. "Just like I don't need yours."

"Fair enough."

Looking around at the dark street and the

rapidly thinning crowd, Caleb still felt like he was charging forward on the back of that wild horse. This time, at least, there wasn't anyone chasing him.

35

CHEYENNE, WYOMING TERRITORY ONE MONTH LATER

Sunlight streamed into the sparsely furnished hotel room, to spill onto the floor and bed. Lottie lay on her side, propping her head with one hand while using the other to flatten out a wrinkled newspaper. That paper and the thin cotton sheet beneath it were the only things keeping Caleb from seeing every one of Lottie's natural wonders.

"Can you believe this?" she asked.

Caleb laughed under his breath. "You mean the newspaper or the fact that you're naked in bed and I'm not in there with you?"

"Well, I meant the newspaper, but that other point seems awfully strange now that you mention it."

Sitting on a rickety chair and leaning with his elbows on his knees, Caleb let his eyes drink in the sight of the redhead before finally glancing toward the paper.

"What's that?"

"It's last week's edition of the *Rocky Mountain News*."

"The paper from Denver? Where'd you get that?"

"I found it at the train station. You know what's in there concerning Stakely, Morris, or even you or Doc for that matter?"

"Do I want to know?"

"Nothing," Lottie said. "Not one word. Soon after we left, there was a mention of the fight outside of Babbitt's, but that was about it. There was one sentence about how some of the town's law may have been indebted to Morris, but even that didn't warrant more than any of the other gossip that's in here."

"Would you be happier if there was a public outcry for my and Doc's scalps?"

"No. It's just that . . . I don't know . . . after everything that happened, I thought there'd be more to it once it was over."

Caleb walked over to the bed and sat down on the edge. He took the paper from her, glanced over it, and then set it aside so he could see the inviting curves of Lottie's figure under the sheet. "It's over. That's all that matters. Just because it's not splashed across a front page somewhere doesn't mean nobody knows what happened. And it sure as hell doesn't mean all of this was for nothing."

"I know that," Lottie said. "I guess I'm just waiting for the other shoe to drop."

"Me and Doc got you out of Denver with all of our skins intact. Nobody's interested in trying to collect those idiotic taxes anymore, and it all got swept under the carpet by lawmen who were too far under Stakely's thumb to do anything else but clean up the mess. I'd say that's plenty of shoes dropping for a while."

She smiled and traced her fingertips along Caleb's hand and arm. "When you put it that way, it sounds a whole lot better. It sure will be easier to travel the circuit again."

"There you go." Suddenly, Caleb twitched and said, "Wait a second. What were you doing at the train station?"

"Buying a ticket. I think I'm going to head back east for a little while and take a rest. After that, who knows? I'm sure it won't be too difficult for me to find you if you plan on staying anywhere near Doc."

"You take care of yourself, Lottie."

Nodding slowly, she reached out to take hold of Caleb's half-buttoned shirt. "I will," she whispered. "But I still need to show my appreciation for what you did when things got a little too much for me."

■ ■ ■ ■

A few hours later, Caleb stepped in from the warm night air with a small bundle tucked under one arm. Although the fresh breeze was particularly sweet that evening, he couldn't deny the instinctive attraction of places like the well-known Bella Union Theater. Inside, the smells of smoke and liquor mingled with women's perfume and the sounds of shuffling cards.

Doc sat at a small table facing the front door, sporting a new dark gray suit and eyeing the card games going on around him. Every so often, he glanced at one of the provocatively dressed serving girls making their rounds. Doc cleared his throat and acknowledged Caleb's approach by pushing out the only other seat at the table with his foot.

Noticing that there was no cane anywhere near Doc's table, Caleb said, "I take it you're feeling better?"

"Right as rain. Lottie's not coming?"

"She's getting ready to leave town."

"Are you going with her?"

Caleb leaned back and surveyed his surroundings. The serving girls had noticed his arrival as well and smiled at him from the bar. "Nah. There's still plenty of money to be made right here."

"I'm so glad you said that. There are some gentlemen from Charleston who've heard of me and want to have a game."

Shaking his head and chuckling under his breath, Caleb said, "Poor fools."

Doc grinned. "And that's not all the good news. Arranging to deal faro here wasn't half the ordeal it was back in Denver. Also, there's no taxes beyond the normal house percentage."

"Word travels fast."

"Alas, poor Tiger," Doc said while lifting his glass. "I knew him well."

Caleb placed the bundle on the table and slid it toward Doc. "Speaking of which, I got you something."

"Gifts? What's the occasion?"

"No occasion. Just a little something I picked up before leaving Denver."

When Doc unrolled the dark brown cloth, he found a pistol that was well maintained but obviously somewhat used.

"It's a .38," Caleb explained. "I thought it might suit you better than that big Colt."

Doc picked up the gun and flipped it around his finger. When he tried another twirl, he snagged the hammer on his thumb and nearly sent the gun flying across the room. After managing to catch the pistol, he said, "That'll take some practice." With the gun flipped around, he looked down at the side of it and his eyes went wide. "What have we here?"

From where he was sitting, even Caleb could see the tiger engraved on the side of the gun. "I thought you might like that."

"Is this . . . ?"

Caleb nodded. "From Stakely's own holster. Those lawmen were just going to throw them out. I think they're awfully sick of anything that reminds them of those assholes."

"I might want to get that tiger covered up, lest anyone sees it and gets the wrong idea. Thank you all the same, Caleb."

"Buy me a drink and we'll call it even."

A wry grin snuck onto Doc's face as he said, "Actually, I might have something a little better."

Looking where Doc was pointing, Caleb saw three men at a card table. One of them was Robert Taylor. Just like in Fort Griffin, Taylor sat quietly wearing his fancy suit while sizing up the other players.

"He's been asking for a high-stakes game," Doc said. "Why don't you do the honors?"

"All by myself? What if I need an accomplice?"

"Just say the word, my friend," Doc announced as he held up his glass in a toast. "Just say the word."